Enter The Dark

Chris Thomas

*This book is dedicated to
Nic ... For all your support and encouragement.*

1

'Ladies and gentlemen of the deep web, I bid you welcome!' said the figure striding towards the camera. In one outstretched hand he held a microphone, in the other, a gold clipboard. He wore a dark grey boiler suit, patterned like a tuxedo, and if it wasn't for the white and green clown mask obscuring his face, this could easily have been mistaken for any primetime Saturday evening family variety show.

His footsteps echoed as he walked across the cold grey floor of the warehouse. Behind him, a white glow from the double doors illuminated the cloudy fog of dry ice through which he had just walked. The doors closed. Above them hung a large sign, red letters and yellow light bulbs blinking hypnotically, spelling out *The Red Room*.

In front of him were the camera operator and two others; one tapped away on a laptop, the other fiddled with a small box of controls. The latter turned a small knob on the control panel and the thumping techno soundtrack that had accompanied the man faded out to silence. All three gave a thumbs up. The lights came up and the man stopped.

'Good evening,' he said, holding the microphone to his mouth. 'Welcome to the latest instalment of The Red Room. We're The Brotherhood of the Righteous, I'm the Host, and have we got a show for you tonight! Please say a big hello to our latest "volunteer".'

With that the doors opened again, and silhouetted against the light were two burly masked figures, goons, wearing 1980s-style red tracksuits with white stripes on the legs and arms. In between them, struggling for all his worth, was a portly figure dressed in a tight white t-shirt and white y-front underpants. On his head was a hessian sack marked with a big red 'V'.

They frogmarched him down towards the Host, who spoke into the microphone.

'Here he is, people. Mister Gary Sweetman. You may remember him from twenty-twelve, when he was arrested for grooming and holding hostage two thirteen-year-old boys from the football club where he worked as a youth coach. Because of serious flaws in the police investigation, the judge could only jail him for a maximum of … wait for it … four months. Well, tonight you're going to put that right. Start placing your bids!'

A large monitor descended from the warehouse ceiling on two heavy chains. On it were a list of ten indiscernible nicknames, and next to each was a number.

Slowly, the numbers began to change, and with them the order of names, ranking from highest to lowest. After a few seconds, the screen resembled a stock market trading screen; a flashing, blinking mix of names and numbers as more people joined in, bidding higher and higher amounts.

The two goons sat the man down on a wooden chair and buckled his wrists and ankles tightly to it. As he struggled in vain to free himself, the Host reached out and grabbed the top of the sack.

'Ladies and gentleman, I give you …' and then he quickly pulled the sack off, revealing the face of a chubby man with bruises and dried blood around his eyes and mouth.

Sweetman blinked and shook his head, desperately trying to acclimatise his eyes to the bright light that beamed down on his face. Clearly, he had no idea where he was; this was the first light he had seen since being snatched from outside his house two days ago.

'Where am I? Who the fuck are you?' he spluttered, his eyes wide with terror.

'Gary, Gary. So many questions,' said the Host, sympathetically, as he walked around the chair, placing a comforting hand on the man's shoulders. 'You're here because you're special. A chosen one, if you will. You were convicted of committing the most heinous of crimes and yet you received a punishment that has been deemed unacceptable.'

'What? Unacceptable by who? I served my sentence, I'm a free man, and you have no fucking right to do this,' he retorted, mustering a little more defiance.

'The people, Gary. The people whose taxes had to pay for your charade of a trial. The same people whose taxes will have to pay to support the young boys as they try to recover from the ordeal that you put them through.'

'You can't do this. Let me go!'

'Sorry, Gary. The rules are very clear on this. You have been chosen and you will answer. These good people have paid their bitcoins and there are a few things that they want to know.'

'This can't be—' he started, but was cut off by a hand over his mouth whilst the Host turned to face the screen.

The Host glanced over his shoulder at the laptop operator, who prodded the enter key and gave another thumbs up. Turning back towards the screen, the Host looked up.

'And it is … 'SliderMonkey'. And with a massive seven bitcoins as well, fantastic. Welcome to the show, Slider, what's your question?'

'I'm not answering anything, you bastard,' shouted Sweetman, shaking his head away from the hand. The Host slowly turned around to face the chair, then, quick as a flash, smashed the clipboard around the side of Sweetman's head. Sweetman hissed in pain, then dropped his head to his chest and started crying.

'My apologies, Slider, go ahead,' said the Host, turning back to the camera.

There was silence as the screen behind filled with words, the first question of the night.

Do you have any comprehension of the amount of pain that you have probably caused those boys? Pain that will stay with them for the rest of their lives?

'Good question, Slider,' said the Host, as he scratched the top of his head with the corner of the clipboard. 'Well, do you?'

Sweetman stammered. 'I, I, I was convicted and I served—'

'NO!' shouted the Host, barely two inches from his face. He slammed the clipboard down into the man's lap, causing him to wince in pain. 'That isn't the question!'

Sweetman struggled to talk in between his deep breaths. 'They were ... They ... I loved those boys. They weren't entirely innocent in all of this. They led me on.'

'Oh I see,' said the Host, softly, as he walked around the chair like a buzzard circling a piece of carrion. 'You hear that, folks? I guess it was the young children's fault. It was their fault for just being too sexy in the first place. I've heard enough. Slider, choose your punishment.'

'What?' shouted Sweetman, as he strained to look behind him at the monitor, which once again displayed an incoming message.

The camera panned up so all the viewers could see the statement, *Start with stomping the groin, but leave some for the others.*

Before Sweetman could protest or effect even the vaguest attempt at closing his legs, the Host swung around and planted a boot square in his groin. Sweetman screamed in agony, desperate to grab his crotch to ease some of the pain searing through his body.

The Host swung back round to face the camera and held the microphone to his mouth.

'Time for another question, I think. Let's see who's at the top now.'

The leaderboard on the screen stopped, before flashing up another name.

'Clearly this chap has got a lot of you wound up. The winner, with nine-point-five bitcoins, is CruelJudge.'

'You can't do this. I have rights,' gasped Sweetman, as he struggled to hold his head up.

The Host walked over and gripped him by the throat, smacking his head back against the seat.

'That's what they all say. But just what exactly are you going to do about it? Sue us?' He forced Sweetman's head to face the camera, which started to draw closer. 'There, see that? You're in their hands now. Let everyone take a nice long look deep into your eyes. The window to the soul, apparently. If you even have one, that is.'

Sweetman began crying again, whimpering, 'You can't do this … You can't.'

The question began to materialise on the screen.

Hopefully now you are starting to feel just a fraction of the fear that those boys felt. What I want to know is, did you apologise to them after doing whatever it is you did?

'A very interesting question, thank you, Judge. Not the sort of question that the legal types would bother asking at your trial. As we all know from past experience, some abusers will 'apologise' to their victims after causing them unimaginable suffering. They think it redeems them, causes them to feel less guilt perhaps in the misguided delusion that the victim will forgive them. Is that how it happened, Gary?'

'I can't remember …'

'You can't remember? You can't remember if, after you assaulted two young boys, you said sorry to them?'

'I might have done, I don't know.'

'Of course you do!' the Host roared.

'OK, OK. Yes, I said sorry.'

'What did you say sorry for? At your trial you completely denied any sort of assault took place.'

'And the case was thrown out,' said Sweetman, desperately, spitting out a mixture of tears, saliva, and snot. 'I was jailed for false imprisonment of those boys; I wasn't convicted of assaulting them.'

'Not convicted doesn't mean you didn't do it though, right, Gaz?' replied the Host, calmly. 'You just told everyone that you apologised to the boys and I very much doubt that was for imprisoning them. Judge, pick a punishment.'

'No, no please,' begged Sweetman, who had by now lost control of most of his bodily functions, as clearly visible through his underpants.

The screen went blank before one word appeared: kneecaps.

A track-suited goon stepped forward and handed the Host a baseball bat; he placed the clipboard and microphone down on Sweetman's lap.

'Hold these, please. One or both, Judge?' shouted the Host, to the camera. The words *just one* appeared on the screen behind. 'Well, Gary, looks like someone is being lenient! Aren't you lucky?' He brought the bat crashing down on Sweetman's right knee, causing him to scream out in agony. 'Actually, better do both just to be certain.' The resulting pain was too much, and he passed out.

'Right, we have just about time for one more question. Get your bids in while we revive our volunteer.' As the two goons wafted a vial of smelling salts under the unconscious Sweetman, the Host went behind the camera, lifted his mask, and took a sip of water.

'How're we doing?' he asked the laptop operator.

'This is one of the biggest yet. We've got just over four hundred people viewing, most of them have only paid to watch. But around twenty or thirty are bidding heavily and I reckon they'll follow on to the end,' they replied.

'Good. Let's get this done and get out of here.' He replaced the mask and headed back towards the chair.

A groggy Sweetman raised his head as best he could, but it kept flopping to the side and to his chest.

'Don't worry, Gary. This will all be over soon,' whispered the Host, softly, in his ear, as he stood behind the chair, massaging both shoulders with his hands. He picked up the microphone and spoke to the camera. 'Alright, everybody, this is it, the big one. The final question. Let's see who it is …'

The lights around the screen flashed and up came a name, *Dredhed.*

'With a massive thirteen bitcoins, it's Dredhed. Dred, what's your question, my good man?'

By now, Sweetman was incapable of mustering the energy to even attempt to look at the screen. His knees had swollen up like melons and his underpants were sodden. His once pristine white t-shirt was stained with a mixture of spit, snot, and blood, into which he now added vomit. As the message began to appear, letter by letter, on the screen, the Host read it out loud, propping Sweetman's chin up with the corner of his clipboard.

'Right, the final request is ... 'Firstly, can you tell Gary that I think he is the most wretched, despicable excuse of a man and he deserves every ounce of pain that he is in right now?' Okay, will do, Dred. Gary, did you get that? DID YOU?'

Sweetman gurgled a vague attempt at a reply.

'I can't hear you, Gary! This is what people, decent, ordinary people, think of you and your sordid crimes. You should defend yourself!' shouted the Host.

But Sweetman either couldn't speak or wouldn't speak, as the message carried on coming through.

'OK, let's see,' continued the Host. "Secondly, if you could speak to those two boys right here and now, what would you say to them?' Great question, Dred. Let's see. Gary? Those two poor young boys, remember them? The ones that you kidnapped from their warm, loving families and subjected to who knows what kind of depravity. The same ones that you tried your damnedest to make out in court were liars and fantasists just in order to save your own sorry self. What would you say to them?'

Sweetman raised his head as far as he could, spat out some frothy pink liquid and looked at the Host.

Very softly he said, 'I would forgive them. Forgive them for ruining my life.'

A pause, before the Host turned to the camera and spoke. 'Well, ladies and gentlemen, in case you didn't hear, Gary here said that he would forgive the boys. Forgive them for ruining his life. Time to end this I think. Dred, you have the honour of removing this man. Did you know they're becoming something of an endangered species now, 'Garys', there's not many of them left. Anyway, would you be so kind as to select an ending?'

The message on the screen disappeared and then showed up a single word: *knife*.

'Excellent choice. Well, I hope you have enjoyed another episode of The Red Room with us, the Brotherhood of the Righteous. I think we can all be satisfied that this sad little sicko understands that if the pathetic justice system in this country won't give the people what they want, then we will. We're going to switch the exit nodes on this transmission now. If you want to see the ending of this trial, you'll need to transfer another two bitcoins and reconnect to the settings that will be sent upon receipt of your funds. If you have seen enough, thank you for watching and keep an eye on the message boards for upcoming editions of The Red Room.'

The Host stopped as one of the goons handed him a pristine silver hunting knife. He ran his finger along the blade, pretending to test its sharpness before putting his face up close to the camera.

'See you after the break!'

2

'Heaven's what you make it, I reckon,' slurred Joe, swirling the last warm dregs of London Pride around the bottom of his pint glass. 'The reason people developed ideas of heaven and hell in the first place is because, historically, most of them led piss-poor, crappy lives. The best way to convince them to put up with all the shit was to promise that they would reap some sort of reward when they died.'

'What in the name of fuck is he banging on about?' asked Mike, as he slapped another four pints of ale down in the middle of their table.

'He's reached the usual philosophical stage shortly after the fifth pint and decided to tackle the issue of whether Heaven and Hell exist,' replied Rosco. 'I only asked him—'

'But now,' interrupted Joe, waggling an authoritative finger around the table, 'people have a different view of it. They are open to more options. Like perhaps we are merely vessels for our souls and when the body withers and dies, the soul is free to move on to create its own existence. Or perhaps the whole thing is just a load of rubbish and when we die, boom, nothingness.'

Mike sat down and sipped the frothy top from his pint of ale. 'Create its own existence? So what, people's afterlife is based on what they think it should be? That's probably one of your more interesting pissed-up brain-farts.'

'Interesting is my middle name.'

'So, what sort of heaven would Hitler have created?' asked Rosco. 'One of the most evil men to have ever lived?'

'And he only had one testicle,' said Mike.

Rosco doffed his glass in appreciation, then continued, 'Would his idea of heaven have been more in line with most people's idea of hell? I can't imagine him creating a heaven that I'd want to live in, pristine world full of clouds and angels and singing and so on. Or would his consciousness be inclined to create a "hell" in the traditional sense of the word as some sort of appeasement for his guilty soul?'

'See, now you're on board with the idea. Well, that's the beauty,' continued Joe, 'it means that you don't need to have a picture-book-style definition of what one or the other should look like, but more that each person would ultimately develop it out of their own consciousness. There's no reason to assume, just because visible signs of life are no longer there, that consciousness has completely ceased. Unless you subscribe to the theory that consciousness only exists as a direct result of the physical processing going on in the brain.'

'Great, well, that's my head exploded. Thanks, Joe. I'm going to play on the fruities,' said Rosco, picking up his pint and heading off in the direction of the fruit machines.

'Where's Billy? He was supposed to be here an hour ago,' asked Mike.

'Well, it's ever since he became an *associate vice president*,' replied Joe, accenting the title with as much sarcasm as he could muster. 'He's started working stupid long hours. Saying that, I did just miss a text from His Lordship. He should be here any minute.'

'Still, it's better than when he came back from his twelve months travelling around Asia,' said Mike. 'Remember? He turned into a right fucking hippy. What was it he used to say? "Time has no meaning". Well that's great, Billy, but it's your round and you've turned up five minutes before last orders. Who'd have thought he'd end up in the capitalist world of corporate finance?'

At that moment Billy walked in and stood next to the table, taking his suit jacket off.

'Evening, boys. How are we all?'

Rosco returned from the fruit machine five pounds lighter and gave Billy a massive slap on his backside.

'Billy, you big bender. Glad you could finally make it. Joe can addle your brain now with his pissed up theory of the afterlife.'

Billy picked up the spare pint and drank nearly half of it in one go, wiping the foam moustache away on his sleeve.

'Is this the same theory that when he dies he wants to be reincarnated as a shark?'

'No, it's a new one. I followed it up until the bit where he started talking about consciousness and then my brain melted,' replied Rosco.

'I thought you said it exploded?' said Mike.

'It did both.'

'And where exactly did you pick up this new theory then, Joe?' asked Billy. 'Same place you get all your information – Wikipedia?'

'Piss off. I came up with this one all by myself. Just now. Though I am quite proud of it.'

'Well, Wikipedia's unlikely to give you the most balanced view of life and death given that any moron can edit it. You know, a colleague of mine introduced me to a program called TOR. It allows a much more realistic view of the world. You can download it for free; I'll show it to you sometime,' said Billy, as he finished off the last of his pint.

'Isn't that what paedophiles and junkies use for searching the internet?' asked Rosco, looking slightly disturbed.

'Sort of,' replied Billy, slightly anxious to convince his friends that he wasn't some sort of drug dealing sex pest. 'It's what's known as an 'onion router'. Basically, it enables people to surf the internet anonymously by routing all of their activity through lots of different encrypted layers or 'relays', which hide stuff like their location and IP address.'

Rosco groaned. 'For fuck's sake. First we have him banging on about death and now I've got to try and understand this nerdy internet shit.'

'It's pretty simple, even for you,' laughed Billy. 'To put it simply, the normal internet that you look at on Google—'

'What, Pornhub?' interrupted Joe.

'And YouPorn?' said Mike.

'And PornTube?' said Joe again.

'Yes, very funny,' grumbled Rosco, gesturing to the barmaid for another round of beers.

'Indeed, that sort of thing,' continued Billy. 'Those regular internet sites account for a miniscule fraction of the amount of information and pages that are actually out there on the so-called information super highway. Under all of that is the 'deep web'. The deep web is maybe, I don't know, five thousand times larger than the regular web and never shows up on Google searches since it can't be indexed. It ranges from boring stuff like scientific data and internal company intranets, to your more 'specialised' sites. Within the deep web, you then get the dark web and that's where things become way more interesting.'

'So how come you downloaded this program if it's used for sick shit like you're suggesting?' asked Mike.

'The developers believe in freedom of speech and of information, where people can communicate without fear of being snooped on by the authorities. Or if you're worried about protecting your own anonymity. Doesn't it piss you off every time you look for a new kettle or a new lawnmower and then, within seconds, every page you look at is bombarded with adverts for kettles and mowers?' responded Billy.

'Well yes,' replied Mike, 'but not enough to switch from good old Google Chrome. Surely this TOR thing is just used by nasty people for doing nasty things?'

'They'd find a way to do it anyway,' said Billy, by now feeling slightly like a salesman for the program. 'This just offers an easy way for normal people to have access to the sheer volume of, how shall we say, alternative information that's out there. Of course, some normal people might not be ready for what they see on the deep web, but that's life.'

The barmaid placed another four ales in the middle of the table, which was by now soaked with beer and covered in the crumbs of pork scratchings and crisps.

'Quiz machine, anyone?' asked Mike, as he collected his beer and stood up from the table. Rosco nodded and together they headed over to the brightly flashing quiz machine to lose some more of their money.

Joe leaned in closer to talk to Billy. 'So, this dark web thing. I assume there is some really fucked up stuff on it. Have you looked at much?'

'A fair bit,' he replied, munching on another large, and slightly hairy, pork scratching. 'There's a lot of weird underground horror videos that are both quite cool and bloody disturbing at the same time. It's fairly easy to avoid the really dodgy abuse stuff or the drugs sites like Silk Road, but for quite a lot of it you have to know the precise link, and the web addresses are mostly random gibberish. Why don't you come back to mine after this and I'll show it to you?'

'I don't know, Ellie's got the hump with me at the moment because I've been going out a fair bit recently. I'm probably already in the doghouse for being pissed again tonight,' said Joe, with an air of disappointment. But Billy could see he was tempted.

'Go on, it's Friday night. I've got a bottle of sambuca that we can start on when we get back,' replied Billy, sensing that Joe was in no fit state to refuse more alcohol.

'I fucking hate sambuca. It's almost as bad as Tequila,' slurred Joe. He was by now more or less resigned to his fate. 'Fine, we can pick up some ales on the way back to yours.'

Mike and Rosco came back to the table and placed down four small shot glasses containing a clear liquor, four slices of lime, and a salt shaker.

'We won a tenner on the quiz machine so Mikey here bought a round of Tequilas. Enjoy!' said Rosco.

Joe grimaced, 'Does anyone actually like Tequila? I mean actually like it?'

'No.'

'No.'

'No.'

'So, why the fuck did you buy it then?'

'Because it's nearly last orders and we won ten quid. We would have won some more afterwards but Rosco here thought that Lance Armstrong was the first man to walk on the moon,' laughed Mike.

'I tried to press 'Neil' but my aim wasn't very good,' protested Rosco.

'Anyway, enough of this,' said Billy, as he sprinkled some salt on the back of his hand. 'Gentlemen, a toast. To our good buddy Joe. And, to his impending imprisonment and general ending of anything he could call a life. Sorry, I mean, his upcoming wedding to the lovely Ellie, of course. First one of us to get engaged, who'd have thought it?'

'To Joe. And his ridiculous philosophies on death!' said Mike.

The four friends licked the backs of their hands in unison, then swallowed the Tequila in one mouthful, contorting their faces as the combination of sharp bitterness, salt, and fresh citrus hit. They slammed the glasses back down on the table, finished off what was left of their pints, and started to put their coats on.

'Right, anyone else want to come back to mine?' asked Billy, as they made for the exit.

'Nope. I've got an early start in the morning,' replied Mike.

'I'm going to give it a miss too I think,' agreed Rosco.

'OK, shitface, it's just you and me,' said Billy, as he put his arm around Joe's shoulder, partly as a gesture of solidarity and partly to stop Joe wandering all over the pavement. 'Let's go and see what delights we can find on the deep web.'

* * *

After twenty minutes of stumbling across the pavement, stopping at the corner shop for some cheap beer almost certainly past its sell-by date, and trying to eat two extra-large doner kebabs without spilling most of them over their coats, Billy and Joe arrived back at the flat.

'Right, keep it down,' whispered Billy, at about the same volume as he usually spoke. 'The neighbours get really annoyed if I make too much noise when I come home this late.'

'Late?' replied Joe, spilling most of his kebab as he turned his hand over to try and focus on his watch. 'It's only twelve thirty. What are they? Old retired church types or something?'

Billy turned to face him, still talking in his extra loud whisper, 'No, they're young hard-working church types.'

'Shit, the light's gone on. Hurry up and open the fucking door will you?' Joe whispered back, loudly.

Billy finally opened the door and, as quietly as they could, they barged through, clattering the bottles of beer in their plastic carrier bags against the frame, before slamming the door behind them.

'I'm going for a piss,' said Joe. 'Get this dark net thing going then.'

Billy took off his coat and hung it in the hallway. He pulled a beer from the carrier bag and opened it using a novelty bottle opener that played the Dam Busters theme. Slumping into the large leather reclining armchair in front of his enormous fifty inch television screen, he pulled a laptop out from the side of his chair.

Joe came into the room and sat on the sofa with his beer, whilst Billy tapped away on the computer, turning the television screen into one giant monitor.

'So, this is TOR,' said Billy, waving the cursor over a small icon that looked like a purple onion. 'It works essentially the same way as your regular browser, except it's anonymous.'

Joe leant forward in his seat, staring intently at the screen as he tried to focus his increasingly blurry gaze.

'Go on then, let's see some stuff.'

Billy had a page that he used as a type of directory. He didn't need to click on anything for Joe to see precisely what existed on this part of the internet.

'Holy shit!' exclaimed Joe, as he stared at the variety of links available to them, ranging from the relatively mundane *How to cook a person* to the downright vile, things that didn't require two guesses for Joe to realise covered some sort of sick abuse. In between was everything from hitman services, online drug dealers, videos of human experimentation; amongst all of this a site for 'horror movies' seemed almost like a quiet sanctuary.

Billy clicked on the horror movie link, bringing up an outdated-looking website with a selection of thumbnail images and movie names.

'Why does it look like we're surfing the net in the early nineteen nineties?' asked Joe.

'Everything's stripped down to help with the anonymity. All those programs that run in the background on your regular PC, that make the internet look how it does, they all give away clues to your identity,' replied Billy.

He clicked on the first video at the top entitled *Bloody Nose*.

'What is this shit?' said Joe, his eyes getting heavier now, though he valiantly carried on drinking his beer.

On screen, a man dressed in white with a white hood and bizarre large rubber lips sat close to the camera. What little sound there was appeared distorted, and the man made indiscernible noises until, after a few seconds, the front of his mask became soaked in blood, as if he had suffered a massive haemorrhage. The screeching, distorted soundtrack filled the room through Billy's surround sound speakers, causing Joe to shift uneasily in his seat.

'OK, try this one,' said Billy, clicking back and then on another of the thumbnails entitled *Couple Brutally Run Over*.

On the screen appeared crackly CCTV footage of what looked like a police precinct somewhere in China. Joe watched as two people casually walked up from the bottom of the screen.

'Boring!' he complained.

But his interest piqued as a car careered up from the bottom of the screen, hitting the couple at full speed. One fell to the side and lay motionless whilst the other was carried on the front of the car before finally dropping under the wheels. The man in the car then got out and ran to the first body, the bystanders standing and staring as he stamped repeatedly on the person's head.

'For fuck's sake, turn it off,' said Joe.

'OK, but you did ask,' replied Billy, clicking out of the webpage entirely. 'This is slightly less violent. It's an online marketplace for buying drugs. Amongst other things, of course.'

The site looked like any other online shop where you might buy groceries or clothes or electronics.

'Look here,' said Billy, pointing at what appeared to be a genuine, regular CD. 'Here you can buy the White Album by The Beatles. Except when you get this version, the entire inlay card is a big sheet of LSD tabs.'

'Holy shit,' muttered Joe. 'But how do you pay for it? Surely putting your credit card in will just give you away and leave you open to getting busted by the police?'

'Bitcoins,' explained Billy. 'The online currency of the deep web and you can buy them anonymously. They are traded like regular currency and their value has skyrocketed in recent years.'

For the next half an hour, Billy gave his friend a guided tour of the area of the deep web that even he only just about dared to visit. More obscure horror movies, bizarre music videos, and even one of the most disturbing video games that Joe had ever seen.

'I've had enough,' said Joe, and with a newfound sense of energy, he leapt up from the sofa and ran out to the bathroom. 'I think I'm about to puke.'

Billy laughed as he closed the computer down. 'Lightweight. Don't mess up my bathroom, I had the cleaner in today.'

Joe came out of the bathroom, blowing his nose on toilet roll, before lying down on the sofa. As the room spun around him, his mind raced with all the images and bizarre sounds that he just witnessed over the last hour. But somewhere inside him it had lit a fire, and he fell asleep knowing full well that he would simply have to go investigating this new world for himself. Little did he realise the path it would lead him down and how it would change his life forever.

3

In the bathroom of a modest terraced house in West London, Saeed Anwar wiped the condensation from the mirror and stared intently into the eyes looking back at him. He concentrated closely as the razor edged the immaculately precise outline of his dark facial hair. Even for the unsavoury types of character with whom he now found himself associating, he felt it important to show that he meant business.

Being nasty came easy to him, but being smart was something he had had to learn since arriving in the United Kingdom, especially since being allowed to stay in the country, for which he had his lovely wife Amanda to thank. And he made sure in no uncertain terms that she 'understood' his gratitude, on an almost daily basis. She had borne him two sons for whom he cared very little, but as long as they were here, so was he.

He finished shaving and wiped the last of the foam away from his face. After splashing on some expensive aftershave, he buttoned up his crisp white oxford shirt. Now he looked the part. In his past life in his home country, every day had been a struggle to survive, and he had developed a very self-interested mean streak. Partly through the needs of self-preservation, but mainly because he simply enjoyed it. Since he had sold out his former family and left the old country behind, his new home had treated him well. He couldn't care less for patriotism or loyalty or gratitude to this foreign land, but it had been good to him and he would take it for as much as he could. It allowed him access to the trappings that he had previously envied, the treasures of the Western world that had seemed so tantalisingly out of his reach. Until now.

Admiring himself in the mirror, he straightened his trousers, flattened his shirt, and left the bathroom. He walked downstairs and into the kitchen, where his family sat around the dining room table. His two boys were eating breakfast cereal. The eldest was Mo, who at the age of six felt an obligatory superiority over his younger sibling. Shan was approaching two, still finding his way when it came to eating cornflakes. Their happy, infantile chatter was the shining light for their mother; she lived for it, but it ceased the moment Saeed walked into the room. Even Shan had learned it was sometimes better to stay silent around their father.

Amanda stood up and pulled the last chair out from the table.

'Good morning, Sae,' she said, as she put a cup of tea in front of him. 'You look smart. Do you have a busy day today?'

Saeed said nothing. He sat down, barely even acknowledging his sons' presence.

'Well, er,' stuttered Amanda, the nervousness in her voice palpable. 'Mo's got his Little Kickers at the church hall this morning. That'll be nice, he loves seeing his little friends. And Shan can have a run around as well. He's getting to be quite an energetic little monkey and…'

As Saeed raised the mug to take a sip of tea, he stared at her; which was when she realised.

'No, darling! Don't drink it yet!'

But it was too late. She knew it, and more to the point Saeed didn't even have to taste the tea to know it. In a way, he quite liked it when she got it wrong.

He put the mug to his lips, staring at her all the time, in silence. She stared back, her eyes almost begging him not to drink the tea. Very slowly he took a mouthful, his eyes not averting from hers as he swilled the drink around his mouth. With an exaggerated gulp, he swallowed the tea. Still fixing her gaze, he held his arm out straight, paused for a couple of seconds, and then slowly turned his hand, so that the liquid poured out in a narrow waterfall of tea, which spread all over the floor.

To Amanda it felt like it took minutes for the mug to empty. All the time it was splashing off the floor she knew that it was pointless trying to make him stop. She just hoped that it would be over quickly, for the kids' sake.

For Saeed, the longer it took, the more he enjoyed the sense of helplessness he knew she was feeling. In the big scheme of things it wasn't important, and he could very easily have put the teaspoon of sugar in the tea himself. But that wasn't the point. The point was that she had forgotten, and by making all these little rules, he maintained a control over her. And he knew full well that, at this precise moment in time, she would be desperately hoping that this would end when the last of the tea hit the floor. Mopping it off of the floor was far preferable to the alternative. This, he considered, was her escaping lightly.

Mo started to giggle at the sight of his daddy spilling his tea everywhere. Saeed switched his gaze from Amanda to Mo, barely a flicker of emotion crossing his face, and then finally placed the mug back on the table. He stood up and grabbed the two slices of toast from Amanda's plate before planting a kiss on her forehead and heading to the front door. After taking a big step over the brown puddle of tea in the middle of the kitchen he turned back towards his family.

'Don't wait up for me, I don't know when I'll be back.'

He collected his car keys from the table in the hallway and slammed the front door shut behind him. It always made her jump when she heard the door slam, but less so when she knew it was him going out. For now, she didn't have to worry about him being around the house, and it was this time with her boys that she cherished. She heard the screech of tyres as his black BMW sped away from the house, and she wondered how long it would be before he returned.

As she got up from the table, the boys started their meaningless chatter once again and she set about mopping up the tea from the floor. During mundane tasks like this, her mind had a tendency to wander back to when they had first met. He hadn't always been like this. At first he was charming, his personality warm and friendly, even to the point where she had started to disbelieve the stories of his past. She had stood by him during his short prison sentence and in the years since his release, defiant in the face of the hostility he had faced. They didn't know him like she did. He'd made her feel special and she was unable to reconcile the man sending her flowers and chocolates with the man that the authorities had tried to deport. Perhaps that was the problem.

Once she had become pregnant, that was the start of his meal ticket. And once he was released, his sense of invincibility had grown and, slowly, almost indiscernibly at first, he had begun to change.

4

'Look,' said Joe, holding out his phone. 'I've got five missed calls and seven unread texts, all from Ellie. She's going to rip my bollocks off as soon as I go in there.'

Billy lowered his sunglasses so that he could read the texts, then stared in through the lounge window. They were sat in Billy's silver TT convertible on the driveway of the non-descript semi in a quiet suburban road on the outskirts of London. They had spent the last five minutes shielding their very hungover eyes from the glare of the morning sun, waiting for Joe to muster enough bottle to go inside the house. There in the lounge was Joe's fiancée Ellie, dressed in tight neon lycra exercise clothing, watching what was presumably some sort of fitness programme on the television, contorting her legs into the most painful-looking of angles.

'It's alright, look. She's doing her yoga. She'll be nice and relaxed and probably missed you so much that she'll drag you straight to bed and give you a damn good seeing to,' replied Billy.

'I doubt that very much.'

'Well if you're not man enough to go in there, I'll happily step in in your place. Look at that arse! Fantastic!' said Billy. He had always joked to Joe about having a thing for Ellie. But since he also made a lot of comments about having 'things' for everyone's girlfriends, and their mums for that matter, Joe didn't pay it any notice.

'Thanks, I'm sure I'll be fine,' replied Joe, rubbing either side of his throbbing head. It was about time he went inside and faced his punishment, and he opened the passenger door and started to get out.

'By the way,' said Billy, grabbing his arm. 'Don't forget. TOR browser. Just install it and enjoy.'

'What, so I can watch more videos of people being run over? Great!' responded Joe, grabbing his arm away. The door shut behind him and Billy reversed out of the driveway before accelerating off down the road.

Joe took out his key and tentatively walked through the front door to discover his fate. He walked into the lounge, where Ellie was still doing yoga, walked up behind her, and put his arms around her waist.

'Don't even think about it, you utter wanker!' she shouted, whilst maintaining a perfectly poised vriksasana pose.

'I'm sorry,' replied Joe, sounding like a small child receiving a telling off from their mum. 'I had one too many and Billy talked me into going back to his and then I fell asleep on the sofa and—'

'Not interested,' interrupted Ellie. 'I'm going out shopping with Helen and Lucy once I've finished here. I'm going to spend lots of money and then we're going out in the evening. And if I can be bothered I might come home tonight. Or I might let you see how it feels for once, wondering where the hell I am.'

She finished up her exercises and stormed upstairs to the bathroom. Joe slumped onto the sofa and propped his head up on his arm. He hated it when they argued, and he knew he'd been an idiot. But creeping into his thoughts were all the images and sounds of the bizarre new world that Billy had shown him last night.

Some amount of time later, he was jolted back awake. He had drifted off on the sofa, but for quite how long he couldn't be sure. The noise of a very loud and disgruntled 'Bye' from Ellie, followed by the slamming of the front door, had been enough to drag him back to reality.

Slowly, he stood up, his balance still off, and walked into the new garage conversion via the kitchen, to collect a glass of water and an Alka-Seltzer. They had recently converted their garage into a games room and office. His new man-cave, it had become something of a sanctuary. He sat down at the computer desk and moved the mouse to start it up. He headed straight for Google and searched for the TOR Browser.

It was perfectly easy to find, especially considering how it had something of a reputation for allowing even the most computer-illiterate people like him the ability to access some of the most questionable content imaginable.

He read through the information on the site about how it was important for people to maintain anonymity and how it could protect the user and their family. Blah blah blah, as if that's what people used it for. As if people used the 'In Private' setting on their browser to search for presents for their wives. Whatever. But he still felt uneasy installing what was essentially a portal into an almost unimaginable world. It was as though, on the one hand, he really had no desire to put this on his computer, but at the same time felt strangely compelled to investigate further. He felt as though he was a child heading into a dark cave that he had just discovered deep in the woods.

His hand wavered as he nervously held the cursor over the button marked *Download*. He took a deep breath and clicked the left mouse button. The automatic installer started to work; he skimmed through the disclaimer, barely reading any of it, and clicked *Install*. After a few windows popped onto the screen mentioning something about configuring and settings and so on, most of which he ignored, it said installation had been completed.

Joe sat back in the chair and looked at the new onion-shaped icon on his desktop. He knew that the temptation would be too great, his curiosity would inevitably get the better of him. And with the whole day at home on his own, what better time to start than right now?

5

S winging around the corner, the black BMW pulled up outside a run-down terraced house. Where other areas of the suburbs had shed their poverty-stricken image thanks to the new money of young, successful, trendy types eager to buy up property close to the city centre, this part of town remained a place that few would call desirable.

Saeed opened his car door and placed his designer sunglasses in the central console. As he exited, he grabbed the dark brown leather briefcase laid on the passenger seat. He shut the door and locked it. Even with his reputation, he still wanted to avoid the chance that someone in this dump might be stupid enough to break into or try to steal his car.

He walked to the front gate of the house. A short wall with chipped bricks and graffiti cordoned off the small, overgrown yard, which was more rubbish tip than garden. Even the fridge freezer propped up against the front of the house had become covered in more greenery and foliage than what passed as a flower-bed. Walking up the cracked, weed-ridden footpath, he kicked an empty can of super strength lager out of his way and pressed the doorbell.

As he waited, he admired himself in what little reflection came back from the smoky pane of glass in the middle of the door. The door opened, though a number of chains and security locks stopped it opening any more than a couple of inches.

'It's me, let me in,' said Saeed, quietly.

The chains and locks clinked as the man inside released them and, after quickly glancing up and down the row of houses, Saeed went inside.

Inside the house, the dim lighting cast eerie shadows as it shone through the smoky haze hanging in the air. Loud music pumped through the walls from the floor above. He walked past what would have once been the living room. The television screen was smashed, and the wallpaper peeled off in large chunks. A stained brown sofa sat in front of a glass coffee table covered in beer cans, burnt-up spoons, syringes, and cigarette lighters. On the sofa lay a young girl, barely older than sixteen. She was seemingly unconscious, wearing nothing but white knickers and a soiled white vest top. Her arms were a mess of red scars and scabs, permanent badges of her drug abuse and self-harm.

Saeed smiled. Another broken home, another vulnerable young girl. They were easier to control in this country than back home. Give them a mobile phone and some nice clothes and they start to worship you. They didn't need to be promised much, since whatever it was would almost certainly be better than what they had. And then you had them and there was nothing they could do.

The stairs creaked as he followed the man up into a large bedroom that had been turned into a makeshift office. In the room, his new informal business partner sat on a large, comfortable-looking sofa.

Saeed threw the briefcase down onto the table in front of him. The man stood up, arms outstretched. The display of tattoos showed his standing within his gang and the slashes showed the number of his victims.

'Brother,' said the man, embracing Saeed in a hug.

'Aleksander, my friend,' returned Saeed, before turning to Aleksander's accomplice.

'Saeed, this is my cousin, Janusz.'

Saeed shook his hand and the three men sat down.

At that moment, a door into an adjoining room opened and two men left. They were followed by another young girl, not much older than the one downstairs, wearing only her underwear.

She was crying. Not loudly or dramatically, just sobbing. As she stumbled out of the room, she held out an arm to balance herself against the wall. Amongst the tattoos, bruises, and bright red scars were fresh red pressure marks on her wrists. Bright purple bruises stood out all over her pasty white legs. She slumped against the wall and slid down into a heap. Her head rested on bent knees while her arms crossed in front of her ankles. She rubbed her wrists to try and ease the pain. She continued crying.

'Did they pay?' asked Saeed, staring at the girl with as much compassion as a man examining a delivery of car parts.

'Of course, twenty each. Did you bring the drugs?' replied Aleksander.

Saeed leant forward and opened the briefcase. Inside were small plastic bags containing a variety of drugs, including marijuana, cocaine, and heroin.

As Aleksander reached forward to take one of the bags out, Saeed slammed the briefcase shut.

'Where's my fucking money from the last lot? I know those pathetic children you call dealers have sold it all.'

'Sae, Sae, Sae. I thought we trusted each other,' replied Aleksander.

Janusz sat up tall and leant forward on the sofa.

'You get me drugs and girls,' Aleksander continued. 'I get you money.'

'So where is my money?' replied Saeed, through gritted teeth.

'Tell you what. Why don't you let Janusz look through this little selection that you've brought us, while you have some fun next door,' said Aleksander, reclining back into the sofa, with his arms folded.

Saeed stared at the two men. Aleksander stared back, before glancing in the direction of the girl and holding out his hands.

Pulling the briefcase towards him, Saeed rotated the numbered wheels on the combination. As the clasps flicked open, he turned it back towards them and stood up. Janusz took it and began opening the bags. He dabbed a small amount of the white powder and snorted it up each nostril before looking at Aleksander and nodding.

'I think we should be okay. Go on, have some fun,' said Aleksander, in a mockingly friendly tone.

Saeed walked over towards the girl.

'Get the fuck up,' he said to her.

She groaned in pitiful protest. Saeed grabbed the girl by the hair and dragged her to her feet. She screamed, a mixture of pain, which the alcohol did little to mask, and of fear, which the drugs were now failing to numb. Ignoring her pleas, he threw her onto the grotty, stained, damp bed. As Saeed stood in front of her, unbuttoning his trousers, she turned over, trying to cover her eyes in a futile attempt to hide. He cared little for her ordeal, or what she had just been through; her sobs actually made him feel more powerful. She screamed again as he slammed the door shut.

After ten minutes or so, the door opened and Saeed walked out, tucking his shirt back in and fastening up his trouser button. Behind, the girl lay on the bed semi-unconscious, a pool of blood by her face and another by her crotch.

'Get cleaned up and get this fucking room changed. You'll have customers soon,' said Saeed, as he shut the door behind him.

He went back over to the coffee table and sat down. Aleksander reached into his jacket pocket and pulled out a folded wedge of twenty pound notes, which he tossed onto the table in front of him. Keeping eye contact, Saeed leant forward and picked up the notes.

'Is this some sort of fucking joke, you stupid little Polish prick?' demanded Saeed, as he thumbed through the notes, mentally totting them up as he went. 'There's easily four times this in the suitcase, plus you owe me my cut from the girls.'

'When we sell it, you get more,' replied Aleksander, unperturbed by Saeed's aggression. 'As for the girls, these pointless skanks will be of no use in a week or two. You get us more girls, you get more money.'

'Fuck you, we had a deal. I can get better than this for these drugs,' said Saeed. As he reached forward to snatch the briefcase, Janusz leapt forward, grabbing his right hand, but before the Pole had time to react, Saeed reached into his sock and pulled out a butterfly knife. Deftly spinning it open, he pulled his right arm away and plunged the knife through Janusz' hand, pinning it to the table. Janusz screamed as he pulled the knife out, giving Saeed the time he needed to plant his foot straight into Janusz' face. He collapsed, out cold, onto the floor.

Turning his attention to Aleksander, Saeed walked around the other side of the table and grabbed the man by the lapels, pulling him to his feet.

'Saeed, Saeed, this is not necessary my friend. Don't do something even more stupid, something you will regret,' said Aleksander, keeping a cool and calculating tone.

Saeed swung him around, pinning him against the wall, and stared him coldly in the eyes.

'You have fucked with me for the last time. This is my show now.'

Aleksander winced as Saeed's forehead cracked him on the bridge of his nose, once and then again. Blood ran down his face as the back of his head was smashed against the wall. Aleksander fell to the floor in a heap. Saeed spat on the crumpled body and walked over to Janusz, who had started to come around. He slammed the heel of his boot down on Janusz's stomach and then kicked him in the groin. Janusz writhed in agony.

Opening the small drawer in the coffee table, he pulled out a brick-sized pile of bank notes and placed them in the briefcase. He walked over to Aleksander and knelt down beside him.

'Be grateful that I went easy on you, Aleksander, my friend.'

'Fuck you,' he replied semi-consciously, spluttering specks of blood all over Saeed's white shirt.

Saeed stood up slowly and walked away. He had barely gone two footsteps before he swung around and kicked the prostrate man in the ribs.

'That's for messing up my shirt,' he said, smirking.

As he turned away, he noticed the door into the adjoining room was ajar. He could see the bloodshot, tear-filled eyes of the young girl through the gap. For a moment their stares locked, and he could practically taste the fear, the anguish, the confusion, the total and utter despair. It was just how he liked it. One side of his mouth raised as he snorted a sound of complete contempt for the sorry figure in front of him; he now considered it a waste of his time to even bother intimidating her further.

He left the house, in his own mind, untouchable.

6

Louise sat in the brown paisley armchair in a corner of the living room, whilst a black and white cat curled up on her lap. As her favourite soap opera played on the television, she tapped the overhanging ash from the end of the cigarette into the Coke can ashtray perched on the arm of the chair. A second, ginger cat circled in and out between her ankles, meowing and rubbing its head on her as it went.

'I suppose you all want feeding then?' she said, to no-one in particular, stubbing the cigarette out and heaving her not-insignificant frame out of the armchair. She walked slowly towards the kitchen; the weight that she had acquired in recent years had begun to play havoc with her knees and ankles. As she walked past the sideboard, she peered at the row of photo frames and the pictures of small children inside them. Every time she walked past them, they reminded her just how lonely and quiet the house felt, but it was something that she had been forced to get used to.

As she reached the larder cupboard containing the cat food, three more cats ran in through the flap in the back door, eager for their evening dinner. She spoke to them as if they were people. Some considered cats to be cold and selfish creatures, but to her they were the only ones she could truly call friends.

After filling the bowls, she went and sat back down in the lounge and lit another cigarette. She checked her mobile phone. It was a very basic handset, with none of the bells and whistles of modern 'smart' phones, but it was enough for her. Plus, it was all she could afford with her meagre benefits. No messages. No missed calls. The story of her life in the last few months. She had hated this small town in what felt like the middle of nowhere ever since she moved here.

It had led her to wallow in self-pity; the soap operas on the television offered her a small opportunity of escapism, to pretend she wasn't her for just a short while. She hated some of the characters as if they were real people. She despised how some characters always seemed to come out smelling of roses, regardless of how they treated other people. And that was how she felt, as though she had been treated unfairly. If people only knew how difficult her life was, perhaps they might feel just a little bit sorry for her.

She extinguished the last of the cigarette, shuffled in the seat to get more comfortable, and shut her eyes. Doing nothing but smoking and eating pie all day was tiring work and very soon she dozed off to sleep.

* * *

In the Carpenters Arms, Barry was king, an alpha male among mortals. He had only moved to North Yorkshire about six months ago but had spent so much time in the pub that he had become part of the fixtures. All of the regulars knew that he had previous form. His total lack of discretion mixed with his low intelligence led, after a few strong lagers, to many nights of boasting to anyone within earshot about his tough man credentials.

He liked to speak to people barely a few inches from their faces, his six foot five frame intimidating even the hardiest of drinkers, even when he was trying to be nice to them. Which wasn't very often. He usually had something to moan about, something that had happened to him that just made him angry, like not enough salt on his fish and chips, or too many people in front of him in the queue at the off-licence.

He sat by himself on a bar stool near the pool table. Two men, barely in their twenties, approached the table and placed a pound in the slot.

'Oi, mate. Can't you fucking read?' he snapped at the men, pointing to a small blackboard nearby. On it, in very childish handwriting, was scrawled 'Player 1 – Barry, Player 2 –'.

'So what?' replied one of the men.

'I won the table last match. If you want to play, you got to beat me.'

The two men laughed. 'Says who?'

Barry took a sip of beer and slowly got up from the stool. Shoulders back, chest out, he walked up to the taller of the two men, put his face about two inches away from the man's, and whispered,

'I do.'

The other man thrust his arm in between them and said, 'Fine. Look, we don't want any trouble, just a game of pool. I'll play you.'

Barry turned to face him, his hard features all of a sudden changed to a beaming, slightly psychotic smile.

'Rack them up then.'

He then stood watching in silence as the man proceeded to pot every ball apart from two on his first go. He bent down to take his first shot and fired the white ball straight off the table.

'Fucking hell.'

The men could barely contain their laughter, 'Who the fuck did you beat to win the table, Stephen Hawking?'

Barry snapped. Grabbing his pool cue with both arms, he pushed the man up against the wall, the wooden stick pressed firmly under his chin. The friend tried to grab Barry's arm and pull him away but he was too strong. The noise had prompted the landlord to rush out from behind the bar and try to maintain some order.

'Barry. Just let him go,' the landlord pleaded. 'Look, I've poured you another beer, on the house. Just let the chap go.'

Barry released his grip as the man clutched at his throat.

'Jesus, you've got serious issues,' the man said.

But Barry ignored him and walked off to a quiet table at the other end of the pub, snatching his pint from the bar as he passed.

He sat at the table and drank almost three quarters of the pint in one go. He had missed the taste of lager during his time inside. It had to be lager, none of this real ale nonsense – that was for old people. Reclining in the slightly sticky upholstery of the bench, he stared vacantly at the rest of the pub. This was his domain, his new world, and he would rule it in the only way he knew how.

* * *

Louise stirred as she felt a cat paw stroking the side of her face. As she came to, something felt wrong. She couldn't move her arms; they were pinned to the arms of her chair. And that wasn't a cat stroking her face, it was a gloved finger.

As panic set in, she shook her head and blinked her eyes to try and clear the haziness from her vision. She saw two men with balaclavas holding her tightly by the arms.

Across the room sat another man, gently stroking the cat on his lap. He wore a smart suit, a tie, and shiny black patent leather brogues.

'Hello, Karen,' said the man, gently, his voice sounding almost distinguished, though slightly muffled by the fabric of the balaclava.

Louise's heart pounded and she began to hyper-ventilate, struggling to get the words out. 'My name's not Karen, it's Louise. Louise Simpson. You've got the wrong house. Please, I don't have no money. Take what you want, just don't hurt me.'

The man gently lifted the cat off his lap and placed it on the floor, shooing it away with his hand. He stood up and walked over to the chair.

'We don't want to hurt you, my dear. In fact, we're under strict orders to take extra special care of you.'

'But I'm not this Karen, whoever she is.' She spoke quickly, desperately trying to make herself understood. 'I told you, my name is Louise Simpson. I'm thirty-six years old and I—'

'No, but you're not, are you, Karen?' the man interrupted, with a firm, icy cool calm.

He grabbed her right wrist and turned it over. There on the underside was the faded pink scar of a poorly removed tattoo. '*Charlie 20.05.08*'.

'You are Karen Parker, aren't you? And as much as you can try and hide from your past, the evidence of it is all around you,' said the man. 'Come, my dear. We have a very special reunion to take you to.'

The man stood up and turned to leave as the two men either side placed a hessian bag over her head. Her pointless struggling made no difference. The men just about managed to pick her up and quickly bundled her into the back of the black transit van waiting outside.

* * *

As time was called at the Carpenters Arms, Barry downed the last of his pint, collected his coat and phone, and stumbled towards the exit.

'Sorry,' he said to the landlord in a slightly childish voice, smacking the palm of his hand down onto the bar. 'Sorry about earlier. It won't happen again, I promise. Scout's honour.'

He tried to make a three-figured Scout salute, but just stared at his hand wondering precisely which three fingers it was supposed to be. Eventually he gave up and just gave an exaggerated full salute accompanied by,

'See ya tomorrow.'

'It had better not happen again, Barry. I can't have you scaring away my punters,' replied the landlord.

But Barry had already staggered to the exit, waving a hand over his shoulder as he pushed the door open. As the cold night air hit him, the mixture of strong lager and whisky chasers zapped his ability to focus on anything.

He wandered down the street, weaving from side to side on the pavement. Bumping into lampposts and litter bins, he flung his fists around in thin air, determined to fend off his imaginary assailants.

A little farther down the road he walked past a side road leading to a disused warehouse. Parked down the street he could see a black transit van and was just able to make out the blurred form of an old man kneeling down by the front wheel. The man was struggling and making sighing sounds as he tried to release the wheel nuts.

'You alright, geez?' Barry slurred loudly down the alleyway.

'Oh yes. I've got a flat tyre and I can't get these blasted nuts loosened,' replied the man.

Barry approached. As he came into focus, the man appeared to be in his late fifties, with a swept back silvery grey bouffant hair style. He reminded Barry a little of his father. The beatings, the drunkenness, the shouting, the swearing all came back to him from the depths of his drink-addled memory. But it wasn't his father, and for some reason he felt compelled to help.

'Here you go, Gramps. Let me have a go of that,' said Barry, taking the wrench.

As he knelt down, his drunken hands struggled to aim right, the wrench clattering against the hubcap. He managed to catch one, but as he did the tyre came into focus.

Slowly he stood up. 'Not sure what your problem is, geezer, but that tyre looks fine to—'

Before he could finish his sentence, he felt a large cloth cover his face. He tried to fight, but his arms were pinned around his back and he was pushed towards the back of the van by a forceful knee pressing into the base of his spine. The three assailants increased the pressure on his limbs as he started to thrash around, but slowly the chemical on the cloth began to make him even more drunk and drowsy. His scream was muffled, and eventually, he could no longer fight it. The men laid him down in the back of the van, got in, and slammed the door behind them.

As the van began to drive away, the last thing he saw was the old man leaning over him. 'Mark Rankin. Have we got a surprise for you.'

The words just had time to register before, finally, he lost consciousness.

7

Alistair Goodfellow leant against the oak panelling of the bar and poured a large slug of 1990 Macallan single malt into each of the cut crystal tumblers that sat on the felt-lined top. He dropped a large ice cube into each.

'No ice for me,' said Jarvis, from across the room. 'You'd have to be some sort of utter philistine to even consider diluting a classic vintage like that with ice.'

It was this kind of unrelenting pedantry that Alistair admired in Jarvis, and also what made him the single best computer expert he had ever met.

'Well I prefer it,' replied Alistair, fishing the ice cube out of Jarvis' tumbler. 'And I paid good money for this bottle, so I intend to enjoy it however I see fit.'

'It's your shot,' Jarvis offered.

Alistair took a small sip from his glass and collected his cue. It had always been his dream to own a house large enough to have its own classically styled billiard room and now he did. He had survived the early boom–and-bust years during the explosion of internet technology companies in the early 2000s and sold his online mobile phone company for a huge sum. It was never publically disclosed how much he received for his company, but when asked, his stock response was 'Nine figures, and the first digit isn't a one or a two'.

He wandered around the table, his hands sliding along the smooth dark mahogany rails of his championship snooker table as he eyed the position in which Jarvis had left him. His colleague was a far stronger tactician than he was ball potter, and Alistair was left with very little option other than to attempt a long red into the far corner.

'Ha, terrible shot,' said Jarvis, enthusiastically, as the red ball missed the corner pocket by a good six inches.

Alistair didn't really care though. While he wasn't in the middle of taking a shot he could sit back and admire this work of art of a room, which he had lovingly designed practically from scratch. The high vaulted ceiling, the enormous chandelier that lit the playing surface, the huge bay windows that were large enough to sit in and admire the view down the long winding driveway which snaked away from the main entrance to the house. Of the dozens of rooms in this house, this was his favourite and where he felt most at ease with the world.

Jarvis was down taking his next shot when Alistair noticed the bright lights through the front window. They were just small specks at the moment and had stopped briefly. He picked up a small black remote control from the mantelpiece and pointed it at the wall behind the bar. A large oak panel separated to reveal a huge plasma screen divided into a display of twelve CCTV monitors, each covering different areas of his huge estate. He clicked the cursor over the monitor displaying the entrance gate by the road and the twelve screens became one. The enormous gold A.G. monogram that graced the centre of the two wrought iron gates split in half as the entrance opened, and in drove two black transit vans.

At that precise moment, the double mahogany doors into the billiard room swung open and Gilbert, Alistair's part-butler and part-personal assistant, ran in, breathless.

'They're back,' he said to the two men. 'But there might be a problem.'

* * *

The three men talked as they walked down the seemingly endless corridor from the billiard room to the entrance hall. Usually, Alistair liked to take in the expensive works of art that adorned the walls in between the vast ornate mirrors, or to admire one of the priceless sculptures that lined the wall like some sort of guard of honour. But not this time.

'How can there be a problem?' asked Alistair. 'We planned this meticulously. Even to the point where, despite travelling two hundred miles from opposite ends of the country, the two vans pull into my driveway at precisely the same time.'

'Everything was textbook,' replied Gilbert. 'We tracked them down, we captured them, we were in and out in no time at all. The local CCTVs were taken care of and the handover went like clockwork.'

'So what's the problem?'

'She has an ankle tag.'

The three men stopped.

'Is that it?' asked Jarvis, adjusting his glasses.

'Well you can't just rip them off, can you?' replied Gilbert, somewhat offended. 'That's if the police haven't already worked out that she's missing and tracked her location to here. I've read about that trilat... trilater ...'

'Trilateration,' interjected Alistair.

'Yes, that thing. I thought we were going to wait until she had it removed?'

'No need,' said Alistair, placing a comforting, brotherly arm around his shoulder. 'See we have the greatest technology-slash-gizmo-type-fellow right here. Jarvis devised a way of cloning electronic tags eons ago. We leave our tag at the house and sync it with the one on her ankle. Then before we leave, we fry her one with a large dose of electromagnetic awesomeness. So, all that the police will have seen on their monitoring screens was a very short blip, a fraction of a second, and then the usual transmission will have resumed. That's if they even noticed. Which I doubt they will.'

'Right, fine. Well, it would have been nice to have been informed about this.'

'Sorry, but we needed to work on it in secret,' replied Jarvis. 'The fewer people who knew about it the better. You know how it works. Anyway, we were keeping an eye on the transmissions from the control room just to make sure that everything went smoothly.'

Gilbert nodded. He had become very protective of Alistair and the organisation over the last couple of years and had come to see himself as some sort of 'consigliere', a voice of reason amongst the fervent activity that went on in this place. The last thing that he wanted was for this project to be put to an end because of some stupid little careless oversight.

But then he should have known better than to doubt for even a second that Alistair Goodfellow would risk destroying everything he had striven to build. For the last few years, this had become his raison d'être, and his success and vast wealth afforded him the luxury of being able to attract the best people. The Brotherhood was growing in strength and reach and would very soon be a force to be reckoned with.

The three men carried on walking until they reached the top of the grand staircase. Outside, the gravel crunched under the wheels of the two vans. A swathe of light flew across the walls, illuminating the vast entrance lobby as the vehicles swung around the yard out front.

'Well, gentlemen,' said Alistair, putting an arm around each. 'Let's go and meet our guests.'

* * *

'Shouldn't we keep them separate?' asked Jarvis, as they walked out of the house. 'It would make for a much better show if it was all one massive surprise.'

Alistair stood on the gravel driveway, stroking his goatee in deep contemplation, shuffling in his velvet and gold Hermès loafers as the light wind swept up his silk dressing gown.

'Yes, good idea,' he said, finally. 'Get her out first and put her in the holding room in the east wing.'

Jarvis went over to the furthest van and motioned for the window to be opened. He leant in to tell the driver the plan and request that they hold their position for the time being.

'Suits me,' said the driver. 'This bloke's absolutely sparko anyway.'

The driver-side door of the other van opened and out stepped a large-set man, well over six foot tall, with shoulders like an ox. Out of the passenger side climbed a smaller, older man. He walked purposefully over towards the three men and held out his hand.

'Alistair, good to see you. We have your merchandise.' He spoke with a distinguished, gentlemanly tone.

'Thank you, Eric,' replied Alistair, as he shook the man's hand.

Eric Wolfe, ex-security services and an expert in breaking and entering, smiled back. The shock of grey hair swept back over his head revealed wrinkles across his tanned forehead. Years of experience from his work in covert operations had found its perfect partner in a man of Alistair Goodfellow's moral standing. And with the resources now at his disposal, his new company had become a trusted part of the Brotherhood.

'I trust you took care of her?' Alistair asked.

'Of course,' came the almost indignant reply. 'I would have considered it a grave dereliction of duty if she had arrived here with even a hair on her head harmed.'

'Indeed, how rude of me. And the tag?'

'It worked like a charm. That kid really does know his stuff. As far as the police are concerned, she's probably just sat on her fat lazy arse watching television. I was tempted to attach it to one of her cats, but they'd probably become suspicious if they traced her to a neighbour's flowerbed.'

The men laughed and motioned to the large man to open the back of the van. He reached inside and grabbed the pasty, chubby arm that was sticking out from underneath a blanket. As the woman struggled, he leant further inside and, with an almighty grunt, heaved her rotund frame out through the back doors.

'Christ al-fucking-mighty. I think my back's gone,' the man groaned, his grasp of English belying the thick Eastern European accent with which he spoke.

'Language!' shouted Alistair. 'There's a lady present.'

'Lady my arse. You should have heard some of the language coming out of her mouth all the way here; it might as well have been a rugby-playing squaddie in the back,' he replied, as he handcuffed her arms behind her back.

The woman stood fixed to the spot, shivering, the hessian sack still on her head, cloaking her in darkness.

'What's going on?' she stuttered. 'Where am I? Who are you people?'

'Slow down, slow down,' laughed Alistair. 'So many questions. Well, it's quite simple you see. We're the Brotherhood of the Righteous. You're at our house. And you're going to be the very special guest on our little gameshow.'

She started crying, and a trickle of warm wetness ran down her bright pink jogging bottoms.

'Why? I didn't do nothing. You can't do this.'

'My dear, we'll take good care of you until it's time. After that though, well, I can't promise you anything,' said Alistair, patting her on the head. 'Take her to the holding room in the east wing, but do not remove the cover from her head until she's there.'

The large man took her by the arm and marched her into the house.

'Pathetic,' said Alistair, shaking his head. 'Even after everything she's done, she's still utterly devoid of any comprehension of anything. As though this is all just one massive mistake and *she's* the victim.'

'Indeed,' said Jarvis, nodding in agreement. 'I think she might attract quite a large audience though.'

The empty van drove off to the workshop at the side of the house, where it would be resprayed and its number plates changed.

'Right, let's have a look at our second volunteer.'

Jarvis motioned to the other vehicle, which reversed to meet them. Out of the front seat climbed another man with slicked back grey hair, almost identical to Eric.

'Stan my man, good to see you,' said Alistair, holding out a hand.

Eric's twin brother, Stan, reciprocated the handshake. Along with his brother he had vast experience in covert and 'black' operations from their time serving together in the security services. Being twins also added an extra dimension to their ability to deceive and evade, something which was very useful in the line of work in which they now found themselves.

'Evening, boss,' he replied. 'We've got ourselves a feisty one here.'

'Is he secure?'

'Of course he is, what do you take me for?'

'OK, let's get him out.'

Two more burly goons opened the back doors to the transit van, which was the cue for the prisoner inside to start thrashing around wildly, kicking his legs at everything and nothing. Once they eventually managed to grab a leg each, the two men pulled the body from the van. The large passenger landed face first in the gravel and shouted a muffled profanity through the sack that covered his face. Once a knee was planted firmly in the small of his back, he stopped thrashing around and let out a painful cry.

Alistair knelt down next to him and caught sight of the fastenings that held his wrists together.

'Cable ties? I thought you said he was secure,' he asked, dubiously.

'Of course he's secure,' responded Stan. 'There is nothing, repeat nothing, in this world that cannot be secured with cable ties.'

'Well I get that cables can, obviously. But this is a rather violent six foot stocky man we're talking about. Couldn't you have used cuffs like a normal person?'

'God, you're so boringly practical, aren't you?'

'How do you think I got all this? Use cuffs next time, please. We need to keep them apart, so put this one in the north wing. And put some bloody cuffs on him,' said Alistair, adopting a more managerial tone.

The two men hoisted him to his feet and made sure they kept a firm grip on both his arms. Stan led the way into the house.

'It really is freaky how similar they look, isn't it?' said Jarvis, as he sidled up to Alistair. 'Which one do you think is the evil twin? There's always an evil one.'

Alistair looked him in the eye. 'They both are.'

As the remaining van started up and drove around the side of the house to join the first, the two men walked back into the house and shut the huge wooden front doors behind them.

'Gather everyone in the drawing room, Jarvis,' said Alistair. 'I think a celebration is in order.'

8

'Are we going to talk about this?' asked Ellie, as she slid a plate of pork chop, peas, and potatoes in front of Joe.

'Talk about what?' replied Joe, taking a mouthful of cabernet sauvignon and trying hard to look as though he had no idea what she was talking about.

'God, you can be so fucking annoying sometimes. You know precisely what. We're supposed to be getting married in a couple of months and you haven't spoken to me for the best part of a week.'

'What, when you stormed out of the house and didn't come back until the following day you mean?' said Joe, as though he had only just that second worked out what she meant.

'You can't talk. You'd only just stumbled back into the house from not coming home that night as well,' Ellie replied. 'And anyway, it's not as if—'

She was cut off by the familiar, yet all of a sudden infuriating, *beep beep, beep beep*, of a text message arriving on Joe's phone. She sighed and looked away as Joe picked his phone up and held it in front of his face. He sniggered at whatever it was he had just read, put the phone back on the table, and took a mouthful of chop.

As Ellie chased a potato around the plate with her fork, she raised her gaze to meet his.

'As I was saying, it's not as if I haven't mentioned this to you on god knows how many occasions. You know exactly how I feel about the amount you go out with Billy and those other dickheads that you call friends.'

'Don't call them dickheads. And don't try and blame everything on Billy like you always do. It's not like he's my boss.'

'But he is a tosser. I can't believe it's simply coincidence that every time you don't manage to make it home, you're always with him,' she replied, trying to hide her increasing frustration by keeping a relatively soft tone. 'I've asked so many times for a bit of respect—'

'I do fucking well respect you,' he protested, but the severity of Ellie's crossed arms and pout suggested she believed otherwise.

Beep, beep! Beep, beep!

'Sorry,' said Joe, picking up his phone once more and laughing again at the new text.

'See what I mean? It's just ludicrous. It's like trying to have a civilised conversation with a demented five-year-old.'

'What?' replied Joe, incredulously. 'You get texts way more than me.'

'Yes, but I ignore them when we're trying to have a reasonably important conversation about the state of our relationship. Anyway, it's not just the going out thing. You seem to be spending more and more time in the garage.'

'Jeez, that's what we had it converted for, isn't it? To spend time in it?'

'Yes, of course,' she replied. 'But whenever you're in there, you're sat at the computer desk. If I come in you quickly shut whatever windows you had open. And I looked up that TOR browser thing you installed the other day. Jesus Christ, Joe! That's what fucking paedos use!'

'Oh, so now you think I'm a paedo as well then?' said Joe, in the belief that, if he slammed his cutlery down either side of the plate in order to ram home the sheer indignation that he felt, this argument was in the bag.

Weirdly, it didn't seem to have worked. 'Well, are you?'

'Of course I'm fucking not.'

'So what the hell do you use it for then?'

'Just stuff.'

'Stuff?'

'Yes stuff.'

'Like what?'

He knew it was true; paedophiles did use the browser, as did drug dealers, supposed hitmen, human experimenters, the worst kind of conspiracy theorists, and the odd cannibal. But he used it to explore the boundaries of creativity, to experience the visceral head-fuck of what passed for entertainment down there. He'd seen independent horror movies that made the latest Hollywood blockbuster scary films seem like a Jane Austen novel. The CCTV footage he could access was of real life suicides, murders, accidental deaths, rather than teenagers crushing their testicles on railings after falling off a skateboard or cats falling into a fish bowl. He was opening his eyes and opening his mind to real life and real creativity. The way he saw it, this was only for the truly enlightened. The Google-fed zombies of the comfortable surface world were probably not ready to have their minds messed with in this manner. No matter how hard he could try and explain it to Ellie, he doubted she would ever understand.

'Just, you know, stuff. I doubt you'd ever understand.'

'So porn then.'

'If that's what you want to believe then fine.' He was getting bored of this now.

'Want to believe?' she stressed, sarcastically. 'How could you possibly think that I *want* to believe you are watching *anything* on this 'deep web'? It makes my skin crawl.'

Beep, beep! Beep, beep!

'Aaaargh!' she screamed, clutching her hair in both hands and then grabbing Joe's phone before he could pick it up. 'Great, it's Billy. 'Got some ales. Be round about nine-ish. See you then you big fucking poof',' she read aloud. 'Well if he's coming here, I'm going out. That way you two can cuddle up in front of the computer, jerking each other off to whatever filth you're watching on your new nonce channel.'

She threw the phone in his lap and collected up the half-eaten plates of food from the table. Joe placed the phone on the table and rubbed his eyes with his hands.

'Look, this is ridiculous. I promise you, I am not a paedophile, nor would I ever look at that sort of thing. If you really think that I am – no, actually – if you really think that there is even the slightest possibility that I might be, then you shouldn't be fucking marrying me,' he said, quietly.

At last a breakthrough. No-one in their right minds would either want to knowingly marry a sex-offender or believe that they were stupid enough to marry one without knowing it. Ellie put the plates on the worktop then came and sat on his lap.

'No, of course I don't think you are. I just read some pretty horrible things about that deep web stuff. And we seem to be spending less time together. We need to make more of an effort together, if we're going to make this marriage work. But if he's coming here tonight, I'm going round to Helen's.'

She snuggled into him and he reciprocated her cuddle by rubbing her back with his right hand. He looked over her shoulder, picked up the phone in his left hand and, as carefully and quietly as he could, texted back,

Cool.

She fell on top of him in a sweaty naked heap, breathing heavily as he lay there making circles on her back with his finger.

She rolled off to lie next to him.

'I love you,' she whispered in his ear.

'I love you too,' he replied, staring, exhausted, at the ceiling.

After a few minutes of lying next to each other in restful silence, she sat upright and grabbed her dressing gown from beside the bed.

'Hopefully that will take care of any need you had to go looking at grown up material with Billy later.' She leant down and kissed him on the forehead. 'I'm going for a shower.'

As she walked out of the bedroom, Joe picked up his phone from the bedside table and pressed in his four digit passcode, *8008*. It always made him chuckle inwardly. He swiped across to *Apps* and then across two more screens until he got to *File Commander*. He opened the app and swiped across another screen until he found the file called *Work*. Pressing on *Work*, he scrolled past the PDF documents and spreadsheets, a couple of blank screens, until he arrived at the grey and purple onion icon for OrBot, the mobile app instance of Tor. As he clicked on it, he noticed a small red circle with a *1* in it bobbing up and down at the top of the screen. He had synced his mobile home page to a deep web message board that he had begun visiting. It was like a marketplace where people could advertise their sites, services, and worse. It also provided forums where people could post links to other like-minded visitors. He had once made the mistake of inadvertently clicking on a forum called '*True Love Doesn't Wait*'. It only needed the first two or three thread titles for him to realise that this wasn't somewhere he really wanted to be.

He dragged the red circle down. Usually, the icon would indicate a private message or a profile update or something similar. But in this world it meant that a new post had been added in the main forum. As the forum opened up on his screen, the new thread flashed at the top, entitled '*TRATD*'. He clicked into the thread and it simply posted a link, *http://tratd39058nfdn.onion*, with a statement, *Access 1 XBT*.

He quickly exited and loaded up Google, typing in *XBT*. The top result was from a currency exchange website with the title '*XBT – Bitcoin rates, news and tools*'. Clicking on the link, it brought up a page with a drop down menu to convert bitcoins into various other currencies. After selecting GBP – British Pound, he pressed the *Convert Now* button and up came the result, *1 XBT = 667.92GBP*.

'Bugger me,' he whispered to himself. It seemed a lot. But for some reason the idea of spending over six hundred pounds to access an anonymous website that he had absolutely no idea about was still tempting.

He switched back to the thread, which had already received close to thirty replies, mostly simply stating *Done*.

Hearing the shower turn off and the door to the bathroom open, he quickly took a screenshot of the thread, closed everything down on his phone, and put it back on the bedside table.

Ellie sauntered back into the bedroom with a towel wrapped up around her body, drying her short blonde bob with another. Joe stood up and collected another towel from the radiator. Before he could walk out of the room, Ellie stood in the doorway, blocking his exit. She reached up and grabbed the frame, allowing the towel to slip off on to the floor. Joe had always loved her body, and her recent interest in yoga had made it even more toned and desirable.

'Just remember,' she said, staring straight at him. 'This is yours. It should be all the 'adult entertainment' you ever need!'

Joe lassoed his towel around her waist, dragged her from the door, and pressed her naked body against his.

'Get off me,' she protested, feebly. 'I'm all clean and you stink.'

'You love it really,' he replied, softly. 'Go on, you'd better get ready. My dickhead friend will be here soon and I'm sure Helen's already opened a bottle of prosecco that'll be warm before she's had the chance to tell about her latest failed relationship with someone from work.'

'Don't be nasty about her,' replied Ellie. 'Come to think of it though, she did mention something about a bloke called Tim from her accounts department.'

'Well there you go,' said Joe, as he slid past her. 'I'm going for a shower. Have a nice evening.'

They kissed a final time before going their separate ways for the evening. But as soon as she heard the shower start up and the door to the cubicle close, Ellie picked up his phone and swiped the screen to unlock it. She always cringed at his immaturity every time she put his passcode in. The phone lit up with the screenshot he had taken of the forum.

Access 1XBT,.onion. None of this made any sense. She grabbed her own phone and quickly brought up a new Google page. Slowly, she started typing the web address into the search field, double checking the seemingly random string of letters and numbers. Pressing the magnifying glass icon, she waited for the buffering to stop. The Wi-Fi was always rubbish up in the bedroom. After a couple of seconds, the result appeared on the screen: *Your search - http://tratd39058nfdn.onion - did not match any documents.*

She thought it was a little weird, but was at least relieved not to find some hideous, unimaginable website at the end of it. After dressing, she left the house slightly more relaxed about what he may or may not be getting up to.

9

Finally, the doorbell rang. Joe opened it to find an outstretched fist in his face, at about mouth level. He jolted back slightly in fear that he was about to be mugged on his doorstep. Then he saw that the fist was in fact grasping a bright orange carrier bag, clinking with the unmistakable chime of ale bottles.

'Evening, fuckface,' said the voice behind the bag, as Billy barged past Joe into the hallway.

'Nice to see you too,' replied Joe, as Billy started loading bottles into the fridge. 'What took you so long?'

'I was watching one of those baking competition programmes that have become so inexplicably popular recently. Normally I don't watch that shit, but I was just flicking through the channels and there was this proper fucking tasty bird on one of the teams. I think they were paramedics or something,' said Billy, as he poured himself one of the beers.

'Even so, that doesn't really sound like your kind of thing.'

'It's not. But they had these judges who took the competition so seriously that I found myself compelled to watch it just to see what kind of bullshit they'd come up with next. I mean, if I ever found myself spouting some of the crap they were coming out with, especially the blokes, I would seriously question my masculinity. "The fondant filling in these truffles is far too sweet for my liking", "Are you trying to upset me? I can clearly see a join between the two halves of my chocolate spheres", "If there's one thing I hate, it's not enough hundreds and thousands on my fairy cakes". Fucking get a life, they're just cakes. Although one thing I did learn is that apparently macaroons and macarons are two different things. Who knew?'

'Or cared? Fascinating stuff. I'll make sure I won't look out for it next week,' replied Joe, disinterested.

'So I see that you've been making yourself very much at home in the deep web then?' asked Billy, as the two made their way into the newly converted garage. 'I told you that once you'd tried it you'd want more.'

Joe pulled the black leather office chair away from the computer desk. He moved the mouse backwards and forwards across the desktop, and the large monitor of his all-in-one PC turned itself on to the log-on screen.

'Grab one of the bar stools from down the end.'

'Thanks a lot. I'm the guest and you give me the uncomfortable chair,' replied Billy, placing his beer down.

Joe was too busy quickly clicking through all the icons and links he had saved to answer. Eventually, he arrived at the message board he'd looked at earlier on his phone.

'So what is it you wanted me to see?' asked Billy.

'It's on here,' said Joe, speaking as he stared directly at the screen, clicking through various links. 'Well it was. Where the fuck's it gone?'

'Where's what gone?'

'There was a thread on here. It said hardly anything, just a web address and a price. Barely an hour before you got here.'

Billy slouched on the uncomfortable stool, trying to work out a way to prop his head up with one arm and hold his beer in the other.

'So what? A thread goes up and then gets taken down, it must happen all the time.'

'No, this looked different,' replied Joe, still hunting around the various forums trying to find it. 'It just said that access was one bitcoin and loads of people saying 'DONE'.'

'You know that one bitcoin is the best part of six hundred quid, right?' asked Billy.

Joe turned and looked at him. 'Seven actually. Well, six hundred and sixty-seven to be precise. That's why it looks good.

Also, if it only stayed for a short time … Come on, don't you want to see what it is?'

Billy was taken aback by the slightly sinister grin on Joe's face and was starting to wonder whether it had been a good idea to introduce him to the browser.

'Ah, hang on!' said Joe, excitedly. 'I took a screen dump of the address on my phone.'

'You installed OrBot on your phone? And the Pidgin messenger? Bloody hell, I didn't realise you would take it all this seriously.'

'Right. You read this address out and I'll type it in,' said Joe, handing Billy the phone. He started typing as Billy read out the seemingly random list of letters and numbers. 'OK, let's see where this takes us,' he said, as he hit the Enter key. As soon as he pressed it, the screen went black.

The two looked at each other. After five seconds or so, a small box appeared in the centre of the screen with the words *Wallet ID* above.

'Is that it?' asked Joe. 'What are we supposed to do here?'

'It's asking for your wallet ID so it can connect to your bitcoin exchange for you to authorise the transfer,' replied Billy.

'I don't have a wallet ID.'

'You need to sign up with a bitcoin exchange or wallet provider. Then you get your wallet and you can purchase the coins through them, which are then applied to it. But it's not a quick process, some can take over twenty-four hours to verify.'

'Bollocks. Have you got one?' asked Joe.

Billy held his hands up and spun nervously on his stool. 'Yes I have, but there's no fucking way I'm putting my details in there. We don't even know what the hell it is.'

Joe was starting to look disappointed. 'Come on, I'll transfer the real money to your account to cover the bitcoin. Right now. I'll do it now on PayPal. Plus a bit.'

'No way.'

'Don't be a pussy. I thought you said these bitcoins are anonymous? You put your wallet ID in and do the transfer and I'll transfer you eight hundred pounds this instant.'

Billy nearly choked on his mouthful of beer, spitting half of it over the desk in the process. 'Fuck me, you really are getting into this, aren't you? You do realise that there could be anything, *anything*, on the other side of this?'

But Joe wasn't paying attention. He had already opened up a new browser window, logged on to his bank account, and started inputting a new transfer for £800.00.

'Just give me your account number and sort code. You know you want to. What is it the kids say? YOLO!'

'It just sounds weird when you say it though. Fine. Here you go,' he said, resigning himself to losing at least one of his hard-earned bitcoins as he handed over his debit card. 'But, we only go on and view this thing from your computer, your house. Anything bad comes of this, I don't want any part of it.'

'Whatever,' replied Joe, hitting confirm on the transfer screen. 'There, funds transferred.' He closed the banking window and went back to the black screen.

'I can't believe you paid that much money to me just like that, as though you're lending me a fiver. Ellie will absolutely do her nut if she finds out what you're doing,' said Billy.

'Who are you, my mum all of a sudden? Anyway, she won't find out, it's my personal account,' replied Joe, standing up out of the chair and motioning for Billy to move.

'Ooo, do I get the comfortable chair now? I am honoured,' said Billy, as he placed his beer down on the desk and moved out of his stool.

Joe stood behind the chair. His heart was now beating quite fast and he began to bite the skin on his thumb, a nervous little tick that always showed he was worried.

'Are you alright?' asked Billy. 'We don't have to do this.'

'Just put the wallet ID in,' replied Joe, impatiently.

'Alright, calm down,' said Billy, as he pulled a small piece of paper out of his real-world wallet. He started typing, a mixture of small letters, capital letters, numbers, symbols. Joe wouldn't be able to memorise it even if he tried. 'Shit, wait a second.'

Billy stopped abruptly and started rifling around in the desk drawer.

'What?'

'Well I heard somewhere that it's a good idea to cover the webcam,' he replied, tearing a small piece of paper from a notepad and sticking it over the small lens in the centre of the top edge of the screen with a piece of tape. 'It's just a precaution, but apparently there's a small risk that people at the other end somewhere in the world can hack into the webcam software and view you on their screen. Then that's your anonymity down the shitter.'

Joe chewed harder, to the point where he started to draw blood from the side of his thumb. Billy typed in the last of his wallet I.D. and hit the enter key. The display changed to a very basic white screen, with two entry fields, one titled *Quantity* and one titled *Key*. Billy typed *1* in the first box and then proceeded to copy another long string of letters and numbers from the same slip of paper into the second box.

'Here we go, seven hundred quid into the unknown,' he whispered, as he hit the 'confirm' button.

Joe took a deep breath and stared at the screen.

Awaiting authorisation.

One minute passed, then another. Billy drummed his fingers on the desktop and Joe paced around the pool table, rolling balls around it with his hands.

'Why does it take so long?' asked Joe. 'I thought you had the bitcoins in your wallet?'

'I have, but bitcoins don't work like regular currencies,' replied Billy, folding his arms and swivelling the chair to face Joe. 'They don't exist in the real sense of a 'coin'. They're more just a record of a transaction. A starting address, a destination address, and a quantity. I don't really understand the ins and outs of it.'

'But what's the delay for?'

'From what I gather, every time you put a transaction in, it adds it to a public ledger. There's then a bunch of nerdy computer types who check all the transactions at their own computers and authorise them. They're called miners. It's all a bit beyond me. Anyway, I'm going for a shit whilst this is doing its thing.' Billy got up and walked out of the garage, to the bathroom.

After opening another bottle of ale from the fridge, Joe sat down and stared at the screen. The long wait had allowed his heart rate to return to normal, and he was now becoming slightly bored. It also wasn't helping that Billy had left the door open and the silence in the garage was being broken by a loud cacophony of exaggerated straining noises, splashes, and paper rustling.

Just then, the page changed back to the black screen with a message: *Thank you. The Brotherhood looks forward to your attendance at our next event. 2 bitcoins to view. Friday 24th July 21:00pm GMT. http://tRaTd84uhg0f023785h.onion*

'Billy!' he shouted out of the doorway. 'Get your fat arse back in here.'

'That was quick, I've not finished yet,' he shouted back, grabbing handfuls of toilet paper.

Joe stared at the screen, trying to assimilate all the information, or rather the lack of it. For over six hundred pounds he had expected a little more. He hit the Print Screen button on the keyboard and copied the screenshot into an email. Billy came back in and stared at the screen.

'Is that it? Two bitcoins to view. View what and who the fuck are the Brotherhood?' he asked, somewhat despairing at the notion that he had just paid a bitcoin simply for the privilege of spending another two. 'Look, I'm not spending any more of my money on this. That's nearly one and a half grand. Save your money, or put it on Croatia to beat Spain. At four to one against, you'd be five grand up if they win. You're on your own now, buddy.'

Taking another photo on his phone just in case, Joe turned to Billy. 'See you on Friday then, my shout. Make sure you bring some ales, but don't tell anyone else about this. I'd better sort myself out one of those wallets then.'

10

Pete Harris pulled the chair away from his desk, dropped a copy of the Daily Mail on his keyboard, and looked around the office. It had been nearly two years since he last even set foot in this building, let alone this office. The force had kept him on the payroll in a 'consultancy role' during his sabbatical, but it amounted to little more than a couple of telephone calls every other month to keep the Inland Revenue happy, and left him unfamiliar with the new day-to-day workings of the unit.

His colleague, Grace Brooks, approached with two white polystyrene cups, steam rising from the coffee, which would be too hot to drink for at least ten minutes.

She handed one to him. 'Feel a bit strange being back after so long?' she said, putting her hand on his arm; in a caring, friendly manner, nothing more.

'A little,' he replied. 'I'm sure it'll be just like riding a bike. Thanks for the coffee.'

He sat down at the desk and turned on the bank of three twenty-four inch monitors that spread across his desk. As the PC whirred into its start-up routine, he carefully placed the cup down on the coaster. *World's Best Dad* adorned the top in a childish scribble, with two small stick figures underneath. He stared at it. It had been with him ever since his transfer to the unit and frequently provided him a brief mental respite from some of the tough, soul-destroying content that he was forced to endure in the line of duty.

It made him realise that he was a father first and foremost, and he found that this mindset helped him switch off when he left work and easily switch back to just being 'Dad' when he arrived home.

During his time in the C.I.D., his skill and patience in monitoring website activity, coupled with a sneaky skill in hacking that he had developed during his time at university, had won him many cases. Very soon, he had come to the attention of the Metropolitan Police Force's Cyber Crime Unit. He was offered a transfer and, with a young child plus another on the way, it was an offer he hadn't been able to turn down. This new work came naturally to him; there was just something about the way people worked and acted online that he understood.

The internet had changed since he first sat at a yellowing grey IBM personal computer in his university's 'IT suite', navigating the infant super highway on an apparently cutting-edge Netscape browser. The current web was unrecognisable from its early incarnation; it had grown organically and exploded into the single most important facet of everyday life. And he had grown with it. But as with everything ingrained in everyday consciousness, the web was abused, and it was now his job to stop people from doing just that.

He felt strong hands on each shoulder, which began to give a deep muscle massage.

'Down a bit,' he said. 'That's it, just there.'

Without looking, he knew that it was Detective Chief Inspector Robert Smith, the man who had essentially head-hunted him into his current position and had been a huge source of support during the last few months.

'Pete,' he said, in his cigarette-hardened voice. 'It's good to have you back.'

'It's good to be back, sir,' replied Pete. 'I just want to get back into the swing of things as quickly as I can.'

'Excellent. How's Olivia doing?'

'Coping. Now she's started school, things are a lot easier. She still has her moments, but she's getting there slowly.'

'Good. Anything you need, you let me know. In the meantime, take a bit to get reacquainted with everything. There are a few new procedural protocols in place since you were here last, but

I'll have Grace go over them with you. Anyway, as I said, good to have you back. I'm going for a fag.'

'Thank you, sir.'

As the chief inspector walked out of the office, Pete turned to look at the computer screens, moving his mouse around the desktop to refresh his memory as to where everything was.

'Right, let's see what's been going on whilst we've been away,' he whispered to himself.

'Started talking to ourself now, have we?' said Grace, as she pulled a chair up to his desk and sat down. 'This is the new program we've had installed. It pulls cases that are being investigated across all forces throughout the whole country. Everything that gets flagged as potentially having some sort of cyber element to it will appear in this. That way we can cross-reference much easier with anything that we're working on here.'

'Cool,' he replied. 'Anything interesting going on?'

'The usual mix of World of Warcraft players having their virtual battle-axes stolen, old age pensioners sending money to the widows of Nigerian politicians, and teenage girls reporting their boyfriends for posting those nude pictures that he took whilst she was pissed up on cherry Lambrini. Mixed in, of course with one or two more serious issues.'

'What's that one,' said Pete, abruptly, almost cutting her off. He tapped the end of his retractable pencil on the glass of the screen, on a case file titled '*Karen Parker – MISPER*'. 'Isn't she…?' he asked.

'Correct,' interrupted Grace, before he had time to finish. 'The local force down in Cornwall noticed from her tag movements that she appeared to have, how shall we say, not moved. For quite a while.'

'Not moved? What, dead?' said Pete, as he continued scanning over the case file.

'Well that's what they thought at first. And when they went round to her house, the fact that she didn't answer the doorbell seemed to confirm it, so they smashed her front door in. When they went in, after being accosted by some very hungry cats, they found the house empty.'

'So she was nowhere to be seen, but the tag locator was still showing her as being there,' he pondered, whilst chewing the end of the pencil.

'Indeed. They found it stuffed underneath one of the sofa cushions.'

'She'd removed it?' he said, as if sharply snapping back out of a daze. 'How?'

'We don't know. She was as thick as shit, if not thicker. She was also a complete lard-arse. But it's definitely hers; the serial number matches, they've pulled the history from the memory and it matches exactly. It was the one she was wearing, prints, DNA, the lot.'

'And no-one's seen her since?'

'Nope, not since she last went to the local convenience store where she purchased two tonne of cat food, cigarettes, three cakes, and a load of magazines,' replied Grace.

'Are we aware of anyone in the local area having knowledge as to who she actually is?'

'I doubt it very much. It was one of the most closely guarded new identities I can remember. When you consider the media furore that accompanied her trial, it's not surprising. To most of her neighbours she was probably just another jobless wonder who had chosen their pretty, and cheap, little corner of England to live out her benefit-scum lifestyle.'

'So, why was it flagged up as potential cyber interest?' he asked, intrigued by such a high profile missing person, despite cases of this nature being a little out of his area of expertise.

'Not sure, maybe one of the investigating officers just got a bit over-zealous and clicked every department in the hope that someone might be able shed a little light.'

'Interesting,' replied Pete, clicking out of the case file. He took a sip of coffee. Finally, it had cooled down to a temperature slightly less than molten iron. 'I'll have a look through the rest of these, see if there's anything I can help with.'

'Right,' said Grace, lifting herself out of the chair. She started to walk away but then turned back and leant on the desk beside him. 'Look, Pete, it's really good to have you back, but if you need to take some time out, or you need anything for you or Olivia, just say so, OK?'

'I'm fine,' he said, unconvincingly. He could tell from her slanted facial expression that she wasn't convinced. 'Honestly. I'll let you know if I need anything. I promise.'

Grace patted him on the shoulder and walked off. Taking another sip of coffee, he settled back into his desk. Numerous questions about the MISPER still bothered him. Having worked on various cases involving suspects with electronic tags, he had become very familiar with the technology. It shouldn't be possible to just remove one. Especially for someone as mentally simple as her. And where had she gone? Someone as fat as she appeared to be would barely be able to walk ten yards outside her front door without breaking out in a semi-asthmatic wheezing fit, drenched in sweat.

He opened a new Google search and typed her real name in. The countless news stories about her crime were nothing new; he remembered them vividly from when the country was first informed, months before her name was made public. There would have been few people who weren't filled with rage and disgust when the details started to emerge.

But he knew what it was like for the victims of crimes when the perpetrators went missing; the worry that they could be out there somewhere. Now she was missing and he felt obligated to try and find her.

11

'Good morning, sir,' said Gilbert, as he placed a silver serving tray on the coffee table in the corner of the bedroom.

Alistair was already awake, sat at the writing desk typing away intently on the laptop in front of him.

'Ah, breakfast. Excellent. Thank you, Gilbert. Most important meal of the day you know.' He stopped typing and walked over to the coffee table.

Breakfast was always the same on the day of a show. Three rashers of bacon, two sausages, sautéed potatoes, black pudding, and two fried eggs. A freshly brewed pot of kopi lewak coffee sat to the side, along with a shot glass of whiskey, just to finish it all off. Usually, breakfast was a lot healthier; granola, natural yoghurt, a mixture of berries of some description, but this alternative set him up properly for the day. A little later, when he needed some adrenaline and energy, he would work it off with a thumping heavy bag workout in his gym.

'Today's the day then,' said Gilbert, as he poured a cup of coffee. 'This is going to be a big one, I feel.'

'Absolutely,' replied Alistair, as he dipped a potato in the runny yellow yolk. 'Planned down to microscopic levels. I assume Jarvis has completed the extra encryption algorithms?'

'I believe so, yes. Having two people will invariably take a little longer, so he's strengthened all the firewalls and increased the levels of encryption. Not even the CIA, GCHQ, NSA, or any other letter-based organisation will be able to trace it.'

Alistair chuckled. 'Good man. And the venue?'

'Eric and Stan are down there now. The set itself is all ready to go. They're just going over the final security arrangements, sorting out the entrances, local CCTVs, that kind of thing.'

'Excellent. Thank you, Gilbert.'

Gilbert nodded and made for the exit. After a few steps he paused and ran his hand through his wavy brown hair. He turned back towards the table, to Alistair, who had yet to notice that he was still there.

'Alistair?' he asked, tentatively.

Looking up and chewing on a mouthful of meat, Alistair mumbled a muffled, 'Yes?'

'Can I talk to you about this one?'

Alistair finished his mouthful and dabbed the corner of his mouth with a pristine white serviette. He motioned with his hand for Gilbert to sit down; he duly obliged.

'What's up?' he asked, casually.

'Well, there's just something about this one that's bothering me,' replied Gilbert.

'Oh?' asked Alistair. He stabbed a piece of bacon with his fork, then a piece of sausage, then some black pudding, and finally an eggy potato, before putting the whole lot in his mouth and settling back into the sofa to listen.

'It's probably nothing, but I'm just wondering whether people might object.'

Alistair put his fist over his mouth to prevent spraying food all over the place, whilst simultaneously trying hard not to choke.

'Object?' he asked, once his mouth was clear enough.

'I know that sounds strange, given the nature of what we do here. But this woman is an utter fucking retard, excuse my French. Don't get me wrong, I can't stand her and thinking about what she did makes me want to put her out of her misery right now—'

'So what's the problem?' interrupted Alistair.

'Do you think there is a risk that our viewers might, I don't know, feel sorry for her? The paedophiles, rapists, and other scum of the Earth that we dispatch, I couldn't care less for, nor would I expect the viewers to. But I just wonder whether some people might object to our treatment of her on the basis that she isn't sufficiently intelligent to have any comprehension of either what she has done or what is happening to her.'

'Don't worry about it,' replied Alistair, frankly. 'We do what we do because it is right, it is making good an injustice. The people who subscribe, they want the same thing. If they don't agree with what we're doing then they don't have to watch. It's a little late in the day to start having doubts about the morality of this operation.'

'I'm not,' Gilbert hastened to add. 'I just don't want to put our group and its goals at risk. We've all worked too hard to make this work.'

'I agree,' said Alistair, softly, as he stood up from the sofa and walked behind Gilbert. As Gilbert tried to stand too, he placed a reassuring hand on his shoulder. 'I'm the last person in this world who wants to jeopardise anything. We're not doing this for the money, right? We're not doing this for the publicity, right? The only way we can carry on doing this is by putting in place a sheer number of measures to stop us ever being found. Even if a viewer or two had some bizarre pang of conscience, what are they going to do about it? They can't really go to the police because they will be indicting themselves, but if they did, we'd be long gone and all history of the show online would have been destroyed. Plus, I doubt very much that they would have come across our little programme if they weren't of a certain personality persuasion. Anyway, I think we're safe with this one. People were so repulsed with her crime that I can't see anyone raising objections.'

'I know you're right, of course. I didn't mean to talk out of turn,' said Gilbert, standing. 'What we're doing is ground-breaking and long may it continue. To the Brotherhood!'

'The Brotherhood,' replied Alistair, embracing him in a hug.

'I'll go and see to the arrangements for our guests, make sure they're ready.'

'Thank you, Gilbert.'

Gilbert turned and walked through the large ornate double doors that opened from the bedroom out on to the landing, closing them behind him. Alistair took his cup of coffee from the table and sat back down, cross-legged, on the sofa. He stared at the doors for a few seconds before pulling a mobile phone from his dressing gown pocket. He scrolled through the list of last numbers dialled and pressed one.

'It's me. Has Gilbert spoken to you about tonight's show? Oh OK ... No, just something he mentioned to me ... I'm sure he'll be fine. Ha ha, no, I don't think there will be any need for that! ... Just checking, but it might be worth keeping an eye on him ... Of course I trust him ... OK, I'll speak to you in a bit. I'm going for a swim.'

With that, Alistair hung up the phone. Swimming on a full stomach was generally frowned upon, but Alistair had never understood it. If anything, he swam better on a full stomach, especially a full English. He slid his feet into his slippers as he left the bedroom. Just outside, on the landing, he unplugged the Segway from the charging point and quietly rode off down the corridor in the direction of the swimming pool complex. The countdown to show-time had begun, and it was time to start preparing.

12

After what seemed like miles, Daisy finally stopped running. The last of the alcohol had ebbed from her system and the effects of withdrawal were starting to kick in. As she walked through the park, her heightened sense of paranoia made her see objects that weren't there and hear people talking to her who didn't exist.

In the distance was a wood. She recognised it as a place where she used to play as a child, a 'happy place', as her therapist would call it. Running towards it, she remembered an old disused caravan that had been abandoned long ago. It had previously belonged to the owner of a house on the edge of the wood who'd used it as a sort of 'man cave', where he could go to escape the wife. It must still be there, she thought to herself, as she gingerly climbed over a stile. No-one ever went in it when they used to play near there, so it was doubtful that anyone would know about it now.

As she ran farther into the increasingly dense oaks and beech trees, the moonlight illuminating her way diminished, and she stumbled more frequently over roots and fallen logs. But just before she lost the light altogether, she reached the small clearing where the caravan was. It was small, with a single door in the middle of one pale green oval side. Each of the small windows had been smashed long ago and a square of hardboard covered the opening. Instead of a door handle, there was now a shackle with a rusty-looking padlock, more of a token gesture than any sort of actual security. She gave the lock a few yanks, but despite its age, it wouldn't budge, and the corners dug into her hand. Scrabbling around on the floor, she picked up a cricket-ball-sized rock and smashed it against the lock. The sharp metal cut into her hand as she hammered in desperation, until eventually the whole latch gave way and the door swung open.

A small ray of moonlight broke through the shredded paisley curtain that once covered the rear window, illuminating the small space enough for her to work out where the bed was. She might have been sharing the caravan with any number of small, rabid critters, but neither that nor the overpowering musk that hung in the air mattered.

The mattress was cold, but it was dry, and she had no hesitation in making it her bed for tonight. As she lay on it, the shivering began, along with the cold sweats. She pulled a dusty blanket from the bottom of the bed up over her and rested her head on her arm. This small, rusty tin can was the safest she had felt in weeks. Its physical strength was insignificant against its isolation; there was no way she would be found here.

As she lay down, her head thumped and the room spun around her. She closed her eyes and her mind began to drift back to the house from which she had escaped. It was so full of painful memories – but she was free of it now. Sadness filled her heart, at the fact that, despite her best attempts, she had been forced to leave the other girl in the clutches of those monsters. A small window of opportunity had presented itself, and she thanked her stars that, from somewhere deep within her soul, a survival instinct had kicked in and afforded her the clarity to act decisively. In a strange twist of fate, the well-groomed man with the smart clothes who had gained and then utterly abused her trust had helped her escape the hell that he'd dragged her down into.

She had looked him square in the eye, peering through the crack in the door. Having heard the commotion that had just happened, she'd hoped it would be safe to leave the bedroom once she heard the front door slam. As the two men lay bleeding on the floor, she ventured into the room, trying to clear her head. The cuts and bruises on her face were nothing compared to the pain that she felt in her stomach and back.

Limping across the floor, she surveyed the scene. She drew strength from seeing her captors lying semi-conscious and bleeding. The bigger man was groaning on the floor. With a rush of adrenaline, and as the pain subsided, she kicked him, hard. She kicked him again and again and again, each kick making her feeling more powerful.

Once satisfied that he was incapacitated, she moved over to the smaller man. He was the one who made her do things. Things that made her hate herself. She stood over him; he looked pathetic, like a spoilt child crying because someone had stolen his sweets. Before she could react, his eyes opened wide and he reached out to grab her ankle. Stumbling backwards, she shrieked as she fell against the coffee table and a bolt of pain shot through her back. He pulled her by the leg, reaching out with his other hand, trying to catch her flailing ankle. Daisy had shouted at him to stop, kicking for all she was worth, but he kept grabbing at her. He pulled her by the leg and she slid off the table onto the floor. Now he had her in both hands and dragged her closer to him, switching his grasp to her arms. He pinned them to her sides, holding her face a few inches from his own, blood and saliva dripping from his mouth.

'You stupid little piece of shit,' he spat. 'You will pay for this.'

As her mind spun, she instinctively leant forward and bit Aleksander as hard as she could on the nose. He gritted his teeth, trying to resist, but it became too much and he let her go. As he grabbed his face, she crawled backwards to try and escape. Frantically looking around, she spied the small penknife, used to cut the drugs, sitting on the coffee table behind her. Reaching back with one arm she picked it up and plunged it as deep as she could into the top of his thigh. He screamed in pain as she pulled it back out. Before he could grab the wound, she plunged it into the other leg. This time, she gave it a twist before removing it.

'Fuck you, arsehole,' she whispered.

The writhing blood-stained mass of Aleksander grasped his legs to try and ease the pain, as blood continued to run from the wounds left by Saeed's beating. Dragging herself to her feet, she hunted around the debris in the room, keeping one eye firmly on the two men lying on the floor. In a drawer, she found a small folded pile of twenty pound notes. Taking it, she went back into the bedroom and pulled some relatively clean clothes from a drawer. She struggled to dress herself, the mixture of panic and pain making her lose control of all her limbs. There were some shoes in the wardrobe, which she put on as quickly as possible before she made for the door.

Holding tight to the banister, she crept down the stairs, keeping an ear out for any noise coming from the bedroom. As she walked past the lounge, she looked in to see the other girl lying half-naked and semi-unconscious on the sofa. She ran in and knelt down beside her. Rubbing her shoulders, she whispered to the girl, trying to rouse her, but it was no good. The girl let out a soft groan as Daisy tried to pull her to her feet. The girl wasn't heavy, but Daisy had nothing like the strength needed to lift her.

'Come on,' she said, with urgency. 'We can escape, but you need to wake up and get moving.'

But all the other girl could muster was more groans, and she fought to make Daisy let go.

'Get off.'

'If you want all this to stop, we have to go now!'

'No,' she mumbled, turning her body away. 'He loves me.'

'He doesn't. He's just using you. Come on!'

Daisy tried one more time to roll her back over and pick her up, but was met with more resistance.

Suddenly, the quiet was broken as a gun fired from upstairs, shattering the coffee table in a shower of glass. The shock sent Daisy reeling backwards onto the floor, and she scrabbled towards the wall. Another shot rang out, kicking up a cloud of foam and dust as it hit the side of the sofa. She edged around the door frame and peered up the stairs. On the landing, Aleksander's bloodied hand grasped the bottom of the banister, pulling his broken body around to the top of the stairs. In his other hand was a gun.

He groaned with the effort of each pull, until he was facing directly into the lounge door. Daisy knew she needed to run now; she had no choice but to leave the girl. Waiting until she heard him pulling himself along, she ran out into the corridor. Aleksander raised the gun, aiming as best he could through blood-encrusted eyelids.

'Stop!' he shouted.

Daisy froze at the bottom of the stairs and put her hands in the air.

'You stupid little bitch, I've got you now,' he said, straining to get the words out as she turned slowly to face him up the stairs.

They locked eyes, and Daisy's breathing became heavy as sweat ran down her face. Time slowed down, tunnel vision engulfing her sight.

'Bye bye!' he said, mockingly, squeezing the trigger. *Click!* He squeezed again. *Click!* And again and again.

Daisy felt a wave of instant relief and side-stepped through the kitchen door. She leant back out into the hallway, smiled, and stuck her middle finger up at Aleksander.

'Fuck you!'

'No!' he shouted, smashing the pistol repeatedly on the floor as the anger exploded from him. 'Get back here!'

But she was gone, out through the side door and into the back garden. At the end of the garden was a gate which led to a back alley running along the railway lines. As the pain in her body eased, she made her way as quickly as she could, in any direction that was away from the house. A couple of hundred yards and she would be in the town centre, where there were people and shops, a place to blend in and disappear.

She stopped briefly to buy some food and a bottle of water, then ran, as quickly as her body allowed, as far away as she could.

And now she found herself in this caravan, finally able to rest. Soon she would have to keep moving, but for the time being she would call this small tin can home.

13

The phone sat in the central console of the BMW vibrated and then rang. Despite travelling at more than sixty miles per hour along the winding country road, Saeed picked it up in his left hand and held it across his face to his right ear. He recognised the number.

'What the fuck do you want? I thought we finished our business,' he said, steering one-handed around an old couple on bicycles.

'She's … gone …' came the exhausted response.

'Who's gone?'

'Your piece of skirt. Thanks to you, she escaped.'

'You useless fucking prick!' he shouted, holding the phone in front of his face, the speed of the car increasing in line with his anger. 'Then you need to find her.'

'No chance,' replied Aleksander. 'She left days ago.'

'Days ago? Why didn't you tell me this?'

'I wanted it to be a nice surprise for you. We are lucky to be alive. Also luckily, no-one heard the shots and called the police.'

'Shots? You idiot!'

'Fuck you. If you hadn't left us how you did, this wouldn't have happened. Have a nice life, Saeed. I hope the girl doesn't cause you too much bother. Goodbye.'

The line clicked and went dead. Saeed squeezed the phone in his hand and smacked it repeatedly against the steering wheel. As his attention switched back to the road, he slammed his foot down on the brake pedal; a junction was fast approaching. As the car skidded to a halt, he lay back against the headrest, his heart pounding as he tried to control his breathing. Aleksander would never grass him in to the police. Even if he did, Saeed already had numerous alibis, people who would say anything for him. Plus, he had already ditched the drugs. But this was a massive annoyance; he couldn't risk being seen returning to the house in case the police did end up being involved and the girl was out on the loose. Not that she could do anything to threaten him either. She wouldn't have the guts to go to the police and chances were, with her past, they wouldn't believe a word she said even if she did.

He pulled out of the junction, driving more calmly now. No point giving the police any reason to pull him over.

* * *

In the lounge, Mo and Shan were sat on the floor, watching Tom and Jerry videos on the television. Their mother was lying down on the sofa, filling in Sudoku puzzles on a small tablet. As soon as she heard the car door slam, she sat bolt upright, the nervousness making her stomach tighten. It seemed to take forever for him to walk up the path, but a few long seconds later she heard the key in the front door. The kids stayed staring at the cartoons; it was a relief to her that they hadn't yet developed the same nervous reaction to his returns.

As the front door closed, Saeed placed the keys back on the hallway table and made his way into the lounge.

'Hello, darling,' Amanda said, hopefully, as she straightened some scatter cushions on the sofa. 'Did you have a nice day?'

Saeed said nothing. He walked past his sons as if they weren't there, stopping only momentarily to stoop down and grab the television remote from Mo's chubby little hands. Dropping like a boulder into the sofa, he switched over to a hip-hop music channel.

Amanda joined him on the sofa, perching as close to the edge as she could without sliding onto the floor. Tenderly, tentatively, she placed a hand on his knee.

'Is everything OK? Did you have a nice day?'

Before she could react, he swiftly grabbed her wrist and lifted her hand from his leg, twisting it as he did so. The speed scared her and she gasped loudly.

'Ta and Jelly,' shouted Shan. 'Ta and Jelly.'

'Quiet, Shan. It's OK, Daddy's had a busy day. It's time for him to watch his programmes.'

'Ta and Jelly! Ta and Jelly!'

'Shan, shush, please,' she begged.

Saeed stared at her. 'I heard you the first time,' he said, menacingly, and threw her arm back in her face.

As she sat, hunched over, rubbing her wrist, Shan began to cry. Saeed raised his eyebrows, which was enough for Amanda to leap from the sofa and pick Shan up to comfort him. As Saeed casually flicked through various other channels, Mo got up from the floor and walked over to his dad.

'Daddy, Daddy, guess what I did after school today?' said Mo, with an innocent optimism, slapping his dad on the leg. Amanda's heart started to beat harder as she struggled to calm Shan.

Saeed slowly placed the controller on the arm of the chair and then placed both hands on his knees.

'Daddy, guess what I did?' he repeated.

'I don't think Daddy wants to hear about that, sweetie.'

'Guess what I did?'

Saeed just stared. A brief moment of tense silence as Mo stared back at his dad with a huge grin on his face.

Saeed lunged forward, pinning Mo's arms to his sides with his hands.

'No!' whispered Amanda as she took a deep intake of breath, the word barely coming out.

Saeed hoisted Mo up into the air and threw him down onto the sofa.

'What did you do, you little monkey? Eh? What did you do?'

Mo giggled uncontrollably, arms flailing, as Saeed lifted his t-shirt up and blew raspberries on his tummy. Amanda realised she had been holding her breath and let out a long sigh of relief, at least for the moment.

'Ha ha ha, stop it, Daddy! Stop it!'

'What did you do then? Come on, tell me.'

'I can't,' shouted Mo, in between laughter. 'You're tickling me!'

'I'm not!' replied Saeed, tickling him harder. 'Let's hear it then!'

'Mo, remember what we said,' interjected Amanda, with a forced laughter. 'Just tell Daddy about the colouring book.'

'Said about what?' said Saeed, blowing another raspberry.

'Grandad...' said Mo, struggling to speak.

'Mo, that's enough.'

'Grandad what?' said Saeed. He continued tickling, but slower now, the smile dropping from his face.

'Mo, no.'

'Grandad came round with a colouring book,' answered Mo, now able to speak. 'I coloured in a fat man and Grandad said it looked like you.'

Silence. Amanda held Shan closer, tighter into her body, with a hand wrapped around the back of his head.

'Did he?' said Saeed, finally, after a few tense moments.

Mo's grin never left his face during the pause, but Saeed's had vanished completely. With his head still, he turned his gaze to Amanda and slowly raised his eyebrows in silent query.

'Well, isn't he a silly grandad then?' he said, the statement being aimed more at Amanda than Mo. 'Go to your room, boy, I need to talk to your mother.'

'But I want to watch—'

'GO!'

Mo jolted, a look of terror suddenly washing over his face, quickly followed by tears. He rolled off the sofa and Amanda came to him, taking his hand and helping him up. She bent down to share her hug with him, to reassure him.

'Take your brother as well,' Saeed murmured.

'No,' replied Amanda, holding both boys close to her.

'Take your brother,' he started, softly, building to a crescendo, before sending the remote controller crashing against the far wall, 'and go to your room! NOW!'

'It's OK,' whispered Amanda, smothering both boys with kisses as though she may never see them again. 'Take Shan and climb into bed. Sing the nursery rhymes you learnt at school, he likes them.'

Mo took his little brother by the hand, the two of them crying, and led him out of the room.

'Sae, I didn't know he was—' she pleaded with him, but was cut off by the crash of a door slamming shut. '…Coming.'

'Really? I've told you before about him coming here,' he replied.

She took steps backwards as he walked towards her, until eventually the bookcase stopped her moving any farther.

She turned her face away from his. 'I didn't realise he was coming. He was waiting on the doorstep when we got home, I swear.'

He squeezed her chin with his thumb and index finger, turning her face back towards his.

'But you let him in.'

'Of course, I couldn't tell him to go away. He's my dad.'

'Every time he comes here, he tries to poison your mind against me.'

'It wasn't like that, he just wanted to see—'

'Don't lie to me!' he shouted, slapping her around the cheek.

'I'm not,' she said, trying not to burst into tears.

'And now he's trying to turn the boys against me as well.'

'He's not. It was just a joke.'

'Oh, a joke was it? Well let's see how funny he finds this, shall we?'

Upstairs, Mo and Shan sat up in bed, the duvet resting like a tent on their heads, illuminated by the small wind-up torch. Mo sang to his brother.

'Mary had a little lamb. Its fleece was white …'

He paused as the sound of screaming pierced through the floor below.

'… as snow.'

A crash from downstairs made him grip his brother's hand tighter.

'And everywhere that Mary went …'

The floor shook again.

'… that lamb was sure to go. It followed her to school one day …'

The muffled shouts of their daddy now resonating up through the house.

'… which was against the rule. It made the children laugh …'

A smash of something glass caused the walls to vibrate. The boys stared into each other's eyes as tears streamed down their faces.

'… laugh and play. To see a lamb at school.'

Finally, there was silence. The front door slammed again.

14

The door to the stark, white-washed holding room swung open, and a burst of daylight flooded in. Mark Rankin sat upright in a large leather recliner in the corner, the only piece of furniture the room contained. Even with the sack over his head he could tell the room had become lighter.

'Good afternoon, Mark,' said Jarvis, as he entered the room, flanked by two burly goons. 'We hope you've enjoyed your stay at our little hotel, but check-out is at three and we really need to start servicing your room.'

The goons grabbed him by the arms and lifted him to his feet. His body squirmed like a worm in a bird's beak. It was pointless, since the straitjacket was tied so tightly he would be more likely to slip a disc than to escape. But he tried anyway.

'Fuck you! Where are you taking me? What day is it?' he shouted through the sack.

Jarvis walked alongside the men as they dragged Mark out of the room and into the courtyard.

'We're taking you out, you've got a big date. Don't worry about getting ready for it though, what you're wearing is fine. And what day is it? Well, if I was going to be melodramatic, I would say something like 'It's your judgement day', but as I'm not I will simply say Friday. Not that it really matters.'

Mark heard the van doors open before he was bundled onto a mattress in the back. The engine was already running, and as he lay down inside, he felt a foot in his back, pressing him down onto his front. Very quickly, he gave up struggling. He had no idea how many days he had been there, but he was tired and hungry, and simply didn't have the energy to fight any more.

'Hello again, Mark,' said the goon. 'We really should stop meeting like this. I hope you're sitting comfortably with your seatbelt on and the chair in the upright position. Well, sort of.'

Jarvis climbed into the passenger seat. 'Just drop me off around the other side, will you?'

'I realise you techie types hate any sort of exercise,' said Stan, as he slowly pulled away, 'but surely even you can manage a short walk across the courtyard.'

'I need to preserve my energy.'

'I can imagine,' replied Stan, sarcastically. 'Tapping away on your ZX Spectrum must burn hundreds of calories.'

'It's a Commodore Sixty-four, actually. Stop me if this is getting too technical for you. But let's face it, if you get something wrong it doesn't really matter. If I get it wrong, this whole game comes to an end.'

'Who'd have thought we would end up in a world where the nerds hold all the power,' replied Stan, as he brought the van to a halt around the west side of the house.

'I know, it's wonderful isn't it?' said Jarvis, excitedly. 'See you at the gig.'

The two men clasped hands and nodded to each other. Jarvis trotted over to the other holding room and waved for the door to be opened. As he walked into the room, the stench hit him like a smack around the face.

'Jesus Christ, what is wrong with this woman?' he asked, pulling his t-shirt up over his nose.

'She went a bit berserk, demanding pizza and curry. In the end we got her some just to shut her up. It did the trick, but then the flatulence started. Plus, she already stinks from the amount she sweats,' replied one of the goons who'd been guarding her, pointing at the empty takeaway containers that littered the floor.

In the corner of the room, Karen Parker sat sobbing into the sack that covered her head.

'Well, I think it's time to put her out of her misery,' said Jarvis, as he walked over to her. 'Hello, Karen, it's time to go.'

'I keep telling you, I'm not Karen,' she said, unconvincingly, through the sack.

'Christ, where do we find these people?' Jarvis said to himself. 'It's time to leave, Karen. We've got a big date lined up for you.'

'Is there food there? I'm hungry,' she replied.

'Er, yes,' answered Jarvis, shaking his head as the goons sniggered into their hands. 'As much food as you can stuff down your fat, sorry, waste-of-space neck. If you would just like to stand up and come with us, we'll do the rest.'

'Are you taking me home?' she asked, as the goons helped her to her feet.

'Sort of, yes. We just need to ask you some more questions and then it will all be over.'

She padded to the van, hands cuffed in front of her, the sack still covering her head. Obligingly, she stepped up into the back of van, with a little helping shove from one of the goons.

'I wish the other one was this easy,' Jarvis whispered to himself, going around to the front of the van.

Eric wound the window down. 'Where to with this one, guvnor?'

'The warehouse on Dean Street.'

'Ooo no, I don't go south of the river, not at this time of the day.'

'Go on, I'll bung you an extra twenty.'

'Done. See you later.'

Eric wound the window up and drove off. As Jarvis watched them go, he heard the crunching of footsteps behind him. Alistair and Gilbert walked across the gravel driveway towards him.

'Everything ready?' asked Alistair.

'Certainly is,' replied Jarvis. 'Set is all ready to go. Our volunteers are fed and watered. Eric and Stan have taken care of the security arrangements. I just need to send the log-on details out to the subscribers, but I can't do that until the encryption program has run its course. It'll be completed once we get to the warehouse.'

'Good. I think this one is going to be big. I'm looking forward to it,' replied Alistair.

Gilbert reached into his pocket and pulled out a walkie-talkie. 'Bring the car around, please.'

The large black Mercedes saloon car drove up the ramp from the underground car park and pulled up in front of the men.

Alistair opened the rear door and put his arms around the two men.

'Gentlemen, it's time to go meet the Host.'

15

'Look, I know we're late, Mister Johnson, but there's not a lot I can do about it,' said a very bored Joe, holding the phone to his ear. The words were coming out but whether or not in the right order, he had no idea. He'd been on the receiving end of this phone call bollocking for over eight minutes now and as he stared at the computer screen, switching brightly colour sweets into lines of three, a chime sounded on his phone.

He opened his email app whilst mumbling randomly placed responses to his caller.

'Uh-huh', 'Yep', 'Can I look into it and get back to you?', 'No, of course we value your account.'

It was the email he had been waiting for.

From: CoinFX
To: Joe
Subject: New Account Registration
Dear Joe,
We are pleased to confirm that your recent application to open a wallet with CoinFX has been approved. The account set-up has been completed and you will be able to access your wallet using the log-in details that will be sent on separate emails.

Thank you for choosing CoinFX for your online currency trading.
Yours sincerely,
New Account Team

'Yes! About fucking time … No, no, no sorry, Mister Johnson, I didn't mean you – we, er, just had a delivery turn up to the office.

Yes, I realise it would be nice if it was your order. OK, look, leave it with me a little longer. I promise I will get to the bottom of it and let you know its progress. Alright, bye.'

He hung up without even waiting for Mr Johnson to sign off. Joe had worked for his family's metal supply business for the last fifteen years. He had seen it grow from a small office in his parents' house into a large scale outfit operating out of a twenty thousand square foot warehouse situated in a leafy countryside area just out of town. It paid him a good salary but he'd become bored with the seemingly endless paperwork, export regulations and, worst of all, the staff.

Finally, he had a diversion. Something raw and brutal that made him feel alive. The sense of the unknown was something he hadn't felt for a long time.

He closed down the accounts program on his computer and logged into his shiny new CoinFX account. This was it, his ticket to a brave new world. He stared at the *Buy bitcoins* page. He had used websites to look up currency exchange rates before, but this was unlike anything he had seen before. A conversion table flashing up the exchange rate of bitcoins into Dollars, Euros, Pounds, and other currencies flickered red and blue. The values changed every second, up and down, red and blues switching place like some kind of dysfunctional Christmas tree. It mesmerised him. Eventually, he clicked on *Buy Now*. He pondered the quantity. Dealing in a currency where one solitary coin cost over six hundred pounds just added to the intensity. Two was the least he would spend, but he had a feeling he would need, or rather want, more. He entered '6' and it calculated the cost.

£4057.52– do you wish to proceed?

He hovered over the *Proceed* button. Hesitating slightly, he glanced around the office and out into the warehouse.

Fuck it, I can afford it, he thought to himself, and he clicked the mouse button.

Transaction confirmed – 6 bitcoins have been transferred to your wallet.

He clicked to log out and sat back in his chair, taking a deep breath and a sip from his glass of water. Pulling out his phone, he opened up an instant message chat with Billy.

Billy. We're on. Proud owner of 6 spangly new bitcoins.

6? Ha ha!! You dickhead. C U @ 8.

16

The two black vans parked side by side in front of the warehouse shutter doors. Standing outside, drinking water and puffing on cigarettes, stood four large men in red tracksuits. A loud clattering came from inside one of the trucks as it rocked from side to side. One of the goons banged on the side of the van with his fist.

'Give it a rest! We'll let you out in a minute. Jeez,' he said. 'I'll be glad to see the back of this one.'

'She's not much better, but at least she's quiet,' replied another.

Jarvis appeared from inside the warehouse.

'Five minutes, gentlemen. Let's get into position.'

The goons took a last drink, stubbed their cigarettes out on the floor, and all pulled balaclavas down over their faces. Two went to one van and two to the other.

'Take her in first,' said Jarvis, as he walked back inside.

The goons opened the van and dragged her out by the arms. 'Time to go, Karen.'

'But I'm not Karen.'

'You really are a – how do you English say – fat waste of space aren't you?' replied the goon as they dragged her inside.

'Your turn, Mark. Get out!' shouted another. As they muscled him out of the back of the van, he kicked and struggled, but he was no match for the goons.

'Fighting to the end?' one whispered in his ear. 'It's cute but I really wouldn't bother.'

'Screw you,' came the muffled reply, drawing cheers of laughter from the goons.

'Screw us indeed!'

'I hope you know what you're doing,' said Billy, pulling a comfortable chair up to the computer desk.

'Nope, no idea,' replied Joe, as he copied the web address from his phone screen into the address bar.

The site appeared. A large sign with blinking lights saying *The Red Room* sat in the middle of the screen and beside it a picture of the Host, giving a thumbs-up. Underneath were written the words *Appearing tonight: Mark Rankin and Karen Parker.*

'Bugger me,' said Billy. 'Aren't those the people who killed that kid?'

'I think so,' replied Joe, unable to pull his gaze from the screen. Underneath were the words *Click on the Red Room to enter.*

'I'm not sure about this, Joe,' said Billy, somewhat perturbed.

But Joe had already clicked on the big red sign which led him to another payment page, requesting another two bitcoins.

'It's thirteen hundred pounds, mate.'

'I know. Look, I just want to see what it is. I'll be sensible.'

He entered the details into the payment page and clicked 'enter'. Another black screen appeared with the Red Room logo and the statement, *Welcome to the Red Room. Transmission will begin in 5:00 minutes.*

'Just enough time for a piss. Do you want a beer whilst I'm up?'

'Please. I think I'm going to need one.'

Jarvis and his assistants sat around the computer console, checking and rechecking all their connections, modems, and the broadband signal. As Alistair and Gilbert paced up and down the set in the warehouse, spotlights flashed, chains clattered, and the sound system came alive with shouts of 'Testing, testing'. In front of the double doors sat two wooden chairs complete with restraints, facing each other. Covering the entire floor was a thin layer of blue adhesive plastic film.

Standing next to one of the chairs, Gilbert shook it to check its stability and pulled at the fabric restraints. Alistair walked up behind him and placed a hand on his shoulder.

'Ready?' asked Alistair.

'Absolutely,' replied Gilbert, taking a deep breath. 'The more time I've spent with this woman, the more I can't stand her. I'm going to enjoy this.'

Jarvis watched from his seat as the two men shook hands, then walked over to the computer set up.

'Everything ready, Jarvis?' asked Alistair.

'Of course,' he replied, with an air of overwhelming confidence in his own ability. 'The secure fibre optic line is running out to the local junction box, the scrambler is all set and ready to go. I reckon we'll have a good clear forty minutes before we need to even think about calling it a day.'

'Good. And how have our subscribers responded to the front page news of tonight's volunteers?'

'It's gone ballistic. Last count was at least four hundred and fifty spectators, so that's the best part of half a mil.'

'Then we should make sure this is a show to remember.'

Alistair and Jarvis embraced in a hug.

'Everyone set?' shouted Alistair, to a chorus of cheers. 'Then let's do this, people. It's show-time!'

17

Finally, the screen on the computer faded to black, and thumping techno music started to fill the room. Joe and Billy grabbed their bottles of ale and sat up straight, as if a teacher had just walked into a classroom to begin a lesson. A blurry red image filled the picture and, as the camera began to zoom out, the words became clearer: *The Red Room*. The two of them looked at each other and shrugged in blissful ignorance. As the angle switched to show a pair of double doors, dry ice filled the venue. The music built to a crescendo before, eventually, the doors opened. Through the white light that broke through the smoke, they could see the silhouette of a person. He had his back turned and his arms held out wide.

As the smoke started to die down, the man turned around and walked towards the camera, the doors slamming shut behind him.

'Is that a clown in a tuxedo?' asked Billy.

Joe sat with his chin propped up on his hand, staring intently at the screen.

'I think it is. But it's OK, look, he's carrying a clipboard. Not just any old clipboard, a gold one.'

'OK, well so far so fucked up.'

'Good evening, ladies and gentlemen,' said the man speaking into the microphone. 'Glad you could all join us down here in the deep web for another episode of The Red Room with me, the Host. We know that you rely on the Brotherhood of the Righteous ...'

'The what?' interrupted Billy.

'Ssh!' snapped Joe.

'... for all your summary justice needs. And can I say that tonight we have not only gone bigger and badder but, as the eagle-eyed amongst you will have probably spotted, we have two, yes, count them, two shiny volunteers for your enjoyment. So without further ado, let's bring out our first volunteer.'

The music stopped and the doors opened again. Silhouetted against the white back light were two burly goons and one saggy, obese-looking figure in a pink tracksuit with a hessian sack over their head. As the pair marched the overweight human whale down to one of the wooden chairs in the centre of the room, the Host faced the camera.

'Ladies and gentlemen, here she is. At one point she was quite possibly the most hated woman in the country. She was jailed for a mere five years for, and I quote, 'causing or allowing the death of a child'. It was only once the sentence was passed that the world learned of her crime and the unimaginable suffering of her son, Charlie. After her release, she was very kindly provided with a new identity, a new house, and a new life. But we found her. I give you ...'

Once the goons had finished strapping her into the restraints of the chair, the Host grabbed the top of the sack, then paused for a moment before snatching it from her head.

'... Karen Parker.'

The spotlight shone down on her face and she blinked as her eyes slowly grew accustomed to the surroundings.

'Where am I?' she sniffed. 'I want to go home now.'

'You can't I'm afraid, Karen, those are the rules.'

'But I'm not Karen. I keep telling you, I'm Louise.'

The Host turned to face the camera. 'Seriously, folks, she has been saying this ever since we borrowed her from her house. Just so no-one is in any doubt that this is who *we* say she is, here is the badly removed tattoo from her wrist saying 'Charlie'. We all saw it in the tabloid photographs of her leaving the courtroom, the ones where she's giving the bird to all the hacks.'

The camera panned to her wrist, to show the red scars of the tattoo. The Host stood behind her, massaging the top of her head.

He leaned in near her ear to softly explain what was about to happen.

'Well, Karen, you have been specially selected to take part in this TV show, OK? The rules are that you sit there whilst all the viewers at home pay money for the honour of asking you a question. If you answer the question incorrectly you will receive the punishment of their choice. If you answer correctly then you will also receive the punishment of their choice. Alright?'

'What? That's not fair, I don't want to do this. I want to go home. I haven't done nothing,' she replied, sniffing as her nose began to run and tears started to roll down her face.

The Host gripped her by neck, constricting the carotid artery, whispering as he did so, 'You have no choice, Karen. We'll see whether the people consider that you 'haven't done nothing', shall we?'

He let go and strolled up to the camera. 'OK, people, let's get this going. Start placing your bids while I tighten the restraints around her cankles. Seriously, we should have used some longer straps.'

The leaderboard lowered from the ceiling, names and bids already flashing up, switching places as the values increased.

'This is royally messed up,' said Billy. 'Why are we still watching again?'

'Because it's cost me nearly two thousand pounds. I want to see what happens. I remember her. If what I think is about to happen *is* about to happen, I want to see it.'

Karen turned her head, following the Host as he circled her chair.

'You don't mind, do you?' he said, as he perched on her knee, staring up at the screen. After a few seconds, the bids stopped increasing and a name was left at the top.

'OK, Karen. The winner of the first bid tonight, with eight-point-seven bitcoins, is Pokerfaced Killer. Good work, Killer, although I thought we might have seen you later on in this process, if I'm honest. And what is your question?' The Host got up and stood underneath the monitor, reading as the words appeared on the screen.

"Karen. I hate you.' Nice start, straight to the point, I like it. 'Never have I felt such revulsion as I did when I heard what you did. I want to know, do you still think about Charlie and what you did to him?' Cracking question to kick off with. Well, Karen, Mister Killer would like to know if you still think about Charlie.'

'Why are you asking me this? I've done my prison for what I done. An' it wasn't me. It was my boyfriend.'

'But you admitted his death. It is only by some pathetic re-wording in this country's laws that technically you only admitted 'causing or allowing his death'. But to us and the people who are watching, you ... murdered ... him ... Karen. Nothing more, nothing less.'

'I didn't murder him. He was my boy.'

'So why didn't you protect him? Anyway, that's not the question. Killer wants to know if you still think about him.'

She started crying. Pulling her head back by the hair, the Host smacked her hard around the face and she started crying even more.

'Don't, you're hurting me! I can't talk about Charlie, it upsets me too much. When I was in prison, everyone hated me, I had to be kept in a cell on my own.'

'Right,' said the Host, scratching his head. 'Are you saying that you don't like to think about Charlie because it has made your life worse? Or are you looking for sympathy for how badly you've been treated as a result of your actions?'

'Well, it's just that—'

'I think that's time on this one. Killer, pick a punishment.'

'No, please. I just want to go home.'

'Seriously, Karen, I'm going to start bidding myself if you keep saying that. Now sit quietly and wait for your punishment.'

'I've been punished. I done prison for years.'

The Host swung back around and grabbed her by the neck, forcing her head back against the chair.

'Not punished by us you haven't.' He paused, staring deep into her eyes, the clown face reflecting back off her dark brown irises. 'I'm going to enjoy this.'

The message appeared letter by letter on the huge monitor. *Break her fingers.*

'What in the fucking name of …' shouted Billy. 'Surely they can't be about to do that?'

Joe sat mesmerised. It was as if this was all perfectly normal and made complete and total sense. He whispered, barely audibly, 'She deserves it.'

Billy covered his face with his hands, peering through a gap in his fingers. On the screen, they watched as Karen shook her head violently from side to side while the Host casually stood over her and, one by one, snapped every finger on her left hand. The screams that came through the speakers cut through Billy like fingernails down a blackboard, and he held his head in his hands. He hadn't realised, but sweat was dripping down his face, though Joe still just stared.

Back on the screen, the Host once again faced the camera.

'Ladies and gentlemen. I told you we had two volunteers for you today and I think it's time to bring out the second one. Please give a warm Red Room welcome to volunteer number two. But I warn you, he's a little bit feisty this one.'

The double doors separated and three goons wrestled with the writhing figure in a hood. Eventually, they muscled him into the chair and fastened the restraints around his wrists and ankles, but still he fought to free himself.

'Don't worry, Karen,' the Host said. 'Those restraints will do their job. So, earlier we told you that we had a hot date lined up for you. And here he is, the man you once called your Stud Muffin, and I can see why because he really is a catch – it's Mark Rankin.'

He whipped the sack off to reveal a sweaty, red face covered in strings of saliva; the man looked as though he might explode at any minute.

'What the fuck is going on? Let me out of this chair you sons of bitches or I'll—'

'What, Mark? You'll what? Call your case worker?' asked the Host, calmly, leaning in close to Mark's face. 'Or will you wait until you're out of here and take it out on a small defenceless two-year-old?'

Mark's anger rose and he fought, shaking the chair as much as he could manage. As the expletives rained from his mouth, the Host turned to the camera.

'Sorry about this, ladies and gentlemen, won't be a moment,' he said, before smashing the clipboard around the side of Mark's face and then dropping his knee hard into Mark's abdomen.

Finally, the prisoner quietened down, except for a couple of choking coughs as he struggled to regain his breath.

The Host turned to face Karen, who was by now sobbing uncontrollably, the pain in her hand overtaken by the sight of her former lover sat just yards away.

'Well, this is a lovely little reunion, isn't it, Karen?' asked the Host. 'Why, the last time you two probably saw each other was when one, or both of you, were committing the final act of violence against your small son. The one where his fragile body and soul finally said "enough!" and gave up trying to fight. What would he be today? Ten? Eleven? Probably playing football or rugby, riding his bike with his friends. But he's not, is he? He's dead. Today, Mark, you are going to pay for it. Start the bidding for Mark's first question.'

'Screw you. I served my time for what that bitch did. It was her son, not mine,' shouted Mark, defiantly.

'It?' asked the Host, swinging around to face him. "It" had a name. Charlie. I think you'll find that the people watching this show see things slightly differently. If you would like to look up at that monitor there, you'll see all the people offering to pay huge sums of money for the right to punish you.'

Mark looked up at the screen, at the names and numbers blinking hypnotically as more and more bids poured in.

'Let's see who the winner is, shall we, Mark?' said the Host. 'And it is … 'Housewife Superstar' with ten-point-six bitcoins. That is incredible. Great to have you with us tonight Superstar, what is your question for Mark?'

The words slowly started to materialise on the screen. *I have seen some horrendous people appear on this show but you are without doubt the lowest, most cowardly piece of scum of all. You tell me this; if you could go back to when you met Karen, would you do the same again?*

'The classic "if you could go back" question, thank you, Superstar. Well, Mark?'

'Fuck you. I'm not answering that,' shouted Mark.

'Yes you are, Mark,' replied the Host.

'No, I'm—' but before he could finish the sentence the Host twisted his body and connected a vicious lightning-quick roundhouse kick squarely to Mark's ear.

'Boom! Get in!' shouted Joe. 'He's certainly got some skills this guy.' But Billy remained silent, hand over his mouth, shaking his head.

The force of the impact blurred his vision and the ringing in his ears drowned out all noise around him. As the fuzzy figure of the Host circled around his chair, he felt as though he was drowning, staring up at the sun through the water as he sunk further downwards.

He was snapped back to a vague semblance of reality as a goon wafted smelling salts under his nose, but the pain of the kick was making his head throb.

'Just answer the question please, Mister Rankin,' said the Host, calmly.

'He was a little shit,' stuttered Mark, groggily. 'Always crying, always following me around, always shitting himself. He needed to man up and—'

The Host lurched forward and gripped Mark by the throat, crushing his head against the chair.

'He was two years old. He was two foot tall. It sounds like you're the one that needs to man up. Are you enjoying this? The sense that your existence is now entirely in my hands? I can do whatever I want to you and you can't defend yourself against it.'

'I looked after him,' Mark spat though gritted teeth. 'He just got in the way.'

'It's true,' piped up Karen. 'We never got no time together because Charlie always wanted something.'

'So you punished him?' said the Host, softly, releasing his grip. 'He was in the way, an inconvenience, and your cuddle time with Mark was more important. You are a sad excuse for a human being. And as for you, I think it's clear that given the time again, you would probably be exactly the same cowardly bully.'

'I'm not a coward, you arsehole.'

'Mark, you're six foot two. And you are trying to make out that the beatings, the injuries, the pain you inflicted on a two-year-old are in some way brave and tough? Not only that, but that they were his fault as well. I've had enough. Superstar, make it a good one.'

I really want this monster to suffer, he's laughing at what he's done. Make him smile forever and give him matching fingers.

Joe and Billy watched the screen as the Host stood in front of the chair, slowly pulling each finger backwards and then snapping it sideways.

'I think he's enjoying this. Look how close his face is to the bloke's,' said Joe, as he sipped from his bottle of beer.

'I think it's sick and I think you're sick,' replied Billy. 'I fully get that these people are scum-of-the-earth, but I can't watch this.'

As he got up to walk out of the garage, he was stopped dead in his tracks.

'I'm going to bid on the next one,' said Joe, already opening a CoinFX screen on his mobile whilst watching the Host finally finish off the last of Mark's fingers.

'Are you fucking mad? They're bidding dozens of bitcoins on this, that's thousands. It's bad enough you've already paid over one and a half grand for the privilege of witnessing this torture,' he replied, grabbing the back of Joe's chair as if trying to shake some sense into him. 'Don't. Seriously. You have no idea what you're getting yourself into. Look, we took the red pill and jumped down the rabbit hole. Let's just chalk this up to experience and walk away. If you start bidding, think of the ramifications. Could you live with yourself?'

'Why should we care about these people? They've done horrific things and weren't punished enough. I don't think anyone is going to miss them. Anyway, who will ever know?'

Billy cast his eyes back to the screen.

A goon held Mark's head back in the chair as the Host hovered over him, holding the clipboard against his lips. He dropped a knee into Mark's groin, causing him to open his mouth wide in agony. As he did so, the Host removed a cover from the bottom edge of the clipboard, revealing a glistening sharp blade that he forced sideways into Mark's mouth. Mark's eyes opened wide with terror as the Host slammed the heel of his palm against the top of the clipboard, slicing it through the soft tissue of his tear-soaked cheeks. He screamed as the blood poured down his mouth, soaking his top.

'I'm not watching any more of this,' said Billy. 'Joe. Joe! Turn this off!'

'No way, I've paid for this, I'm watching to the end,' replied Joe, unperturbed by his friend's concerns.

'Then you're on your own. I'm going.'

But Joe didn't answer.

'Time for one more question, maybe for the both of them,' said the Host, as he wiped the blood from his clipboard using the sleeve of his boiler suit. 'Start placing your bids.'

The camera panned around the stage, first showing Karen frozen, staring wide-eyed at the sorry figure of Mark, who had by now slumped forward as much as he could, a frothy pink line of bloody saliva dripping from his mouth. As it zoomed in for a close up of Mark, the Host came off-camera and went around to talk to Jarvis. The two men discussed the bidding and amount of time left, as more and more bids poured into the leaderboard. The Host lifted his mask up and wiped the sweat from his brow with his sleeve before running back to stand next to Karen. He grabbed her face and forced it up towards the screen, pointing with the clipboard.

'Right, Karen,' he whispered into the microphone, as she shook her head weakly, tears and snot running down her face, 'let's see what's next, shall we?' The names and values carried on changing until they finally settled on a last late bid.

Charlie20508 – 198 bitcoins

There was silence in the room; Jarvis and the computer operators looked at each other. The Host stared at the screen, for once lost for words, then turned to Jarvis, who shrugged his shoulders in bewilderment. No-one had ever bid an amount this large before. As Karen looked up at the screen, she read the words and started crying.

'Is that my Charlie?' she cried. 'He's trying to speak to me.'

'Don't be a moron, Karen. Of course it isn't. He's dead, remember, you killed him. Anyway, folks, we have just had the single largest bid ever received here in the Red Room. We'll just need a couple of minutes to confirm the transaction. While we do that, we should probably switch transmission nodes just to be on the safe side. So, click on the link that's about to appear on your screen and we'll be right back with you.'

With that, the screen reverted to the picture of the Red Room logo and a new link appeared.

'Billy, did you see that? I think something big is about to go down. Billy?' Joe turned around, but Billy had already left without him noticing. 'Your loss then,' he said, to no-one in particular.

Clicking on the new link, he got up to go to the fridge for another beer while it loaded. It would have been nice to have Billy here to share the experience, but if he didn't have the guts, then that was his problem. Joe's mind was racing, a wild mixture of excitement and apprehension. The more he thought about precisely what he was watching, the more he needed to justify it to himself. For some reason, that was fairly simple. He'd found somewhere that he understood. So much of the deep web content he had seen up until the last twenty minutes seemed contrived, gruesome for the sake of being gruesome, evil for the sake of being evil. But this, this had a purpose and he felt honoured to be witnessing it. For most people, including the friend who had introduced this 'tool' to him in the first place, it would be too much. They just wouldn't 'get it'. Joe got it though, the morality entirely justified it, and it made him part of something special.

Joe returned to the desk with his beer and some peanuts. He was going to need sustenance for this next part, and his heart pounded in eager anticipation as he waited for the show to resume.

18

'Welcome back to the Red Room,' said the Host, as the transmission resumed. 'After that fantastic bid from Charlie, we just had to double check a couple of issues with the transfer, but now we are back and good to go.'

Behind him, the goons were mopping the volunteers' faces and pouring water into their mouths. Karen still stared up at the monitor, convinced that her boy was talking to her from beyond the grave. Mark sat with his head slumped into his chest, the crusty blood around the corners of his mouth making it hard to drink. He stared at his crumpled fingers, shoulders going up and down as he fought against the pain. Every now and again he looked up at Karen and shook his head. His energy was fading fast and he just wanted whatever they were going to do to him to be over.

'OK, so let's see what Charlie wants to ask you two, shall we?' said the Host, crouching down between them and placing a hand on each knee. 'Given how much he's paid, he can pretty much do whatever he wants. Good eh? Charlie, let's have your question.'

Hello, Mummy ...

Karen burst into tears as the Host read the words appearing on the monitor.

I want to play a game. It's called 'Name that injury'. You two have to name the injuries that you caused me, whoever loses gets it.

'Yes, yes, yes!' said the Host, excitedly standing up and punching the air. 'That is a brilliant idea. A bit like Rock Paper Scissors. I'll count to three and then one of you has to shout out an injury that your boy had on his body when it was found.'

'No, I can't do this,' sobbed Karen, sniffing.

'Yes you can, Karen,' said the Host, pinning her head back against the chair. 'Let's face it, you've got plenty to choose from.'

A gurgled 'Fuck you, you're sick,' came from the other chair, as Mark somehow mustered some energy to at least try and act defiant. A goon stepped forward from the back and handed the host a shiny, golden baseball bat.

'Don't worry, Mark, all you have to do is cast your mind back to when that happy little boy, who looked up to you for protection and to her for comfort, found himself on the receiving end of some of the worst punishment which could be dished out to a human being. Let alone a two-year-old. Come on, it's easy. Just imagine how you used to kick him, punch him, pick him up by the throat and slam him against the wall. I'm sure all the injuries will come flooding back. Let me start you two off. Ready? One … two … three … Fractured wrist!'

The two looked up as the Host swung the baseball bat, bringing it down with a crack on Karen's right wrist, causing her to scream in agony.

'Sorry, you were both too slow.' He switched attention to Mark, who took a deep breath and closed his eyes in helpless anticipation, before the host dished out the same.

Amongst the pained cries, now in stereo, the Host continued.

'Right, now that you've got the hang of this, let's play for real. OK, one … two … three …' A pause, silence. 'Come on, one of you!' said the Host, twirling the baseball bat around.

Eventually, Karen quietly mumbled into her chest, 'Broken eye.'

'Yes, quite right, a point to Karen. When he was found he had a fractured eye socket. Well two, actually, but who's counting?'

Like a batter facing a vicious curve ball, the Host swung around behind him and smashed the baseball bat into the side of Mark's head. A red mark appeared instantly around his temple. He groaned in pain and, were it not for the goon with his vial of salts on standby, would probably have passed out.

'Next round. One … two … three …'

Despite the pain that was already crippling his body, Mark knew he didn't want any more.

'Broken leg,' he spluttered, as best he could.

'No, please,' begged Karen.

'Sorry, Karen, but he's right. Don't you remember, your boy had a broken tibia? Not only that, you also manage to fracture his femur. Now that takes some doing. He must have done something really serious for you to punish him that much.'

'Don't, please, I …' But before she could finish the sentence a wave of pain cut through her body as the baseball bat connected with her shin. It sent shockwaves up her body, the pain so intense that she started to lose feeling in her right side.

And so it continued; cracked skull, dislocated jaw, broken ribs. The pain they were already in acted as some sort of operant conditioning, making them answer instinctively until eventually neither could find the energy to speak. As the Host looked at the two crumpled, soaking, black, red, and blue figures in the chairs in front of him, a goon took the bat from his hand.

'Well, ladies and gentleman, I think we can safely say that these two are starting to understand the suffering that they caused. It's just a blessing for them that it's all happening so quickly, not prolonged …' the Host said, propping Mark's head back by the chin '… over a matter of months. Unfortunately, we need to be gone soon, otherwise we would dearly love to make these two suffer a little more. But I think we have time for one more, for which I am going to turn to the main man himself, Charlie. Charlie, pick an injury and who you want to be the lucky recipient.'

The words appeared on the monitor. *They forgot this one. Shattered pelvis. Mark.*

With that, the Host placed the microphone and clipboard down on Karen's lap, before spinning around, leaping into the air and stamping his foot down as hard as he could on Mark's hip bone. There was an audible crack as he landed. Even the bystanders who had witnessed the last ten minutes had to wince. Finally, Mark gave up the ghost and passed out.

'Thank you, Karen,' said the Host, collecting his belongings from her lap before facing the camera close up. He looked at Jarvis, who held up his hands, fingers spread wide. 'OK, we've only got ten minutes before we need to finish this. You've got one minute to start placing your bids.'

The names flickered and changed, before stopping with a winner. 'Well, no-one was likely to better Charlie's bid from the previous round, but twelve bitcoins is still pretty good. Let's hear how you want this to end ... JoltinJoe!'

Joe sat back in his seat, took a long sip of beer, and wiped his brow. There was no turning back now.

19

His fingers trembled as he slowly typed the letters in one by one, the keyboard one big fuzzy mess of black and white. He felt like a sniper in a war zone, hidden away, anonymous, looking at someone whose life he held in his hands. He stared at the murderers on the screen, oblivious to his presence and the fate that was about to befall them. The sense of power Joe felt overwhelmed him, despite the internal conflict that welled inside him. But it was just a show, it might not even be real. Worse things happen in movies or in video games.

And anyway, he wasn't actually committing the act, he was merely making a suggestion. Even if the authorities wanted to track him, it was all anonymous and they would probably be more interested in finding this Brotherhood, the ones orchestrating the whole website. They were the ones doing the killing and making money out of it. They were under no obligation to do what he said. He convinced himself that it would be fine and, really, he was actually doing the world a favour by ridding it of these two monsters.

He rubbed his eyes, took another sip of ale, and continued typing. He could have done with a bit longer to think about this, to make it really special.

'I'm going to have to hurry you, JoltinJoe,' said the Host, into the camera.

This is my first time in the Red Room. It's been a real pleasure to see these two monsters get what they deserve.

'That's great, Joe, but I really need you to hurry up or I'm going to have to choose myself.'

Suffocate him. Slit her with the clipboard.

He hit enter and sat back to watch. A goon held Mark's forehead back as the Host positioned himself side-on, just in front of the chair. He raised his right knee and then thrust his leg out perfectly level, landing the edge of his foot in Mark's throat. The years of martial arts training allowed him perfect balance, and he held his leg in position as Mark fought for breath. Raising the microphone and clipboard above his head he gave one final thrust of his leg, crushing Mark's windpipe. As the Host lowered his leg, Mark let out a final breath, before his head slumped forward, motionless.

Behind him, another goon held Karen the same way. The Host threw the clipboard up in the air; it spun two or three times, then as he caught it by the top, he spun around and slashed the edge across her throat. Blood sprayed from the wound and she gargled a pink-white froth before finally falling forward, caught only by the restraints on the chair.

As the Host wiped the blood from the bottom of the clipboard, a pair of goons unbuckled the lifeless bodies from each chair and lay them on the floor. The Host turned to face the camera.

'Ladies and gentlemen, that is all from the Brotherhood of the Righteous. I hope that you have enjoyed this episode of the Red Room and we—'

But he was cut off by Jarvis, waving his arms wildly and making a 'cut' gesture across his throat.

'Just a minute …' the Host told the viewers.

Joe swivelled from side to side in his chair, trying all he could to calm his heart rate down after what he just witnessed. He had taken one massive leap into the murky unknown and had become part of the legacy of the dark web. And it was something he liked the feel of. No longer was he just the director of a medium-sized family business, with a girlfriend and a mortgage, he was part of something out of reach to the average man in the street. A member of the so-called Brotherhood.

And then he noticed it. A Chrome session flashed orange in the toolbar at the bottom of his screen. He clicked on it and as the status box popped up in the middle of the screen, his heart sunk lower than it had ever before.

Transaction failed

'Oh my fucking god, no. Please, don't do this to me. Not now,' he said out loud. Frantically, he began clicking at random links in the hope that it would somehow fix this situation. But it was no use, his transfer had failed. He didn't know precisely what this meant, but given what he had just seen, he knew it wouldn't be good.

'What's the matter?' the Host asked Jarvis. 'I can't be doing with any problems.'

'That last transaction bounced. Whoever this JoltingJoe is, he's done us,' replied Jarvis, continuing to tap away on his laptop keyboard. 'We're checking all incoming filters for any hint as to who and where this guy might be. He seems like an amateur, I'm sure he'll leave some sort of trace.'

'Find him. We need to get this moved out,' the Host replied, returning to the camera. 'Well, ladies and gentlemen, sorry about that, it seems that our last viewer decided he wanted something for nothing. For all you genuine Brotherhood members out there, thank you for watching. Once again, the world is rid of another couple of monsters this country did not see fit to punish suitably. I think we can all be assured that their debt to society has now been settled with interest. And hopefully the spirit of Charlie will be able to rest in peace a little easier. Remember to keep an eye on the message boards for the next instalment of the Red Room. Thanks for watching and goodnight!'

He walked away, but then paused and turned back to the camera, 'Oh and, JoltingJoe, whoever you are, if you're still watching … We are coming for you and we will find you.' And with that, the cameras cut off and the screen went black.

The goons continued with the clean-up operation, the chairs were dismantled, and the plastic covering peeled from the floor. They had already moved the bodies into the back of one of the vans and now were removing the remaining traces from the warehouse.

The Host removed his mask and threw it into one of the sacks with the rest of the rubbish, shouting over his shoulder as he stormed out of the warehouse.

'Jarvis? Found him yet?'

'Nearly, I'm just running a tracking program,' replied Jarvis, collecting his laptop and scurrying after the Host. 'We managed to download nearly all the sub-links before we cut transmission and then it'll just be a case of working through them until we find the open window.'

'OK, do it in the car. We've got to go, now. The boys are getting twitchy.'

'Fine. I'm going. Don't worry, we'll find him.'

Joe's sense of power and ego had been short-lived. He had closed the website window down and exited the browser altogether. But he had a feeling it was a futile gesture, little more than burying his head in the sand. He paced up and down the garage, throwing pool balls randomly around the table, trying to make sense of what had just happened. How could the transaction have failed, there was more than enough credit to cover it. He wished that he could go back in time an hour and never become involved in this, just watch instead. Or that he'd wake up and realise he was still pissed, lying on Billy's sofa.

At that moment, he heard the jangle of keys in the side door, closely followed by a giggling, stumbling Ellie.

'Shit,' he whispered, as she propped herself against the wall, trying to remove a knee-high leather boot and failing miserably.

She finished removing the boot whilst lying on the floor, then crawled into the garage on her hands and knees.

'Hello, big boy. What are you doing in here? Playing with your balls?' she slurred, giggling at her own wit.

'Hilarious,' he replied, struggling to muster even a half smile. 'You look a tad pissed. Good night, was it?'

'Brilliant. Helen's got a new froybend and—'

'A what?'

'A froybend, you know a … Ha ha, I mean boyfriend. She's got a new boyfriend and it turns out he's got two kids and she didn't know until he turned up at her house covered in Peppa Pig stickers. And then she went ape-shit at him but then said she'd forgive him because he's got a massive cock.'

'Sounds delightful. Anyway, probably best if you went to bed isn't it?'

'What? Don't be so boring! Come on, let's dance,' she shouted, flinging her arms around his neck.

'Look, I'm really not in the mood at the moment.'

'Where's Billy? I thought he'd still be here.' she said, looking around the room, before grabbing both of Joe's cheeks in the palms of her hands and wobbling them up and down. 'Did you two have a little tiff?'

'Stop being stupid. No, he left because he's got an early morning start with football. Anyway, look, I'm going to shut down the computer and come to bed. Why don't you go up?' Joe replied.

'Jeez, you are so uptight. Come on, relax,' she said, grabbing his hand and sitting him back down in the chair.

She hitched her skirt up and straddled him on the chair, while he tried his best to look interested. He placed his hands on her backside and began kissing her as she started to grind into his crotch. At that moment, a program window opened up on the screen behind her. Joe glanced over her shoulder. His heart, which still hadn't calmed down from before and was now in overdrive as his girlfriend tried her best to arouse him, all of a sudden felt like it was about to explode out of his chest. There, on the screen, was the clown-masked face of the Host. Joe let go of Ellie, who was still making all the moves, and stared as the Host gestured to the bottom corner of the window. In it, a small box appeared, showing Ellie's back and his face.

'What's the matter?' asked Ellie, seeing his face frozen. She turned around on his lap and looked at the computer, snuggling into him and trying hard not to fall asleep. 'Oh, hello Mister Clown Face!'

'Ellie, don't,' said Joe, though what good it would do he didn't know.

'Hello, Joe,' said the Host.

'Billy, is that you, you fucking pervert? Get a good eyeful of my arse did you? Better than you'll ever get, you sad little tosser.'

'No, this isn't Billy, is it, Joe? Why don't you inform this delightful young lady who we are?'

'What do you want? Look, I know I messed up the transfer, but I'll pay it, I swear. Just give me a little more time to sort it, the banks will be closed now for the weekend.'

'Oh, Joe, this isn't about the money. You really think that's why we do this? Think about it, what did you feel as you watched? Revulsion? Fear? Justice? Exactly, we do this because our viewers want justice. In the olden days, dispensing justice was a very unpleasant business. These days it's gone soft, but people don't like that. And our Brotherhood has decided to right that wrong. But the only way it can work is with the complete integrity of everyone taking part. And tonight, you failed. We will be coming to get you, to reclaim more than just money. You belong to us now.'

'What? Please, I didn't realise what was going on. I just thought it was ...' begged Joe.

'Thought it was what, Joe? Fake? A joke? It's real, Joe, what you saw was real. You watched it for long enough to understand.'

'I didn't know what it was,' he protested, in the hope that Ellie would believe him.

'Don't bother, Joe. Luckily for you I think your better half is asleep.'

Joe craned his neck back to check that she was. 'How did you find me though?' he replied, turning back to the screen, thankful Ellie couldn't hear.

'Look at the top of the monitor, what do you see?'

The minute he said it, Joe realised what he had done. Or rather hadn't done.

'Shit,' he said to himself. Billy had even warned him specifically about covering up the webcam, and it now became clear why. He stood up with Ellie in his arms and walked her over to the sofa, where he lay her down.

'Look, so you found my computer, big deal. You've got no idea who I am or where I live. The minute I close this window, I'll just disconnect from the internet, uninstall the webcam driver, and you won't be able to find me again,' he said, surprising himself with the level of guts and defiance he had managed to muster, not that he really believed it for one minute.

'I really wouldn't do that if I were you, Joe,' said the Host. 'If you help us and do what we say, then you will be fine. But you should understand the level of influence and reach, as well as resources, that our group has. Pretending we don't exist is not an option. We will—'

Before he could finish the sentence, Joe pulled the network cable from the router and closed down the window. He loaded up the applications and began uninstalling the webcam program before plugging in a hard drive and starting a back-up. Sitting with his head in his hands, he turned to look at Ellie, fast asleep on the sofa. What had he done? For now, she was probably still unaware and hopefully wouldn't remember in the morning.

He needed time to think. There was no way these people could track him. They couldn't, could they? Just from a webcam chat? But they had found him. Or at least they had tracked him to a computer; but still, that was all they had. All he had to do was stay offline for a while and they would probably lose interest. He walked over to Ellie, placed a pillow under her head, and lay a blanket over the top of her. As he walked out of the garage and turned the lights off, a message alert sounded on his phone. Pulling it from his pocket, he opened the text. As he read it, he dropped back against the wall and slumped into a heap on the floor.

'No!' he whispered, banging the back of his head against the wall as he read the two-word text again.

Foolish Boy

20

Daisy walked up the garden path, holding her hands out to the side allowing the soft white heads of the tall pampas grass to glide through her fingers. She looked up at the decrepit terraced house, the dull grey frontage blending in with the stormy clouds that floated overhead. With its faded paintwork, chipped rendering, and cracked windows held together with brown packing tape, it was not the most inviting of places. An empty beer bottle rolled around the front step and stopped against the red wooden door, knocking just enough to push it ajar a couple of inches.

Pushing the door open, she walked in slowly. The woodchip paper on the walls in the hallway had been painted magnolia and was now pebble-dashed with patches of black mould. Down the end of the hallway, a television blared out a hardcore porn movie, and she heard voices. A man came out of a room, lighting a cigarette, and she darted onto the first couple of steps of the stairs, ducking down behind the banister while he turned into the kitchen. She stood up and slowly crept up the stairs. As she arrived at the landing, she peered around the banister at the row of chairs lined up against the wall, two empty and one with a man sat reading the paper. He seemed completely oblivious to her presence, even as she stood up at the end of the landing.

After a minute or so, the door at the end opened and a man left, hastily putting his jacket back on and wiping the lipstick smear from his face. Daisy stood back against the wall as he rushed past, as if she wasn't there, and she caught the sweet overpowering scent of cheap perfume lingering on his clothes. The door opened again and a chubby, nightie-clad woman, probably in her early

30s but easily looking forty, beckoned the remaining man into the bedroom.

'Mum!' shouted Daisy, but the door was slammed shut with the click of a lock fastening.

She ran to the end of the landing and began hammering on the door, but there was no response from inside. Hearing the front door go, she turned around and started back down the stairs. Another man passed her on the stairs. He had a close-shaven head and wore large gold earrings, a heavy chunky gold necklace, and at least three huge sovereign rings on his fingers. As they passed each other, he stubbed a cigarette out on the wall and reach around to grab Daisy's backside. The sound of his arrogant laughter hung in the air as she hurried past and leapt around the bottom of the stairs.

At the end of the hallway, she tiptoed through the open door. Two men in shiny shell suits sat on a sofa. One tapped cigarette ash into an empty can of cider that rested on his bulbous gut whilst sipping from another. They discussed the various attributes and acting abilities of the actress in the adult movie on the television, stopping intermittently to take a drag from the cheap cigarettes or a swig from the super-strength cider.

In the corner of the room, a small girl sat on the floor. She looked no more than eight or nine years old and wore a stained white vest top and shorts. Her long tousled hair hung in dreadlock-like clumps and she had bruises on her arms and legs. Sitting cross-legged against the wall, she held a Barbie doll dressed as a ballerina. It had one leg missing and the girl lovingly brushed its long wiry hair with a small plastic brush. Minutes passed, and Daisy just stared at the girl, watching her repeat the same motion over and over again.

'Hey!' Daisy said, in a harsh whisper. The girl didn't respond, the noise from the television drowning Daisy out. 'Hey, sweetheart,' she tried again.

This time, the little girl turned her head to the doorway, a large clump of hair hanging in front of her face. Daisy knelt down to her level.

'Hi, what's your name?' she asked.

The little girl held up the doll. The face was a hideous mess of wavy plastic and black scorch marks, the result of numerous cigarettes extinguished on it. The girl stared a moment before answering,

'My name is Daisy.'

Daisy lost balance and put her arm down to stop herself toppling over. The little girl let out a scream, and Daisy put a finger to her lips in an effort to make the girl quieten down. But it was too late, and already one of the men had left the sofa. Walking over to the little girl, he grabbed her by the wrist and pulled her to her feet. Daisy reached out to try and stop the man as he brought his hand up, but despite a desperate leap forward with her arms outstretched, couldn't stop the man bringing a forceful slap down across the little girl's face. Daisy lay on the floor, raising her head to look at the girl as the man dropped back down into the sofa and carried on smoking. The little girl sat with her head in her hands, sobbing.

Daisy reached out a hand to place it on the girl's leg.

'Come on, sweetheart, come with me. Let me get you out of here.' As she made contact the girl grabbed her wrist and turned her head. She wiped the hair away from her face, revealing two eyes sewn shut with surgical stitches amongst a mess of bruises, scratches, and scabs.

'Who are you? What do you want?' She spoke in a high-pitched shriek that made Daisy recoil in horror. 'They mustn't let me see. Not allowed to see!' Daisy backed away, thrashing to try and break free. But the small girl kept coming. 'Who are you? What do you want?' she repeated. 'They mustn't let me see. Not allowed to see! Who are you? What do you want?'

Daisy awoke with a start, sitting bolt upright and rubbing her eyes. As her eyes became accustomed to the inside of the caravan, she began to make out the form of an elderly gentleman, dressed in a green quilted body warmer, green wellington boots, and a brown tweed suit.

'Who are you?' he asked, pointing a long walking stick at Daisy. 'What do you want?'

'Sorry ... I must have ... fallen asleep,' she replied, groggily.

'Well, that's all bloody well and good that is, but you've broken my bloody lock, you little rascal. Go on, get out of it before I bloody well call the police.'

Daisy gathered her meagre belongings and ran out of the caravan. She stopped at the step and pulled a note from the wedge she kept hidden in her underwear.

'That's for your sodding lock. Don't worry, I won't be coming back here, the service was shit, there was no room service, and no breakfast.'

'Why, you bloody little monkey, come here and I'll give you a bloody piece of my mind!'

But Daisy had already started running, further into the forest. After a week of sleeping in the caravan eating nothing but takeaway, she stank, but it had been the nicest week of her life for as long as she could remember. The pain in her body had all but disappeared, the drugs and alcohol in her system cleaned out. The cold turkey effects were diminishing, but she still needed to stay as far away from the town as she could.

After a mile or so, she stopped for a rest on a fallen log. The dream started to replay itself in her mind. Memories of her childhood came flooding back, how she used to play with dolls as a coping strategy to block out the events around her. She had always wanted a real dad, not one man after another shacking up with her mum, treating her like she was nothing but a nuisance. Her real dad had – well, she didn't know. She didn't know who he was or why he wasn't around. She assumed he was one of her mum's many tricks but figured he must be out there somewhere. One day, maybe she would try and find him, but that would first mean having to contact her mother, something which she had absolutely no intention of doing.

She stood up and starting walking. This part of the woods was unfamiliar to her, but she could hear the faint hum of lorries and industry in the distance ahead. As she approached, she found a gap in the chain link fence large enough to fit through, but there was far too much activity going on through there at the moment. She would wait until tonight and sneak in to have a look around. For now, she would go and sample the delights of the burger van parked just the other side of the fence and then head off to try and spend some of Aleksander's hard-stolen money on a local bed and breakfast.

21

The banqueting hall in Clifton Manor was enormous. Its high ceilings, art deco architecture, gold gilded railings, and thirty place dining table had led it to be photographed for numerous high society magazines, as well as to be used as a set in many television programmes. What was usually left out of these photographs, however, were the dartboard and vintage retro jukebox that sat in the far corner, by one of the huge bay windows.

Eric and Stan were playing darts while Jarvis sat at the end of the banqueting table with his laptop. The doors to the hall swung open and in walked Gilbert and Alistair.

'Gentlemen, if I could drag you away from your no doubt important game, we've got some urgent matters to discuss,' said Alistair, motioning for Jarvis to vacate his seat at the head of the table.

'We'll carry this on afterwards,' said Stan. 'Please try and remember the score.'

'Shouldn't be too difficult,' replied Eric. 'We both need double one. And have done for the last six minutes.'

The two men sat down at the table as Gilbert poured a round of coffee, placing a pristine white bone china cup and saucer in front of each man.

'Anything to go with it? I could murder a fairy cake or a French fancy,' said Stan.

'Sorry, no, we're all out of girls' cakes, Stan,' replied Gilbert.

'OK, thank you, gentlemen,' interjected Alistair. 'We need to make plans as to how we move from here. We'll carry out the disposal of last night's volunteers after dinner tonight. We need to think about our next volunteer and we also need to think about how we are going to deal with our new friend JoltinJoe. Jarvis, can you give us the run down on last night, please.'

'Certainly. We had a peak audience of five hundred and twelve paid up subscribers. This dropped to four-eight-one after the Guess the Injury round. I think perhaps a few people had seen enough but the majority of those left stayed until the end. Probably because we didn't switch exit nodes before the final round and make people pay another couple of coins for the privilege of seeing the money shot. So when you add that up at three coins each, plus the bids that were made of around two hundred and thirty coins, we made just over seventeen hundred bitcoins. At current exchange rates, that equates to just over one point one million. Take out Stan and Eric's hundred and fifty grand each, although god only knows what they did to earn it …'

'Ha, shut your face, Poindexter,' laughed Eric. 'We're the backbone of this entire bloody operation. If you ask me, you're getting an absolute bargain.'

'OK, fine,' continued Jarvis. 'For driving the vans a bit and doing some dodgy wiring, we take out a hundred and fifty thousand each for Stan and Eric. Plus the goons' pay, that leaves us with around about six hundred thousand.'

'Not bad. Make a donation to the children's hospice in town and tell them I'll come down for a meet and greet soon.'

'How much?'

'All of it. So, this Joe guy that stiffed us, what do we know about him?' asked Alistair, sipping from his coffee as he sat back in his chair.

'Quite a lot, actually, the guy was clearly an amateur,' replied Jarvis, leafing through some papers. 'Joe Henderson, thirty-four, a director in his family's metal supply business. The business is doing very well despite the recession. A girlfriend called Ellie, whose backside we all had the pleasure of seeing. And if you will excuse the excruciatingly bad pun, he's just your 'Average Joe'.'

'That was shit even by your standards,' said Gilbert. 'How did you get all this from just his webcam being on?'

'Put simply, we were able to put a trace through the incoming nodes and track them all back to find anything that looked vaguely similar to the outgoing payment of the bitcoin transaction, which had failed because the bitcoin miners picked up an anomaly in the source wallet. It's all hidden there, deep in the source coding for the transactions, if you know where to look. After that, it was simply a case of looking for anyone who'd left a window open; in this joker's case, his webcam. Once we'd hacked into his PC we could look on his desktop, where we found the browser window still open, showing the failed transaction. Somehow, the gormless buffoon hadn't spotted it. Like I said, an amateur. After that, it was a piece of cake. We now know where he lives, where he works, his friends, his family.'

'The marvels of Facebook I suppose,' said Alistair.

'Indeed. A whole life online for anyone to find.'

'Not just anyone. Us. Now, the only reason that this project works is because of the integrity of our viewers. We cannot have imbeciles like Mister Henderson jeopardising it all because he doesn't know how to bloody well send a few bitcoins. And I think we should waste no time in letting young Joe see that we mean business.'

'Talking of business,' added Eric, 'we ran a little close to the mark during the last one in terms of time. I think it would be wise to do the next episode from somewhere with zero connections to your organisation. It sounds like this little jackass not only has a lot to lose but also somewhere that might be of use to us.'

'Good thinking,' said Alistair, leaning forward with his elbows on the table. 'Let's start slowly, see if he caves early. If not, then we ramp up the hints until he gets it. Clearly, he didn't have the slightest clue what he was signing up for or what a dark place the deep web can be. But we need to lean on him. In fact, put a note in the disclaimer for the next episode explaining what has happened as far as Mister Henderson is concerned and how we dealt with it. Keep out the specifics, but just enough to make anyone else think twice about pulling the same stunt.'

'OK, we'll get to work on it,' said Eric.

'And the final point on our agenda,' said Gilbert. 'Who's going to be our next volunteer?'

'I think it's between the two we spoke about last time. Darren Blundell, really nasty piece of work, just been released from Belmarsh on a technicality. And Cramer McAllister, gangland enforcer and general all round shit,' replied Jarvis.

'Who's the easiest?' asked Alistair.

'McAllister probably. Turns out that along with being partial to removing his victims' manual digits with bolt cutters, he also has something of a secret penchant for rent boys. Should be fairly easy to set up a sting,' replied Eric. 'But saying that, I've always liked the idea of going after Blundell. His drugs operation was responsible for turning so many areas of the finer cities in the country into misery-ridden warzones. He didn't care whose lives he ruined; women, children, pensioners. Like Jarvis said, a real nasty piece of work.'

'McAllister,' said Alistair. 'Leave Blundell for the next time.'

'We're on it,' said Eric. 'Jarvis, we'll need your help with McAllister and young Mister Joe.'

'Eric, I am forever at your service,' replied Jarvis.

'Good. So if there's nothing else, I'm going for a swim,' said Alistair, planting his hands on the table as he stood up. 'Gilbert, if you can make the arrangements for the disposal later, and I'll see you all at dinner.'

Just as the last vestiges of sunlight disappeared over the hill behind Clifton Manor and a quiet stillness fell over the vast estate, the silence was broken as the large metal door to the maintenance area clanked open.

'We really should put some oil on that,' remarked Eric. 'One of these days it'll seize up.'

Eric was driving a small electric utility vehicle, used to travel between the various extremities of the estate. On this occasion, it was carrying a more gruesome cargo than its usual buckets, shovels, or new fence panels.

'Well, at least they'll know that we're coming,' replied Stan. 'Although I never understood why we have to do all this bloody hooded cloak bollocks each time. It's not as if we're New Age mental cases.'

'As long as we get our hundred-odd grand each time, I'd happily wear a Brownie uniform.'

Turning the headlights on, they started along the gravel track that led away from the house, past the formal gardens, before finally entering the woodland. In the distance they could see the twinkling glow of fire. As they approached, the woodland opened out and the fire torches illuminated the form of the large stone folly. Alistair had had it specially constructed from the same Welsh spotted dolerite bluestone that was used to build Stonehenge. Each of its five pillars cleared twenty foot high and were adorned with pagan and Masonic symbols and icons. Not that he believed in any of that, he just put them on as more of a joke, to start all the conspiracy theorists speculating when he was gone.

Around the outside stood Alistair, Jarvis, and the other members of the Brotherhood, who parted as the vehicle approached. Two of the goons entered the centre of the folly and hooked two large chains to metal rings protruding from the ground. Taking the strain as they braced their feet against the stone steps, they pulled hard. A large round stone began to slide across the ground, revealing a deep, dark hole a metre across. The vehicle turned and reversed in between two of the pillars until a bang on the back from one of the goons signalled it to stop. Reaching into the back, he pulled out a large drum and promptly poured its white gloopy contents down into the hole. Another goon emptied a second container.

The bystanders all gathered around the hole as Alistair, dressed in a long black cloak with red velvet lining, stepped forward and lowered his hood. Behind him, Gilbert, Jarvis, and the rest of the goons did the same and were then joined by Eric and Stan. Stan pressed a button on the back of the vehicle and the flatbed started to rise. As the incline became steeper, the limp naked body of Mark Rankin slid down into the abyss. Alistair stared intently as the bruised, battered face turned in his direction. The eyes were shut but the sinister slashed smile still etched into its cheeks grinned back at him. It almost looked happy as it fell into the darkness, before finally landing with a splash in its final resting place some seconds later.

The flatbed continued to rise and the body of Karen Parker clung to the base like a beached whale on a rock. As the flatbed thudded to a stop, the men looked up at it. Alistair in turn looked at Eric and, with a slightly angry face, gestured with his head in the direction of the flatbed.

'Er, that's as far as it goes,' said Eric.

'Then do something about it,' replied Alistair.

'She's too bloody fat, the moisture and the friction. She won't budge,' he said, trying to lever her away from the base with a long crowbar. Eventually, with the sound of a vacuum releasing, the body slid down the flatbed and disappeared into the hole.

'I bet that poor sod is glad he's dead, having that enormous beast belly-flop on top of him,' said Stan.

'That's enough,' snapped Alistair, over the sniggering. 'Let's at least try and maintain a modicum of decorum, they were our guests, after all.'

All the men gathered around and put their hoods up. Two of the goons emptied another drum down the hole before pushing a large pile of rocks in to cover it.

Alistair reached into his cloak and pulled out a small red leather bible, which he threw into the hole.

'I'm not sure if this will do you any good, but it may be your best chance of avoiding the remainder of eternity in Hell. But still, with you two gone, the world is rid of two of the most evil abominations of human creation. Your lives were significant for nothing but bad things and the pathetic justice system entirely failed in ensuring that you paid the appropriate price for your deeds. But we made sure.

'There are lots of people out there who have lost faith in justice and maybe some of them were witness to these two's judgement day. Perhaps we have restored some faith in humanity. As our reputation grows we must become ever more careful. But soon people will realise that there is someone who makes a stand, who rights wrongs and who makes the truly evil face up to their deeds. We are the Brotherhood. We are the Righteous. Gentlemen, the Brotherhood!'

'The Brotherhood!' they all replied, in unison. The men all turned to leave as the stone cover was replaced.

'Eric, you lead the way. When we get back to the house, Jarvis, you rack them up.'

22

Monday morning again. The first week at work since the leave of absence had seemed to fly by for Harris, and he felt comfortable being back in the thick of it all. A cup of coffee sat steaming on his desk, next to the picture of his daughter, while the partition to his desk was adorned with a rainbow of coloured sticky notes. The vast majority were yellow, containing mundane telephone messages. *Ring such and such at, Send reports to such and such, Check database for such and such at ...* In amongst the organised chaos of notes sat the most important colour, the blue ones, reminders to pick up his daughter, pay for this lesson or that, or to print off something for a school project.

'Busy working, I see?' asked D.C.I. Smith, jabbing him in the rib with a forefinger as he walked past.

'Sorry, sir,' replied Harris. 'Olivia's got a school project to complete on ancient Greeks, which basically means that I've got a school project to complete on ancient Greeks. It's got to be in on Wednesday and luckily she only told me about it this morning. So, with Grandma being a complete technology imbecile, I thought I'd better print off some material for them to work with tonight.'

'The joys of single parenthood. Glad those days are behind me now,' said Smith. 'Getting back to the slightly less important matter of police work, there's been a bloody enormous development in this particular post-it note.' He took a pink note off of the partition and slapped it down on the desk in front of Harris. The note read *KAREN PARKER – REVIEW MISPER*

'What kind of development? Have they found her?' asked Harris, holding the note in front of his face with one finger.

'Look on the log. The Missing Persons Bureau running the case have come up against one brick wall after another. It seems to be one massive mystery how this person can just, all of a sudden, disappear into "fat air", shall we say.'

Smith continued as Harris scanned down the log to find the case. 'What the new system enables us to do is automatically link cases that might be connected. So when a case is flagged up for our attention any other case that links to it will be flagged up to us as well. In this instance—'

'Mark Rankin,' said Harris, cutting him off.

'Yes, indeed. You couldn't write it, could you?' he said. 'Like I said, a fairly enormous development. I'm still not sure how this relates to us, but I want you to investigate this a little further, liaise with the team looking into the Karen Parker case. The file on Mark Rankin is very new so there may not be much information on it. But I can't believe this is pure coincidence. Grace has been doing a little digging with regards to the protocols for missing persons. Grace!' he shouted over to Brooks, who picked up some files and pulled a chair up to Harris' desk.

'I imagine this is anything but a routine missing person procedure,' said Harris, as he continued scanning down the case log.

'Quite right,' said Brooks. 'Apart from the obvious dead ends the investigation team have hit, there is also the rather tricky conundrum of how much of this to make public. Both of them were given new identities and new homes about as far away from each other as it's possible to be and still remain in England. Usually there would be enormous press coverage, TV interviews with family, pictures plastered over the newspapers, social media, and so on. But with these two, it's slightly more challenging. We can't go public since then every one of their neighbours would realise that they'd been living next door to child killers. Neither had any family in particular, but even if they did, their relatives either don't want to know or, in the case of the remaining children, are living in secure locations under new identities for their own protection anyway.'

'Presumably, their families or the kids' guardians have been contacted though?' asked Harris.

'Yes, of course. But only along the lines of enquiring whether either had been in contact with them, as is checked periodically anyway.'

'Did Rankin have an electronic tag?'

'No. Technically, he received the lesser charge and was deemed unlikely to try and contact her other kids.'

'Those other children really dodged a bullet there, didn't they?' said Smith.

'Thankfully they were too young to understand,' replied Brooks. 'But getting back to Rankin, or Barry as his name was changed to. He was well known in his new local area as something of a nutter. A loner; not someone that you'd want to be friends with anyway. In fact, it was the landlord of his local pub who called it in. He thought it was strange that a week had gone by without Rankin visiting his establishment, such was the frequency with which he drank there.

'Last time he saw him, Rankin had left the pub at closing time, steaming pissed as usual, having just started a fight with a couple of lads over a game of pool. That was over a week ago. So the landlord rang the local police station, who then did a check of his home address and found him missing. No obvious signs of anything, really. The place was a tip of course, the remnants of his dinner were still sitting on the kitchen table, the calendar on the wall had stuff written in it. At first sight, he had every intention of returning home at some point. But that, for whatever reason, never happened.'

'Anything on his last movements?' asked Harris.

'CCTV catches him leaving the pub, staggering around for quite a while fighting with the beer fairies, and then disappearing down a side alley.'

'Anything on the alley?'

'Nothing. It's a CCTV dead spot. From either entrance.'

'So a fairly good choice for someone who, maybe, wanted to remove him without being seen?' said Harris, suspiciously.

'Indeed. But they would have to be a bit crazy; apart from being over six foot, the guy was a fucking nut-job.'

'Crazy, or professionals.'

'Look, you two work together on this. I realise it's a little outside our remit. But it seems like whatever happened to these two shits is somehow linked, and if there is anyone else involved they seem to know what they're doing. The lack of CCTV coverage, the electronic tag. Something smells, and I'm pretty certain it isn't Grace's BO. I'm going for a fag.' Smith was removing a cigarette from the box in his shirt pocket before he'd left the office.

'He really is charming,' said Grace, sniffing her armpit. 'I think I smell nice today.'

'You smell fine,' replied Harris, not really paying any attention. 'I'm going to request the tracking logs from Karen Parker's tag. There must be something on there that provides a clue. Can you find out anything that's available on these two? Anything from their case workers: email addresses, mobile phone details, any internet history that might throw something up?'

Brooks nodded in agreement and headed back to her desk. Harris turned around and pulled the pile of pictures off of the printer.

'Come on, Archimedes,' he said to himself as he placed the pages into a clear folder and into his draw. 'Give me my eureka moment.'

'Is this seat taken?' Brooks said, as she planted a tray full of salad and fruit down on the table next to Harris.

'Let me just check,' replied Harris, looking around the half-empty canteen. 'No, you should be OK, but if someone better-looking comes along you'll have to move. Still on the diet I see. When do you think it'll start having an effect, eating all this rabbit food?'

'Hilarious. Probably about the same time your heart attack kicks in from eating all that shit,' she replied, as Harris took a huge bite of his cheeseburger.

The food in the canteen wasn't great, but at least he didn't have to worry about cooking for himself when he eventually arrived home. More time to do his Greek project.

'Fair enough. So, did you manage to find anything from the case workers about our two little elusive friends?'

'A bit. Karen didn't really maintain any sort of online presence, kind of a pre-requisite for her new identity. Can't have her shouting the odds on Facebook. She had a basic phone, very little activity. Pretty much, she spent her whole time indoors with her cats, eating and watching daytime television. Mark on the other hand was a lot more active on the internet.'

'Is that a euphemism?' interrupted Harris, chuckling to himself.

'For what?' replied Brooks, somewhat confused.

'Doesn't matter.'

'Right. Anyway, he had a few online profiles,' Brooks continued, 'not on any social media sites, but log-ins for gambling websites, Amazon, and loads of porn sites.'

'I knew it!' Harris said, triumphantly.

'God, you're weird. Yes, porn sites,' she replied, weary at his childishness. 'But he seemed to spend most of his time on a live roulette game run by one of the big bookies.'

'If it's a bona-fide site, they wouldn't allow him to run up gambling debts, so I can't see that being a factor in his disappearance. Did they ever contact each other?'

'Not that we can see. I don't think there was much love lost between them after they were arrested, each trying to blame the other, etcetera.'

Just at that moment, a junior analyst from their team burst into the canteen and made his way hastily to their table.

'Danny,' said Harris, chewing on a mouthful of chips. 'I'd offer you a seat, but I told Grace she'd only have to move if someone better looking came along, and frankly, you look like a pile of crap.'

'Whatever,' Danny Fowler replied. 'Stop stuffing your face, you need to come and see this. Now.'

'Where did this come from?' asked Harris, as six members of the team huddled around Fowler's desk, watching the video play out on his screen.

'It was sent to the general email address just now,' replied Fowler, adjusting some settings on his monitor in an attempt to make it clearer.

'The general email address?' asked Harris. 'Isn't that monitored by Dorothy?'

'Yes, she nearly had a fucking coronary when she clicked on it, poor old mare. She's having a lie down in the common room.'

'But we don't know who sent it?'

'Well, we have a sender obviously, and we can see the return path is somewhere in Russia, as it nearly always is. We haven't started trying to run any traces yet, it literally just arrived,' replied Fowler.

'Is that a clown in a tuxedo?'

'Yes, it would appear so.'

On the screen, a crystal clear but silent video played out of the clown in a tuxedo twirling a knife close to the camera, before it cut to a close up of him slitting the throat of a chubby, beaten, and bloodied figure sat in a chair. The shot then zoomed in to the man's head, blood clearly flooding from his severed artery, focusing in on his eyes as the life slowly drained from them, before they eventually closed.

The team had seen enough videos and supposed snuff movies on the dark web during the course of their work to know that there were a lot of fakes out there. Highly realistic fakes, but fakes nonetheless. Usually, they would be grainy amateurish home movies, shot on a smartphone. But this video was made all the more disturbing by the amount of effort taken with setting and production values. The clip lasted barely thirty seconds, but every bit of detail was played out in high definition.

'It's unlike anything I've ever seen from the dark web,' said Fowler. 'This is a proper serious effort. These guys clearly meant business; they weren't just filming this to send around within their little group of mates.'

'So why have we got a copy?' pondered Brooks.

'Clearly someone wants to make us aware of it. Conspicuously,' replied Harris, arms folded, picking some burger from between his teeth.

'Any idea who the poor sod is in the chair?' asked Brooks.

'I'm just running facial recognition now,' replied Fowler. 'Luckily, the resolution is top-notch, so it shouldn't be too difficult. Unless his injuries are too severe for the computer to bring up a match, that is.'

Harris leant in to the screen and clicked the cursor on the progress bar of the video to make it return to the beginning, then paused it. The clown face stared back at him. Its eyes, the only human part visible through the wrinkly mass of latex, burned themselves into his consciousness. These were the eyes of a murderer. Harris was convinced, after watching it and re-watching it, that this was far too precise and calculated to be a fake. This was a serious operation and these were very dangerous people.

'Got it,' said Fowler, as the computer screen pinged up the word *MATCH*. 'Gary Sweetman. Fifty year old male, arrested a few years ago for grooming a couple of young boys and—'

'Yes, I remember him,' interrupted Harris. 'He was let off largely because of a technicality—'

'Police cock up you mean?' jumped in Brooks.

'Well, that as well,' replied Harris, already sliding around the desks to get to his own. He brought up the crimes log again and typed *Gary Sweetman* into the search field.

Your search returned 0 matches.

'Damn, nothing has been reported. Not in the last month anyway. I'll try and expand the search period,' said Harris, scratching his head. 'Grace, can you access the file for the original Sweetman case, please?'

She had already returned to her desk and was searching for it on the database.

'Got him,' she replied excitedly, after a few minutes. 'Only the search function on the main database is a lot better than on that new system, so it's better at recognising partial matches.'

'I don't really want your life story. What've you got?'

'Alright, calm down. Turns out that Sweetman was his middle name, which he tended to use as his surname, and that's what everyone knew him as.'

'What was his real surname?'

'Cock.'

Harris choked as he took a sip of water. 'I can see why he didn't like it. Actually, you'd think that being a paedophile he would be quite proud of it.'

Harris turned back to his screen and typed in *Gary Cock*.

Your search returned 1 matches.

'Bingo,' he whispered, clicking on the search result, *Gary Cock – MISPER*.

He banged his fist on the desk and stood up. 'OK, listen everyone. This guy is on the system as another missing person. Reported a week or so before Parker and Rankin. I'm not saying they're linked, but I think we would do well to assume the worst. Someone has sent us this file for a reason. Fowler, you work on who, we'll try and work out why. We'll also see if we can find anything down on the deep web involving our two erstwhile lovebirds. Let's get to it.'

Retrieving the pile of papers from out of his drawer, he placed them in the top of his printer and began scanning.

'I'd better get these emailed over to the mother-in-law. It's her project now. Grace, we might be in for a late one.'

23

'So, good weekend?' asked Rosco, sipping the frothy head from the top of his ale.

Billy and Joe looked at each other across the table.

'It was alright,' shrugged Joe. 'We had a few beers around mine on Friday night, stayed in with a curry Saturday night, and then did bugger all yesterday. You?'

'I was working most of it,' replied Rosco, 'hence the urgent Monday night beer club. My dad took a plastering job in some huge mansion just out of town and insisted we spend the whole weekend there, rush job apparently. One of the rooms was in a right state, looked as though someone had been trying to punch a hole through the wall. Still, the money was good. Billy? How's the world of high finance? Did you kill the bear today or did the bear kill you? Or whatever it is you lot like to say.'

Billy had barely taken his eyes off Joe since they got there. The two had not had any communication since he stormed out of the garage three nights ago. Billy had spent the weekend wrestling with his conscience, doing his best to try and block out what they had watched. Deciding that his loyalty to his friend was still of great importance, coupled with feeling slightly responsible for introducing him to the darker area of the internet in the first place, he had opted against telling anyone. But he still felt as though Joe needed to face up to his actions of Friday night.

'Well, my day started rather uneventfully. It carried on equally uneventfully up to and beyond lunchtime and then just as I was about to leave, my wanker of a boss decided to drop a massive file on my desk requesting that I write a report on it to present to the department heads tomorrow morning,' he said, staring into the whirlpool of ale as he rotated the glass with his wrist.

'Ha, so this is you writing a report then? Another couple of pints and you'll fly through it,' joked Rosco. 'Anyway, you never said what you got up to at the weekend. The usual chatting up some tart at Kickers, plying her with cheap alcopops before going back to hers?'

'No, actually. My weekend was way, *way*, more interesting than that,' replied Billy, suddenly looking more animated, much to the uneasiness of Joe, who stared at him wide-eyed whilst trying to subtly shake his head without Rosco noticing. Sensing Joe's unease, Billy continued, 'Like Joseph here said, I went around to his on Friday night. We had a few beers, watched a bit of television. Actually, Joe found this cracking new programme. It's online only—'

'Billy! I don't think Rosco really wants to hear about that. It wasn't particularly interesting,' said Joe, through gritted teeth.

Billy stared at him briefly before smiling at the side of his mouth. 'No, you're probably right.'

'No, go on. I want to know.'

Sensing Joe's eyes on him, and his increasing irritation, Billy decided to continue. 'Well, it's this gameshow where people log on to watch a live feed and they can place bids—'

'Billy ...'

'As I was saying, they place bids and whoever bids the most wins and they get to—'

'Evening, gentlemen, sorry I'm late,' interrupted Mike, dropping his leather man-bag down onto the middle of the table. 'Bastard signal failure on the tube one stop from home. We sat in the dark for about twenty minutes. Anyway, I'm here now. What's everyone drinking?'

Billy cast a final glance at Joe, stood up and went to the bar with Mike to help with the round. Joe stared at them as they walked away, slowly taking small sips from his pint glass.

'So what's this gameshow then, Joe?' asked Rosco, as he sidled onto the empty stool next to Joe.

'It's nothing. Look, it's just a stupid website where you pay to watch a couple of birds doing stuff to each other and whoever bids the most amount of money each round is allowed to tell them what to do to the other one next,' replied Joe, pondering to himself whether he was entirely unconvincing or just mildly unconvincing.

Surprisingly, it seemed to have worked. 'Is that it?' asked a slightly disappointed Rosco. 'You can watch that sort of thing for nothing on late night free-view channels. Anyway, I don't really want to imagine you two bumders cuddling up on your sofa watching grotty websites.'

The other two returned from the bar with a tray of beers and handfuls of crisps and pork scratchings. Just as they were sitting down and arranging the glasses and packets on the small table, Joe's phone chimed with a message alert. His heart leapt and he spun around on his chair, scanning the rest of the pub.

'What is it, dickhead? Did your secret boyfriend text you to say he's coming to sit with you?' asked Mike.

'Ha, no,' laughed Joe, slightly nervously. 'I thought it was Ellie, but it's probably just a wrong number.'

He looked at the text again. There was no number showing for the sender, just the two initials, *BR*.

Aren't you going to offer us a drink?

He swiped to delete the message and put his phone down.

'So, Joe was telling me all about this website that you started saying about,' said Rosco.

'Did he indeed? What exactly did he say?' replied Billy.

'Just that you two were watching some grotty site where you could pay the women to do sex things to each other.'

'Right, yes. A sex site. Like I said, pretty interesting. But Joe, you forgot to tell them all the best part about it. Tell them how much you spent. It cost him a small fortune just to pay for the privilege of entering the site,' said Billy, jabbing Joe in the ribs with his elbow.

'It wasn't that much,' said Joe, twirling his phone around in his fingers.

'It would have been if he'd placed any bids. Luckily, I think I talked him out of it though.'

Joe looked at him and raised his eyebrows, and suddenly it dawned on Billy that he had indeed failed to talk Joe out of it.

'You utter twat,' said Billy. 'How much did you spend? What did you have them do?'

'Not a lot. Anyway, I didn't win.'

'Thank god for that.'

Mike and Rosco stood up from the table. 'This is all very interesting, but I think the fruit machines are calling, so we'll leave you two to discuss your special interest sites.'

Joe's phone received another message.

Don't forget to invite your friends next time.

Joe went white and placed the phone down on the table as he got up from the chair. He started walking around the pub, looking for anyone who might be sending the messages. The pub wasn't particularly full, it shouldn't be too difficult to find them. A couple sat in the corner; he'd watched them having a domestic for the last twenty minutes, it couldn't have been them. An old man with grey hair sat alone on a table for four, nursing a pint of ale in a dimpled glass with a handle. He didn't look like he would even be able to use a mobile phone. Just across the room he saw another couple sitting together; the man tapping away at something on his phone. The man looked up and, as they made eye contact, Joe sensed it must be him. He darted across the room and stood next to the couple's table.

'Did you just send me a text?' Joe asked the man with the phone.

'What? No,' replied the man, slightly bemused. 'Why the hell would I have sent you a text?'

The man turned away to carry on the conversation with his girlfriend, and as he picked up his pint, Joe snatched the mobile from his table. Before the screen lock came on, Joe scrolled through the session windows; but all he found were takeaway apps, Twitter, and Angry Birds running. The man slammed his glass back down onto the table.

'Oi, what the fuck is wrong with you, you freak. Give me back my phone,' he shouted, as he tried to wrestle the phone away from Joe's hand. Joe turned away, shielding the phone from the man as he accessed the messages. Seeing that there did not appear to be anything sent to his phone, he threw the phone back on the table. The man stuck his middle finger up at him, and signed the conversation off with a loud, 'Prick'. He sat back down to a consoling arm around his shoulder from his partner.

'What the fuck was that all about?' asked Mike, as they joined him on the way back to Billy at the table.

'Nothing, just a misunderstanding,' retorted Joe, as he barged past the oncoming old man, who had by now finished his pint, put on his flat cap and trench coat, and was trying to leave the pub. 'Watch where you're going, you old fart!' Joe shouted at the man, as he stumbled against the cigarette machine to regain his balance. The man held out his hand in timid acknowledgment and left the pub without turning around.

'Calm down, Joe, what the hell is wrong with you?' said Mike, shaking him by the shoulders.

Joe shrugged him off and sat down. Looking up, he saw Billy staring at him, his eyes wide, cutting through Joe like daggers. Glancing down at the table he could see why. He turned his phone over and the text from BR was on screen; clearly Billy had read it.

'It's them isn't it, Joe?' asked Billy, knowingly.

'Who?' interjected Rosco.

'No-one,' replied Joe, bluntly. 'Just some people.'

'What people?' asked Rosco again.

'No-one. Rosco, just leave it, it's fine. Who's for another beer? I'll get a round of sambuca to go with it.'

'No thanks. I'm going to call it a night, got an early start in the morning,' replied Billy, picking his hoodie off of the back of his chair. He shook hands with the three of them, staring Joe straight in the eyes as he tightened his grip. Before any of them could protest at him, or call him something along the lines of 'a big girl' for leaving, he walked out of the pub.

After a brief moment of silence at the table, Mike announced, 'Go on, I'll try one of those beer things you keep mentioning.'

'Good man,' replied Joe, slapping him on the back as he got up and walked to the bar. 'I've got at least another couple of pints left in me tonight.'

Joe stood at the bar ordering his drinks. He surveyed the other patrons sat at various tables, wondering to himself if one of them was the one watching him, sending him texts. Just as the tray was placed on the soggy beer-soaked towel in front of him, he heard his phone chime.

Wrong man, Joe. We are coming for you. Nowhere to hide.

* * *

The following morning, Joe sat at his desk, rubbing his temples. He stared through a thick hazy fog that hung in his brain. All he could see were lines and lines of emails melting into one giant jumble of quotation requests, invoices, and other mundane nonsense. The steam from his coffee rose and filled his nostrils, but it did little to clear his mind. Late delivery notifications, shipping exceptions, missing paperwork. It now all seemed so trivial. He had received no further text messages since the pub last night, but the last couple played over in his mind.

'Joe?' The voice from the office door barely registered. 'JOE?' it repeated, louder.

He looked up from his screen to see the warehouse manager standing in the doorway. Past him, at the other side of the building, he could make out two people. In a warehouse of only five, it was fairly easy to spot people he didn't recognise, and these two he didn't recognise.

'What?' he replied.

'There's a couple of blokes here to see you, said they're from a shipping company,' replied the warehouse manager.

'Can't you see them?' Joe said, barely able to conceal his lack of motivation.

'No, I bloody well can't,' came the response. 'We're already behind on the Anderson order, and the lorry is coming in at midday to pick it up. Sorry, tough shit. You'll have to deal with it. Plus they asked for you by name.'

'Fuck me gently, they do my head in, these travelling sales wankers,' he moaned, picking up his coffee and heading for the warehouse.

He strolled out into the middle of the warehouse where the two men stood, trying as best he could to give off an air of being both incredibly important and hugely inconvenienced. They weren't dressed like ordinary salesmen. Instead of dark, pinstripe suits with shiny black shoes, they wore chinos, open-collared shirts, and loafers. Standing in the centre of the large open expanse of breeze block and corrugated metal walls, they conversed in whispers, periodically pointing to various parts of the room.

'Good morning, gents,' said Joe, with an outstretched hand. 'What can I do for you?'

'Mister Henderson, nice to meet you,' replied the first man, in an unseemly, loud voice, reciprocating the handshake. A tall, freckled man with a fast receding line of ginger hair, he gripped Joe's hand firmly and squeezed it hard, looking him straight in the eyes as he did so. 'Thank you for seeing us and please accept my apologies for turning up unannounced. I'm Colin Ziff, sales manager for Britten Rashford Freight—'

'Never heard of you,' interrupted Joe, as he slid the business card that had surreptitiously appeared in his hand during the handshake into his back pocket without looking at it.

'We're very specialised. We only handle very particular cargo for a select group of customers. Anyway, we are obviously aware of your operation from the Government's importation records and, as we were passing, thought we would drop in and introduce our services. My apologies, this is Carl White, our finance director.'

The other man carried on surveying the work that was going on around him, turning only very briefly to shake Joe's hand. This was a completely different handshake, the sort that made

Joe take an instant dislike to him. A wet, flaccid handshake using only the fingers, which said, 'I don't want to shake your hand, but I will.'

'This is quite an operation you've got here,' said White, in a soft, gravelly voice that belied his large frame. 'Yes, yes, this will do nicely. I think we'd able to handle this freight, no problem at all, don't you, Mister Ziff?'

'Agreed. As long as Mister Henderson's finances are as good as they appear and he has no trouble paying his bills. Which I am sure you don't, right, Mister Henderson?'

Joe was starting to become visibly irritated. He set his coffee cup down on a nearby forklift and tried his best at posturing in the hope that these men would just go away.

'Of course we pay our bills. Look, we're not after a new freight forwarder, the ones we use are perfectly good. So, gentlemen, if you wouldn't mind, I am rather busy.'

'Of course, Mister Henderson, our apologies for inconveniencing you,' said Ziff, wiping his freckly forehead with a sleeve. 'If I could just steal a couple more minutes of your time to really explain exactly what it is that we do, you may change your mind. See, most freight forwarders pride themselves on moving cargo quickly and safely, so that it arrives at its intended destination in as good a condition as when it left.'

'Yes, I know how freight forwarding works,' replied Joe, who had now had enough and had turned to walk back to the office.

'But our customers rely on us for taking charge of their cargo and making sure that it is never seen again.'

Joe stopped in his tracks. His head was pounding and now these people had really begun to piss him off.

'Look, I'm sorry, but that obviously has no relevance to my business. Why the hell would I want you to get rid of my freight?'

'To ensure that no-one knows what you've done,' said White, walking over to Joe and placing a hand on his shoulder. To the warehouse workers whizzing past on their forklift trucks and carrying metal bars from one side to the other, it looked as though the two men were old acquaintances having a jovial time. What they couldn't see was the amount of pressure with which White squeezed the back of Joe's neck. Joe's heavy hangover prevented any sort of reaction other than bewilderment at the sudden turn of aggression.

Maintaining pressure, White positioned himself in front of Joe's face.

'But don't worry, Mister Henderson, we charge very reasonable rates. What's more, we accept most forms of currency. British Pounds, U.S. Dollars, the Euro … bitcoins.'

Any strength that Joe felt flushed away as the sense of realisation hit him like a brick to the face. All of a sudden, his hangover seemed to vanish and was replaced with a heartbeat pounding so fast he could hear it in his head. The two men stood silently and stared at him.

'Joe,' came the shout from the other side of the warehouse, temporarily snapping Joe out of his trance. 'Can you come here and sign these certificates please?'

White relinquished his grip and patted Joe on the shoulder. 'Go on then, Mister Henderson, I think you're needed. Tell you what, you go and sort your colleague out. We'll head to your meeting room upstairs and then, when you're done, you can come and join us so we can thrash out the Ts and Cs. OK? Good.'

With that, the two men walked off, leaving Joe stranded in the middle of the large blue expanse of concrete floor. He pulled the card from his back pocket and turned it over to see the large embossed logo, '*B.R.*'

He swallowed hard and whispered to himself, 'Oh fuck.'

Joe could see the two men through the glass partition of the meeting room, helping themselves to a drink from the water cooler. Taking a deep breath, he tentatively opened the door, feeling somewhat like a naughty pupil who had been summoned to see the head teacher. Closing the door behind him, he remained standing in the corner of the room with his hands crossed defensively in front of his body.

'Please, sit down, Joe,' said Ziff. 'There's nothing to worry about. Obviously, if we had wanted to kill you we would have done it by now.'

The two men burst out laughing. Joe laughed along nervously, feeling a bead of sweat drip down the side of his face as he scratched his forehead. He pulled one of the faux-leather black chairs back from the table and sat down, keeping a couple of feet back. As quickly as they started laughing, the two men abruptly stopped, and their demeanours switched from jovial to thoroughly menacing.

'But seriously, please understand that the option is still open to us. And given what you've seen of our organisation, you would be foolish to assume otherwise,' said Ziff, staring at Joe, who was now resting his head in his hands and had started chewing the skin on his thumb.

'Look guys,' said Joe, his voice audibly cracking as he glanced at the two men staring back at him, 'I know that you are proper pissed off with me...'

'Uh-huh,' replied Ziff.

'We most certainly are,' agreed White.

'But, OK, I'm sorry. I don't really know what more you want from me or what more I could possibly give an organisation such as your good selves. I'll pay you the money I tried to send. Right now; I'll go and transfer the bitcoins to your account this instant. And I promise I won't say anything about what I saw. If it helps, I think what you're doing is great. That's why I watched and made my bid—'

'Which failed.'

'Yes, which failed, I get that. But my point is that I'm on your side. I think these scumbags that you deal with deserve everything that's coming to them ...'

'Did he say he was sorry, Mister Ziff?' interrupted White.

'Yes, I believe so, Mister White.'

Joe's eyes flicked back and forth between the two men as they conversed.

'Yes, I thought that's what he said.' White paused. There was a moment of silence before he stood up sharply, slamming his fist down on the desk as he did so. 'Sorry?' he shouted. 'You enter our domain, watch our work, and then by some ridiculous act of fuck-witted buffoonery put the whole thing in jeopardy. Do you realise the amount of work that goes in to doing what we do? The amount of preparation? The amount of care needed? But it's OK, because you're fucking sorry?'

Joe sat, shaking. The original video call and the texts, he could discount those as just pranks, brush them aside as if they weren't there. It's on the internet, it's not real life. But now the reality of his situation was starting to hit home. He chewed harder, and from somewhere found a little of bit of fight, although secretly knew that anything would be largely futile.

'I'll just go to the police after you're gone and tell them the whole—'

'The whole what?' interrupted White, banging his hand down on the table again, causing Joe to look away. 'That you tried to pay money to an online gameshow in which someone was killed on your orders? Come on, no sensible police officer is going to give you any sort of plea bargain for that. The minute you hit enter on your keyboard to send the bid you started your involvement, but you could have still backed out. Instead, you went further. You wrote down a specific method by which to end someone's life. Once you hit enter on that, there was never going to be any turning back. If you hadn't fucked up your transaction, we wouldn't be here and you would have nothing to worry about. You would be free to marry your sweetheart in a few months, safe in the knowledge that you hadn't upset a very powerful group of people.'

'Please leave Ellie out of this,' begged Joe, sniffing as his nose started to run. 'She doesn't know anything about any of this and—'

'Joe, Joe, Joe,' said Ziff, calmly, as he got up from his seat and walked around the other side of the table to Joe's chair.

'It's good that she doesn't know anything about this. It's in all of our interests; the fewer people know about this, the better. What we need to do now is work on a solution.'

'What kind of solution?'

'Well, Joe, we're in it,' replied Ziff.

'What, this meeting room?'

'Give me strength. No, this building.'

Joe stood up instantly and began pacing up and down the length of the meeting table, shaking his head.

'No, no. No way. You are not taking this warehouse, it's my family's. It would destroy my parents, and me for that matter. I can't let you take it.'

'Joe, I realise this situation might be a little stressful for you, but please stop being such a gibbering simpleton for just a second. Sit down,' replied Ziff. 'It's fairly straightforward. We don't want your building, the paperwork would leave an audit trail as long as your arm. No. We just want to borrow it. And if you refuse, we will make your life very, very difficult.'

'Or whatever would be left of it,' interjected White.

Again the two men laughed. Never in Joe's life had he ever regretted anything as much as he regretted clicking on the link to the Red Room. Even going back to Billy's flat; if he had just gone home that night, his life would be normal. The same boring, stuck-in-a-rut routine day in day out. But normal at least.

'What precisely would borrowing it entail?' asked Joe.

'Well, we would have our team come and prepare the venue for the night of the show. Take over your security cameras, tap into your internet ...'

'And your neighbours' ...'

'Yes, and theirs too. Then on the day we bring the volunteer here, we film the show. Well you know how that all works, having seen it. Hopefully, we would be here no longer than about half an hour, forty minutes. See, the last episode took a lot longer, what with there being two of them. Longer than we were comfortable transmitting live to the internet. The longer it takes, the more vulnerable you are to being tracked down. We ran it close to the mark last time. Not so close as to put us at risk, but still close. Hence, this episode we need an entirely neutral location, with nothing to link it to us. This would be a much slicker, quicker episode.'

Joe paced up and down the office, chewing like crazy. 'But then what? What about forensics?'

Ziff sat back down in his chair, pulled another away from the table and put his feet up on it.

'We take care of that. We've been doing this a while now and have become adept at leaving zero traces. Otherwise, we would put our entire operation in jeopardy. Your warehouse will be as it was before the show.'

'But how the fuck can I be sure that you won't just wait until after the show and kill me then?'

'You can't,' laughed Ziff, his laughter echoed by White. 'But I can tell you that it won't happen before then, for certain. After that, well you'll just have to trust me.'

Just then there was a knock at the door. It was Sandra, the lady from accounts. Ziff removed his feet from the chair and the two men smiled at her. She smiled back.

'Joe, are you going to be much longer, only there's a whole load more paperwork that needs to be signed off.'

'I'll be down in a bit,' Joe snapped back.

'OK, don't get your knickers in a twist, but you have been up here quite a while. We've got orders waiting to go out,' replied Sandra.

'Apologies, my dear, it's our fault. Joe's been grilling us on our freight rates. He's quite the master negotiator,' said Ziff. 'We're nearly done and then I promise we'll give him back to you in one piece. Is that Chanel Chance you are wearing? May I just say that it suits you down to the ground?'

Sandra looked flattered that someone in the building had finally paid her any attention that didn't involve asking for photocopying or to make the tea.

'Why yes it is, sir, thank you very much.'

Ziff winked and nodded.

'Yes, thank you, Sandra. Like I said, I'll be down in a minute. I'll have a coffee as well please,' said Joe, trying to maintain a vague air of authority.

Sandra rolled her eyes and closed the door behind her as she left the room.

'So, I think we understand each other then, Joe?' said Ziff, more as a statement of fact than a question.

As the sweat dripped from Joe's head, and a small patch of blood formed around the cuticle of his thumbnail, he drummed his fingers across his front teeth, kicking the legs of the chairs as he paced past them, shaking his head.

'No, no,' he started saying, as a whisper, waving his hand around, before getting louder. 'No, no, no. I can't. You can't do this, hold me to ransom. I don't care what you say, I'll go to the police. I won't do this.'

The two men stared at each other, slightly taken aback by this sudden and unexpected burst of bravado. They stood up, collected their leather portfolios from the table, and made for the exit. As he walked past Joe holding the door open, Ziff gently cupped his hand around Joe's cheek.

'Yes you will,' he said, gently, raising his eyebrows and staring deep into Joe's eyes.

They walked from the office and out into the lobby. As they left the building, Joe slammed the door shut behind them. Turning round, he bumped straight into Sandra.

'Bloody hell,' she exclaimed. 'What's the matter with you? You look like shit.'

'Nothing,' replied Joe, curtly. 'They were just giving it the hard sell, nothing I haven't seen before.'

He watched through the window as the two men drove past, and he became slightly more relaxed. Their words still rung in his head, but at least they were gone and he could get on with his life.

As the car turned out of the trading estate, it drove for a couple of miles and then pulled over in a country lane. Turning the engine off, Ziff tilted his head back, unbuttoned his shirt collar, and began to peel a layer of latex away from his neck. He rolled the thin rubber up and over his face until eventually the whole mask, including hair, separated from his head. White did the same.

'I fucking hate these things,' said Stan.

'I told you, you should have shaved,' replied Eric. 'Ring Alistair while I sort the number plates out.'

Stan pulled a mobile phone from inside his jacket. 'It's me. He's rattled but I think he's going to need a final push ... Yes ... Yes, there's someone we can use to convince him ... We'll get on it straight away.'

Joe pulled up in his driveway and paused for a minute before leaving the car. He looked up at his house, his ordinary, non-descript house. The windows were open and he could hear the television blaring out in the lounge. As he put the key in the lock and turned it, he thought about the men who had come to his office today, about their threats and the mess in which he now found himself. He had so much to look forward to and his lack of satisfaction with his lot had led him to put it all at risk.

And he began to hate himself for it.

Opening the door, he glanced down the hallway into the kitchen. He pushed the door to the lounge ajar to look for Ellie, but she was not in there. As he walked closer to the kitchen, he saw a silver, shiny object lying on the floor.

'No,' he whispered.

It was the large chef's knife that they had been given as an engagement present. Then he noticed the trail of blood. A thin spatter had sprayed up the tiles, all over the white gloss kitchen cupboards and across the tiled floor. His heart began to race and the sweat began to pour, for what seemed like the hundredth time today. He looked around for Ellie, terrible thoughts of what these people had done to his fiancée racing through his head.

He followed the trail of blood out through the kitchen and into the utility room. The door to the downstairs toilet was shut. Holding out a hand to grab the handle, he approached tentatively. When he reached the door, he took a deep breath in expectation at what might be lying behind it. He opened the door.

There was Ellie. She was slumped on the toilet, holding her hand under the running water of the sink next to it. A river of red liquid circled the plughole before disappearing. She looked up at him.

'I didn't hear you come in,' she said, quite normally. 'Look what I did, clumsy idiot.'

As she showed him the gash across the knuckle of her thumb, the relief overwhelmed him and he reached forward, embracing her in a huge hug.

'Oh, thank god,' he said.

'Thank god? I've sliced open my fucking thumb, you dickhead.'

After sticking the two large flaps on her thumb back together with steristrips and covering it with copious amounts of dressing and porous tape, Joe set about wiping up the blood from the kitchen. As he knelt on the kitchen floor, he heard the phone ring.

'Any chance you could answer that, with your one good hand?' he shouted into the lounge.

A few moments later, Ellie walked into the kitchen, an ashen look across her face. Joe looked up at her.

'What is it?' he asked.

'It's Billy,' she replied. 'He's in hospital. In a coma.'

24

'Peter, I think we might have found something,' said Grace, excitedly, rushing into the office in a mixture of panic and relief.

She was stopped in her tracks by the raised finger of Harris, gesturing to the phone tucked under his chin. Grace waited patiently next to his desk as he finished his conversation.

'Sorry, sweetheart, I'm going to be late again … Yes I know I was late last night, but I've got really important work to do at the moment … Hey, Grandma's not boring … Look, I need you to be a really good girl for her, alright? And I'll be home as soon as I can … Yes, fine, I'll take you to Legoland at the weekend, I promise … OK, night night. Love you ... Bye.'

Finally, Harris hung up the phone. 'Sorry about that. What have you got?'

'I've just been down to the lab,' she replied, placing some graph papers down on his desk that looked like ECG traces. 'They pulled all the data from Karen Parker's tag from a week up to the date she was reported missing. Some poor sod has sat there and gone through every minute of data bit by bit.'

'Lucky him.'

'Yep, but it appears to have been worth it, because he found this,' she said, pointing to a ring drawn on the paper in red ink. In amongst the pages of identical traces was a tiny, almost indiscernible drop in the level of the line. 'This line here shows the co-ordinates for her location. That's how they know where she is, or if she breaks curfew and so on. And this line—'

'Is the transmission strength,' interrupted Harris, staring at the graphs. Grace had forgotten that he was well-versed in the workings of electronic tags. 'Bugger, do you know what this means?'

'Well I assume that at that point there, the tag developed a small glitch that messed up its transmissions.'

'Precisely. But what caused it?'

'I don't know. The weather?' she replied, sarcastically.

'It could be,' he replied, ignoring the sarcasm altogether. 'We see breaks in transmission like this when the wearer has attempted to break the tag off of their leg, or smashed it against something, either to break it or even just accidentally.'

'But her tag was found intact,' said Grace. 'So I get that when the tag was removed from her leg, it might have caused the transmitter to jump or glitch, but—'

'No, they're alarmed. If the wearer tries to forcibly remove the tag, or if any of what we just said happens, the tag transmits an alarm to the monitoring station. Even if she somehow managed to unlock it normally, slip it off, and reattached the clasp as if it were still on her leg, the tag would know and it would show up. How long would it take to unlock, remove, and relock one of these? Even with the right knowledge and equipment, you're looking at a few seconds. More than enough of a time lapse for it to trigger an alert,' said Harris, talking and scanning the graphs at the same time.

'So, how would she have managed it, especially given what a useless waste of space she is?' pondered Grace.

'Maybe she didn't,' replied Harris. He scanned the documents for the officer leading the missing person case and then began composing an email. 'I'll ask the local force to have their forensics team re-examine the tag. They'll need to check absolutely everything: prints, serial numbers, the lot.'

'But they already did that. It had all her tracking history and was covered in her DNA.'

'Doesn't conclusively confirm that it is the exact same tag that she was issued with originally though,' replied Harris, hitting the send button.

Grace collected her papers and returned to her desk. She was always secretly impressed by Pete's ability to look at situations from angles that others would never have thought of; not that she would ever tell him as much. His head was far too big as it was.

Harris returned to his screen. The video of Gary Sweetman was an almost permanent fixture on his desktop now. He had watched it over and over again, searching for the slightest hint of its origins. But, depending on your point of view, that was either the beauty of, or the trouble with, the deep web. Apart from the trillions of megabytes of mundane data that existed there, the vast majority of the content was based on the anonymous side of the global internet, mainly because it did not want to be found. It opened up a world of possibilities and was increasing exponentially. Policing it became an almost thankless task. If looking for something on the regular web was like searching for a needle in a haystack, searching for something on the deep web was like trying to find an ant in the Sahara.

Unless you knew where to look. Which Harris did, up to a point. He was experienced in traversing the sea of content on the deep web. Since joining the Cyber Crime Unit, he had become very familiar with it, given its status as the new playground of choice for anyone wanting to commit crime online. But sometimes he needed help, and who better to provide help than someone operating in this very playground.

Harris knew him only by his tag, Mr$pangle, and knew very little about him other than that he ran a site on the deep web offering 'alternative lifestyle events'. Mr$pangle knew Harris was a police officer and was happy to keep feeding him information in return for a lack of hassle over his own activities, provided he kept them legally, if not morally, clean.

Pulling out his smartphone, Harris opened a chat with him under his online pseudonym used for investigations such as this: LostBoy.

LostBoy: Spang?

After a few minutes, his name went green and a response came back

Mr$pangle: What?
Lostboy: Don't be like that! How u doing?
Mr$pangle: What do you want?
Lostboy: I want you to look at something for me.
Mr$pangle: No thanks, see a doctor.
Lostboy: Funny. I'm sending you a file.
Mr$pangle: ......
Lostboy: Got it?
Mr$pangle: Interesting.

After the file had finished downloading, Mr$pangle's icon changed to red. He had gone offline.

'Wanker,' whispered Harris. He hated having to rely on these gutter-crawling weirdos, but sometimes it was necessary to come down to their level.

He went and made himself coffee in the hope that when he returned, there would be a reply. Sure enough, it hadn't taken long.

Mr$pangle: It's a show
LostBoy: A show?
Mr$pangle: Check out the Brotherhood of the Righteous
LostBoy: A one off?
Mr$pangle: No, they do it most weeks.
LostBoy: ??
Mr$pangle: Different people
LostBoy: How do I find it?
Mr$pangle: That would be telling
LostBoy: Perhaps you can tell me at your little gathering in the woods this weekend. I'll bring my dildo collection.
Mr$pangle: Fuck you. enterthedark message board

Harris cursed. He knew the site well; it was a one stop shop for anybody's dark web needs and links. In fact, it was the first place he had gone looking for any information that might shed light on the video, but he had drawn a blank.

LostBoy: Checked there. Nothing.
Mr$pangle: Gotta be quick
LostBoy: Know anything about Karen Parker?

LostBoy: ??

Mr$pangle avoided the question by logging off again, which suggested to Harris that perhaps he had already said too much and was in no mood to divulge further details. But at least he now had something to go on. And the mention of Karen Parker seemed to have struck a nerve as well.

After stopping to eat some dinner in the canteen, Harris returned to his desk. An email had just arrived and it caught his eye instantly. It was from the forensics team looking into the Karen Parker missing person case.

'Yes. I bloody well knew it,' Harris whispered to himself, before shouting over to Grace. 'Grace, look at the email I just forwarded to you. The tag that the officers found at Karen Parker's house wasn't the exact one she was originally fitted with.'

'Great, that's all we need, you on ultra-smug mode,' said Grace, rolling her eyes.

'We can all sit around and talk about how great I am later, but clearly this case is more than just her wandering off on the way to the shops to buy pies. I think we need to look further for anything we can find on the Brotherhood of the Righteous, a group my source mentioned. The fact he cut me off the minute I mentioned Karen Parker's name is also significant.'

Grace had walked over to his desk to see the email for herself. She knew he was probably right but still needed to see with her own eyes that his big head was justified.

'OK, what have we got?' started Grace, as she began writing in her notepad. 'We've got a video of a man being murdered, sent in by someone whose identity we are yet to establish. We have two of the most despised people of recent years going missing, one of whom has had their tag altered. And we have the mysterious anonymous organiser of swingers parties telling us to look into something called the Brotherhood of the Righteous.'

'Exactly, so at least we're further along,' replied Harris, cheerfully. 'Have Fowler scour around on the deep web, see if he can find anything on this Brotherhood. There must be something on there. You liaise with the team from Parker's case, give them all the recent information about the tag and have them check further into her movements and especially anyone seen going in to or coming out of her house. I'm going to monitor the chat rooms, see if anything pops up on enterthedark. Mr$pangle said I needed to be quick, so I'm guessing that these people advertise on there but limit the amount of time so as not to attract too much attention.'

'I'll get on it.'

'Blimey, that was quick,' said Harris, impressed at the ease with which Fowler had managed to dig up some information on the Brotherhood. Impressed, but not surprised.

Fowler had joined the unit direct from university, the next generation of computer experts for whom the internet was like a second home. He had grown up with computers and was able to write code before he could ride a bike. Harris was just glad that he had decided to join the good guys and spend his talents catching similarly-minded criminals who had chosen the opposite path for their skills. A close call, given that Fowler was nearly expelled from his university for hacking into the campus computer system and changing all of his grades to firsts. That and trying, and very nearly succeeding, to access the GCHQ databases. When it came to hackers, usually the best way to catch one was to employ one. So, Fowler was offered a position at CCU and had very quickly become Harris' main point of contact for the more technical side of their work.

Fowler smiled knowingly at Harris, who had pulled a chair up to the desk. He had a huge admiration for Harris and his approach to the work, but he was better at getting down and dirty in the less civilised areas of internet operations. In one hand, he whizzed his wireless mouse across the desk in a blur of red and black. In the other, he squeezed a padded metal grip strengthener.

'Here,' he said, pointing to a page on one of his four monitor screens as Harris leaned in to look closer. 'This group has very little presence, even down on the dark web. Whatever, or whoever, they are, they don't like to shout about themselves. But that doesn't stop others from discussing them.'

Harris scanned down the seemingly mindless chatter on the message board that Fowler had found, a multitude of nicknames, text speak, and general nonsense, but in amongst it all some surprisingly useful detail.

EvilWeevil: Anyone see the red room with the pedo?

Jizzler: Yeah, sick. Asshole Sweetman got what coming to him.

Crazy8: BR are fucking legends. Can't wait for the next one.

EvilWeevil: Get saving. Next one is the big one.

Crazy8: Who they doing this time?

EvilWeevil: Dunno, check enterthedark and find out.

'See, so this is presumably a discussion of the Sweetman video that we have,' points out Fowler, tapping on Sweetman's name with his biro. 'There is then a gap of a couple of days ...'

Jizzler: New TRATD listed. 1BX to enter.

Crazy8: I'm there.

'What's TRATD?' asked Harris. 'One bitcoin to enter? That's not an insignificant sum of money.'

'That's just the start of it,' replied Fowler. 'Jumping ahead slightly, TRATD appears to stand for 'The Righteous and the Damned'. From what I can tell, it's the online calling card of the webcast run by the Brotherhood of the Righteous. Read a few more.'

Harris scrolled down to the messages that started at 20:45pm the previous Friday.

Jizzler: Get to the red room. They've got 2.

EvilWeevil: How much?

Jizzler: 2 to enter.

EvilWeevil: Who is it?

Jizzler: Go see.

EvilWeevil: Yes, yes, yes. MR and KP. This'll be brutal.

Harris patted Fowler on the shoulder.

'My god. MR and KP. Mark Rankin and Karen Parker. This is it, isn't it?'

It became even clearer as posts from later on in the evening appeared on the thread.

EvilWeevil: Wow. That was epic.

Jizzler: Those two fuckers dead. RIP Charlie, your avenging angel sorted it.

EvilWeevil: Can't wait for next week.

'Shit,' exclaimed Harris. 'That explains why no-one has heard hide nor hair of either of these two. They're not missing, they're dead. And it would appear that we have something more sinister on our hands than we thought.'

'Uh-huh,' replied Fowler, in agreement. 'If what these people are saying is right, we're dealing with a serious operation. The Sweetman video looked very professional and it would go some way to explaining why we've hit brick wall after brick wall. These people are clearly advanced in their methods and the security around what they do is immense.'

'I always thought that 'red rooms' were a legend?' pondered Harris.

'They have been, up until now,' replied Fowler. 'The dark web is full of videos claiming to be human experimentation or snuff films. Really dark, totally sinister stuff. Live amputations, live eviscerations; underground, sub-culture concepts. 'Red room' became something of an urban legend, a mystical location where all these websites exist. Nothing has ever been verified, and there has never been any concerted series of videos, just one offs.'

'We need to keep an eye on enterthedark. I want us to be at their next one.'

'Got it. Shall I notify the team looking for Karen Parker?'

Harris sat back, stroking his chin. He had always played the game in strict accordance with the rules, but sometimes the rules changed and he had to adapt to the situation. And this was a situation unlike any the unit had ever encountered before.

'No, not yet. Let's see if anything gets posted for this 'next week' that mister EvilWeevil mentions. If it follows the dates on these messages, there should be something coming up soon.'

25

As Joe and Ellie walked through the front entrance, a pile of letters on the mat stuck to the underside of the door. Ellie bent down to pick them up, whilst Joe snuck past to place his keys on the small box attached to the wall. Neither had said much to the other on the drive back from the hospital. They were relieved that Billy had been brought around from his coma, a miracle by any standard, and hopefully an indicator that he had somehow managed to avoid any serious brain injuries. But he still looked an absolute mess. Ellie had done her best to comfort his mother, who had been sat by his bedside for the last 36 hours whilst Joe sat holding his hand.

Joe pulled his mobile phone out from his jeans and dialled Rosco's number.

'Hello, mate,' said Joe, sombrely.

'Hi,' replied Rosco. 'Did you go and see him? He looks bad.'

'Yes, not good. Not good at all. We didn't get an awful lot of sense out of his mum as to what happened. Have you heard anything?'

'Only what the police know,' continued Rosco. 'He was driving home yesterday afternoon by the looks of it, lost control on that windy country lane he quite often takes to work. You know, the one that goes near the brewery he visits. Shot through the hedge row and slammed into a tree. He had his belt on and the airbag kicked in, but he hit hard enough that it knocked him out completely. The guys at the brewery heard the smash and phoned the ambulance.'

As Rosco talked, Joe heard a message notification on his phone. He held the handset in front of him briefly whilst continuing to listen and saw the preview.

How's Billy-boy doing?

Joe went silent; the sickness in his stomach became palpable.

'Joe?' asked Rosco. 'Joe, are you still there?'

'Er, yes. I'm still here,' he answered, struggling to get any words out. 'Sorry, yes, it's horrific, isn't it? Look, I can't really speak at the moment, something's come up. I'll speak to you tomorrow. Bye.'

'Joe?'

Even though he heard Rosco, he still hung up the phone.

Opening up the text, he read it again. Could they really have caused this? It was just an accident. Billy drove his sports car like an idiot sometimes, and there had been numerous occasions in the past when he was lucky to come out unscathed; this must have just been an unfortunate set of circumstances. He tried to convince himself that this had nothing to do with him, but try as he might it was wholly unsuccessful. His world was starting to come down around him; he prayed that it wouldn't get any worse. But unfortunately, he wouldn't have to wait long for it to do so.

'Explain this, dickhead,' shouted a very angry Ellie, as she threw an email printout down on his lap. She stood there, hands on hips, her face bright red, staring at him as he slowly and disinterestedly unfolded the piece of paper.

'Dear Ms Sellars,' Joe began to read, in an almost sarcastic tone. 'We are sorry to inform you that your recent payment for the hire of our venue was rejected by your bank due to insufficient funds. We tried to contact you by phone but could not reach you. It is with regret that we must inform you that, due to the popularity of the dates you have chosen, we have been left with no alternative but to offer this date to an alternative client. If you would like to contact us, we would be pleased to assist with making alternative arrangements. Because we were able to find alternative clients… blimey, they use the word 'alternative' a lot don't they … for the room, you will not forfeit your deposit for which I enclose a cheque for one thousand pounds. Yours sincerely, blah blah blah.'

Joe folded the piece of paper in half and threw it onto the coffee table. He sat there, rubbing the bridge of his nose, thinking desperately for something to say to explain this. After a few seconds of silence he mustered,

'Well, good news we got our thousand pounds back.'

Ellie could contain herself no longer.

'You total bastard!' she shouted, gesticulating wildly with her hands. 'Is this just some fucking joke to you? This is our wedding, which you were supposed to pay for. 'Leave it to me' you said. 'I'll pay out of my trust fund' you said. Well, where's your sodding trust fund gone?'

'I spent it,' he replied, nonchalantly.

'Oh, that's OK then,' she said, mock sympathetically, before exploding into a shouting fit worthy of a banshee on crack. 'Well we've now lost the wedding of our dreams, thanks to you. What could you possibly have spent that much money on without me knowing? Well?'

'*Your* dreams, you mean. What's the point in me even trying to explain? Whatever I say has happened to that money will be wrong.'

Ellie sat on the corner of the coffee table in front of him, arms folded so tightly it looked like they would cut off the blood supply to her head.

'Go on then, try me.'

'Look, I didn't want to say anything. I wanted it to be a surprise.'

'A surprise? What, that you thought we would get married without a fucking venue?'

'No. Look, we'd said that we couldn't afford a honeymoon, right?' said Joe, slightly more confidently, convinced he could make this one stick. 'So I thought I'd surprise you with an all-inclusive two week trip to the Maldives. I was going to pay for it out of my own savings and then transfer the money from my dividend fund at work to cover the venue hire. But I didn't realise that it was all going to go through at the same time, and obviously it's gone wrong.'

'Prove it,' snapped Ellie.

'What?'

'Prove it. Show me the booking confirmation email or something.'

'I don't need this. Not only is my best friend in hospital, but now you're accusing me of lying to you?'

'Don't play that card with me. You and I both know that it was only a matter of time before Billy ended up wrapping his car around a lamppost or something.'

'How can you be so insensitive?' said Joe, trying his best wounded puppy expression. 'Anyway, I had to do it all with bitcoins so that you wouldn't find out. There is no confirmation email, other than me setting up my bitcoin account. I didn't want you to find out and ruin the surprise.'

'Well it's certainly ruined something. So, just to make sure I understand correctly. You blew the money that you had put aside for our wedding venue on a surprise holiday to the Maldives that you paid for with a virtual currency and therefore have no confirmation of anything. But you forgot that the money was supposed to be for the venue, which they have now given to someone else to have a completely lovely day in.'

'I didn't forget, I just mistimed moving all the money around.'

'The end result is the same. *My* dream wedding is now ruined, thanks to you. How on Earth do you expect us to find another venue this late on? I knew I should have made you pay the whole amount right at the start. Why did I let you convince me to just pay the deposit?' she said, sobbing as tears began to roll down her cheeks.

Joe stood up, wondering to himself if he should try and comfort her. Basing his decision on the fact that if he did nothing she would complain, but that if he tried to show some compassion by putting his arm around her or through some similar act of love she would more than likely bite his head off, he decided to stand back a little.

'Look, I'm sorry. I didn't mean to.'

'Pathetic,' she said, through gritted teeth, 'utterly pathetic. You completely ruined what is supposed to be the happiest day of our lives and all you can do is stand there and say you're sorry. I'm done. I'm going to stay with Mum and Dad.'

With that, Ellie stormed out of the room, slamming the door behind her. A few minutes later, she reappeared at the bottom of the stairs with a hastily prepared holdall overflowing with clothes. She opened the door and stared at the sorry figure of Joe, who hadn't moved since she'd left the room. As their eyes met, she said nothing, and just shook her head.

'Please don't go,' he pleaded. 'I'll make it up to you, I promise.'

But the wet-fish act did nothing to convince Ellie that he would start acting like a proper man, and she walked out of the house and drove off.

Another message popped up on Joe's phone.

Meet tonight at the warehouse. This can all be over.

Joe sighed and resigned himself to the inevitable. Anyway, it wasn't as though his life could get any worse.

Joe pulled into the industrial estate. His company had only moved into their new facility a few months ago, the third of five buildings being constructed on this new park. At close to midnight, the place seemed like a cemetery compared to its hustle and bustle of industry during working hours. Even with only three buildings, there would usually be a constant stream of articulated lorries, delivery vans, and forklift trucks whizzing about the freshly laid tarmac.

He reached into the glove compartment and pulled out a small black box. As he pressed one of the buttons on it, the long heavy green gate rolled to the side. He drove into the yard at the rear of the building. Bringing the car closer to the shutter doors, the security lights on the back wall illuminated the vast expanse of concrete like floodlights during an evening football match.

'For crying out loud,' he said to himself, as he saw the curtain-sided van with Britten Rashford livery parked outside the shutter doors. Leaning against the bonnet drinking from a thermos of coffee was Mr Ziff, the 'freight salesman' from the day before. Next to him stood Mr White. Joe pulled up alongside and got out of the car.

'Good evening, Mister Henderson,' said Ziff. 'We didn't think you would mind if we let ourselves in.'

Nothing these men did surprised Joe anymore. Plus, he considered that letting themselves into his yard was fairly innocuous given what he was beginning to understand they were capable of.

'A fully liveried freight truck and foreign plates as well. You two really have come prepared, haven't you? At least it might look vaguely like we're getting a delivery to anyone watching,' said Joe, as he unlocked the rear entrance.

The powerful LED lights switched on; he shielded his eyes as the cavernous warehouse was bathed in a bright white glow and the two men followed him in. Slamming the door behind him, he was suddenly overcome with a rage which surprised even him. Grabbing a crowbar from the work bench next to the door, he had finally had enough.

'You bastards!' he shouted, as he marched towards Ziff, raising the bar above his head. 'I know what you did to Billy; you've ruined my fucking life and now you want me to help you!'

Ziff spun on his heels and raised his arm, effortlessly stopping Joe's arm dead in its tracks. The two men locked stares briefly, Joe's eyes burning with anger, specks of saliva dotting his chin. The lack of emotion in Ziff's eyes barely had time to register. His other hand reached underneath, grabbed Joe's wrist, and with the slightest of effort rotated, forcing Joe to his knees. With a hand on the back of his head, his arm bent double, he now found himself staring at the hooked end of the crowbar, which hung barely inches from his eye.

'Mister Henderson, this is entirely unnecessary. And if I may say so, completely futile,' said Ziff, coldly. 'It was unfortunate what happened to your friend, but needs must I'm afraid.

Now, if you've got all of this nonsense out of your system, perhaps we could discuss our situation like grown-ups?'

He released all of Joe's limbs whilst simultaneously snatching the crowbar from his hand. Joe knelt on the floor, rubbing his shoulder. He looked up to see Ziff twirling the crowbar around like a tap dancer with a cane, strolling around and casting his eyes over the warehouse.

'What do we think, Mister White?' he asked his colleague, who had taken on the role of some sort of building regulations surveyor. He was taking photos on his smartphone, and he was sizing up the warehouse using a laser measure.

'We can set the doors up over there, and there's some decent ceiling stanchions to hang the prize board off. I'm guessing that all of your comms are in that little room over there, Mister Henderson?'

Joe nodded silently, still kneeling on the floor.

'Excellent. I'll need to see inside if that's alright,' he said, although he had already started to make his way over there, so it didn't really matter whether Joe said yes or no.

'Right, Joe, I'm going to need you to man up a bit now, OK?' said Ziff, grabbing him under the armpit and hoisting him to his feet. 'You don't have anything to worry about. We know what we're doing.'

'You're just going to murder someone in my place of work,' replied Joe, chewing his thumbnail.

'It would probably be better if you didn't think of it like that.'

'Oh right, OK then,' snorted Joe, sarcastically.

'Look, Joe, it's simple,' continued Ziff, beginning to sound like Joe's father. 'It is in no-one's interest for this to go wrong. You know what we do. You know how we do it. If we had been complacent, would we have lasted this long doing it? You sought us out, remember. Now you have the chance to go down in deep web history. Anonymously, of course. But think of it, the thrill you experienced when you first installed the browser and saw what it was capable of showing you. Now you can be a part of it.

Plus, you don't have a choice, so you might as well just roll with it.'

'Fine,' said Joe, rocking sideways as Ziff playfully punched him on the top of the arm. 'But I want payment.'

'Ha,' snorted Ziff. 'You're only in this situation in the first place because you stiffed us for money, and now you want us to pay you?'

'Look, what difference does it make to you?' asked Joe. 'The clown thing said that you don't do this for the money. My life has been more or less ruined by this. If it ever gets out that I allowed this warehouse to be used for your show, I might as well kill myself. Even if the police find me and arrest me, it won't be anywhere near as bad as what my parents will do to me. Plus, my fiancée has already walked out me. I don't want a lot.'

'How much?'

'Fifty bitcoins. Plus, you'd be guaranteeing my silence even further still.'

'You want us to pay you thirty grand?' asked Ziff, who was by now slowly starting to like this kid. In the face of everything, he'd managed to find some balls.

Joe nodded. 'I kind of promised my fiancée an all-expenses-paid, first class trip to the Maldives for our honeymoon. So, if I happen to make it out of this alive and not in jail, at least I'll be able to start to rebuild my life.'

'OK, I'll see to it that fifty bitcoins are transferred to your wallet before the show on Friday,' replied Ziff, moving to square up to Joe. 'But if you do anything to jeopardise this operation, I will personally see to it that we hurt you and everyone you care about. Clear?'

Joe swallowed and nodded.

Ziff slapped him lightly around the cheek. 'Good lad.'

White emerged from the back office, tapping away on his smartphone.

'This all looks good. Very basic security system, shouldn't be too much trouble taking control of it. Internet access is surprisingly fast for out here in the sticks, must be the fibre optic they put in these new estates. Plus, they very kindly put the junction box for the internet just up the road, so we won't even need to leave the estate. Anyway, it won't take us too long to set everything up. A few local cameras we need to take care of, but that's about it.'

'There you go, Joe,' said Ziff. 'I told you there was nothing to worry about.'

'Fine, let's just get it over with,' said Joe, edging towards the exit. 'We close early on Fridays, so there'll be no-one here from about two o'clock. Just turn up in some sort of utilities or tradesman van, will you? At least make it look like something normal to the neighbours.'

'Not a problem,' said Ziff, holding out his hand. 'If I may say as well, you have some really useful props in this warehouse. It's going to be a blast. See you on Friday.'

Reluctantly, Joe shook his hand. And with that, the two men climbed into their van and drove off.

Joe got in his car and drove through the gate. As he watched the large wrought iron construction slide silently across the gap, he couldn't help but feel that a chapter in his life was about to come to an end. Weirdly, the fear he had felt before was still there, but now it was mixed with that same sort of excitement and anticipation he'd felt the first time he went exploring the deep web. He didn't really know whether to laugh or cry at this precise moment, but one thing he did know, as he started to drive home, was that in a couple of days his life would be changing forever.

26

Cramer McAllister piled another fistful of pound coins into the fruit machine. He rested his pint on its top and pressed the spin button. As he felt his phone vibrate in his back pocket, three cherries rolled into a line in front of him and three more golden pound coins dropped into the tray underneath. With one hand, he collected his winnings and fed them back into the slot, with the other he retrieved his phone.

Two messages had arrived. He opened the first from a contact simply called '*Slater*'. The message read: *31 Chapman Drive. Posh boy coke pushers. 2gs unpaid.*

Another job for later on that night. Slater was the drugs kingpin in the area and McAllister was his muscle. He was rarely given any more information than that, not that he needed it. This was the part of his job, if that's what it could be called, that he enjoyed. Generally, the routine involved kicking their door in, messing them up a bit so they knew he meant business, and then, unless they coughed up the money they owed Slater, he would cause them pain in as many imaginative ways as he could think of. Which was a lot. In fact, even if they coughed up he wasn't going to let it ruin his fun or make him miss out on doing them over. And his favourites were the middle class mummy's boys who fancied themselves as some sort of gangland drug lords from the comfort of their plush commuter belt five bedroom houses. He would look forward to that.

But his other indulgence was men. Young men. And the other message was hopefully going to be tonight's other little plaything. The text was from an online dating website called '*Bearz 'n' Boyz*'. Although the term 'dating' was used very loosely. This was a site where men advertised for sex; nothing more, nothing less.

He opened the text. Eighteen, skinny, shaved. Just the way he liked them. He swiped to accept the meet up and replaced the phone in his back pocket. He carried on playing the fruit machine, waiting for his 'date' to arrive.

The phone on the dashboard vibrated.

'He's gone for it,' said Stan. 'That wasn't too hard.'

'Not as hard as he probably is right now,' replied Eric.

'Charming,' replied Stan, climbing over the back seat into the back of the van, where a slight-set boy, barely in adulthood, sat scrolling through his phone. The boy had an armful of tattoos, as well as various body piercings visible through his tight white vest top.

'Right, listen,' said Stan to the boy, as he tried to slide his enormous brick of a phone into the pocket of the tightest pair of jeans Stan had ever seen. 'How the hell do you even walk in those things?' he asked, rhetorically.

'I'm used to it,' replied the boy, as he flicked his head to remove a strand of hair that had fallen over his eye. 'Why, do you like me in them?'

'Shut up,' replied Stan, bluntly. 'Right, all we want you to do is go into that pub and find this man. We've just hooked you up with him on Bearz 'n' Boyz so he'll be expecting you. Whilst I appreciate that you are a very, how shall we say, 'flamboyant' person, I would be hugely grateful if you would try and avoid drawing too much attention to yourself if you can help it.'

'What about my money?' asked the boy.

'I'm getting to that,' replied Stan, impatiently and a little irritated. 'Once you've made contact with him, don't have a drink, just tell him that you're desperate to get into his pants or whatever it is you lot say. Then we need you to tell him that you have a flat just around the corner, which is that one over there, number three, got it?'

'Fine. Do I actually have to fuck him?'

'No, once you're in and he's got his kit off, we'll do the rest. There's a grand in cash for you now and another grand once we're done.'

The boy held his hand out for the cash. Stan pulled a folded up wedge of twenty pound notes out of his shirt pocket and placed it in the boy's hand. Just as the boy grasped his fingers around the money, Stan quickly grabbed his wrist as the boy fought to snatch it away.

'Ow, let go of me, you arsehole,' the boy protested, as Stan leaned in.

'Be clear,' Stan said in a stern, calm manner. 'If you so much as spill a word about this to anyone, we will find you and we will make you wish you had never been born. OK?'

'Alright, sweetie, calm down,' said the boy, rubbing his wrist as Stan let go.

The boy climbed out of the back of the van and shut the doors behind him. Stan returned to the passenger seat just as Eric hung up a phone call.

'I sent a couple of the goons into the pub in advance,' said Eric. 'I've been in that pub before. It's not really a place for a nancy boy like him. It's all hairy arms, shaved heads and neck tattoos. And that's just the women.'

They moved the van to a small alley near the block of flats and reversed next to the gate that joined on to the ground floor apartment's garden. The two men left the van and entered the flat, where two waiting goons already sat, playing cards at a table. They were going around the flat, closing all the curtains, making it look a little lived-in, when the walkie-talkie on the kitchen table crackled. Eric picked it up and mumbled a few affirmative grunts.

'Target is on its way. Everyone take their positions. Remember, this guy is bigger than Rankin and even more of a nasty shit, so we need to be clinical and efficient.'

The other men all nodded in agreement before concealing themselves in various hiding places around the flat and turning off all the lights.

A few minutes later, the door crashed open as McAllister burst into the room. He turned on the light and tossed the boy down onto the floor.

'Get your fucking clothes off now, you little pussy. And get on the sofa,' he shouted.

The boy was used to being treated roughly, but even he looked somewhat stunned at the strength and aggression of this man. He looked back at McAllister undoing his belt and trousers as he struggled to peel his own tight clothes off. A semi-naked and somewhat impatient McAllister then grabbed the boy off the floor and pinned him face-down on the sofa. He grabbed the boy's jeans and yanked them down past his ankles, ignoring the muffled sounds of pain coming from the cushion, and positioned himself directly behind his buttocks.

Just as he was about to start taking what he wanted, he felt a tap on his shoulder. Letting go of the boy, he turned round to see four men in balaclavas stood two feet away. The shock froze him to the spot, giving the boy enough time to make his escape, grabbing his clothes from the floor as he ran behind a kitchen worktop.

'Evening, Cramer,' said one of the men. 'Is that a gun in your pocket or are you just pleased to see us?'

As McAllister looked down at his now flaccid manhood, he all of a sudden felt two sharp stabs in his torso, followed by a hissing crackle as thousands of volts shot into his body. His arms flailed as he tried to fight it, but he quickly lost control of his limbs and slumped to the floor.

'You're going to pay for this, you fuckers,' he shouted defiantly from the floor, as two of the goons pinned his arms to his back.

'That's a good point, actually,' replied Eric, as he tossed another wedge of notes at the boy, who was now practically fully clothed. 'Thanks for reminding me. Go on, get out of here.'

The boy didn't need a second invitation and ran out of the flat.

'Don't you fucking know who I am?' Cramer continued. 'I'll have the lot of you fucking killed.'

'Of course we know who you are, Cramer, that's why we're here,' said Eric, calmly, kneeling down to talk closer. 'You are our very special guest. And we are going to see to it that you get our extra special treatment for being such a valuable member of the human race.'

'Fuck you,' he spat.

'Indeed,' replied Eric, as he removed a small syringe from his pocket. He held it in front of McAllister's face and flicked the glass side. McAllister's eyes darted backwards and forwards as he fought against his assailants. 'Time for night-night.'

As the tranquiliser took effect, McAllister's eyes eventually closed and his body went limp.

Stan took out his mobile and dialled. 'We've got him,' he said.

'Excellent work, gentlemen,' said the voice on the other end. 'Get him back here; he's got a very important job to do.'

27

Daisy lay in her room at the bed and breakfast, staring up at the ceiling. It had been nearly two weeks now since she'd escaped the clutches of Saeed and Aleksander. This place was hardly the Ritz; it was damp, it smelled, and the less said about the other guests the better. Between the half-way house residents fresh out of prison and the emergency housing association benefit cheats that turned up in the middle of the night, she practically felt like royalty. But that didn't stop her almost sleeping with one eye open every night. Throw in one of the most lecherous, overweight slobs of a landlord she had ever seen, and it made the little caravan in the woods seem like a five star hotel.

But it was cheap, and it had meant that the money she stole from Aleksander could stretch further. She was able to buy proper food and medicines to help her body heal. Most of all, its cheapness allowed her to buy clean clothes. No longer did she feel like a child of the gutter, a piece of filth that people would sooner wipe off their shoe than help.

She had even visited the local swimming pool. For most children, going swimming was a fairly unremarkable occurrence, but it was a pastime notably absent from her younger years. She had learned to swim once but she couldn't recall when. But now, it was helping her; once she had learnt to ignore the stares from other bathers when they saw the bruises, scratches, and scars over her arms and legs, that is. Apart from helping her grow fitter and stronger, it also helped clear her mind. The abuse that she'd suffered, the violations at the hands of filthy, repulsive men who would make normal people want to puke; no longer did she feel the need to try and suppress the anger. She could channel it through exercise, focus her aggression into something positive. And she loved the effects. Even after a few days, she no longer felt weak and pointless. More importantly, she had slowly begun to stop hating herself.

She was roused from her daze by a thump on the door. Turning to look, she decided she was too comfortable, rolled her head back, and closed her eyes.

The thump came again, twice this time, and a little bit harder.

'Oi, Daisy,' came the shout from the hallway. 'It's Kev, let us in.'

'For god's sake,' Daisy whispered to herself, before shouting, 'piss off, I'm trying to have a sleep.'

'Go on, I need to talk to you,' he replied.

Kev was one of the pointless benefit cheats, put up in the hostel because he had three children, a girlfriend, and nowhere to live. From the way he talked, she could tell he was barely educated, a jobless wonder who did nothing all day but could somehow afford cigarettes and strong cider. She waited for a moment in the hope that he would just go away, but there was another thump at the door. Cursing to herself, she rolled off the bed and opened the door. It had only just slipped the catch when Kev pushed it open and barged past into her room.

'Fucking hell, Kev. What do you think you're doing?' she asked, angrily.

'Alright darling, calm down,' he replied, walking around her room, picking various objects up, looking at them, and then putting them down again. 'I thought we could get to know each other a bit better.'

'No thanks, you're fine,' she replied, holding the door open and motioning for him to leave.

'Kev?' came a shout from down the hallway.

'In here, mate. Don't mind if Wesley comes in as well, do you?' he asked, as the second man entered the room before Daisy had any chance to object. They looked identical. Black trainers, grey over-baggy sweat pants that sagged well below their waists, topped off with a basketball shirt and endless amounts of cheap gold jewellery. And, still, in their mid-twenties, they were yet to shake off two facefuls of bright red acne.

Daisy sighed and looked at the two men as they shook hands in some overly flamboyant manner involving lots of slapping of hands, twirling of fingers, finished with a fist bump. She couldn't contain a loud snigger.

'What are you to two supposed to be, Bloods or Crips?'

'What did you say, bitch?' said Wesley, in his best West Coast gangster voice, forming a gun shape with his first two fingers and thumb extended, as he walked towards her. He aimed it sideways at Daisy's face, making a gunshot sound, and smirking arrogantly until he felt the hand on his pectoral pulling him back.

'It's cool, bro. She's just messing. Sit down and have a smoke.'

'Do you have to do that here?' asked Daisy, as Wesley sat down and pulled a long, cone-shaped joint from his tracksuit pocket.

'Come on, baby, chill out,' said Kev, swaggering towards her with his arms out wide, crotch thrust forward.

Daisy put her hands up in front of her face in an attempt to make him keep his distance.

'You do know that wearing pants halfway down your leg like that started in prisons as a sign that the wearer was bent and asking to be fucked up the arse?'

Wesley stood up and walked over to them. 'This little whore needs to be learnt some fucking respect.'

Kev reached over her shoulder and pushed the door closed. 'You wanna watch what you say. We bust little pussies like you all the time.'

'Of course you do,' replied Daisy, trying her best to act nonchalant, but inwardly her heart was beating twenty to the dozen. 'Because you're some sort of gangster pimp, right? Not the pointless council estate scratter that you look li–' Daisy let out a scream as Wesley grabbed the back of her hair and pulled her head. He threw her down towards the bed.

'You fucking what?' he said, arms pumped outward in an attempted display of masculine dominance. 'I'm gonna fucking do you.'

He grabbed her arms and pinned them down above her head on the pillow. She struggled, but his weight was too much.

'Grab her trousers,' he shouted to Kev, who, despite a slight reluctance, did what he was told.

Kev started to grab at her belt and undo her button fly, all five popping open at once as her legs thrashed around. He took a strong grip on the belt hooks and pulled. But the jeans were on too tightly and his grasp slipped, causing him to fall back against the wall. Daisy looked up to see him stumble and, before he could regain his balance, she brought her leg back and thrust her foot as forcefully as she could against his head. Catching him straight on the jaw, she smashed his head hard against the concrete wall, knocking him out cold.

Wesley let go of one of her arms and brought his fist up. He punched as hard as he could. Daisy felt the air as his hand brushed past the side of her head and was swallowed by the pillow. Again, he went to strike. She waved her free hand around and moved her head out of the way as the fist landed once more. His aggressive grunts became louder, and he straddled her on the bed, hoping to land a decisive blow.

As he raised his arm one final time, Daisy looked up at him, wide-eyed. The flashbacks began. Of the house, of the abuse, of the other weak pathetic men in the same position. They shot through Daisy's mind. One after another after another, each one making the hatred swell within her. After a split second that seemed like much longer, her breathing calmed and she lifted her leg up as forcibly as she could, straight into Wesley's crotch. Before he could move, she did it again. He screamed a high-pitched scream and rolled off the bed onto the floor.

Daisy jumped off the bed, planting kick after kick between his legs as he writhed around on the carpet, groaning in agony.

'You ... fucking ... little ... bastard!' she screamed, between each kick.

Kev had come to slightly and reached out to grab her leg. She pulled away and ran for the door, slamming it behind her as she ran out into the hallway.

As she ran past the front desk, the landlord shouted out for her to stop, but she ignored him and carried on into the street. She started running, anywhere away from the hostel. There was no way she'd be able to go back in there now.

Eventually, she arrived at the same industrial park she had seen at the edge of the woods. Slowing to a walk, she attempted to appear to any passers-by like a jogger taking a rest as she glanced over her shoulders, trying to take in her environment. Stopping at a bench, she patted her back pocket.

'Shit,' she whispered. 'Shit, shit, shit. No.' The stash of money. She had left it under the mattress in the hostel room.

Darkness was beginning to draw in. The bright headlights of the cars leaving for the day formed spiky stars through the tears that had started to well in her eyes as they drove past.

Rubbing her eyes, she tried to collect her thoughts. She had been in this position before, but now found herself back in it a little quicker than she had anticipated. From the brief exploring carried out the last time she was here, she remembered the covered pallet store in the yard of one of the warehouses. For now, that would have to do.

Shinning over the green metal gate and landing with a thud on the concrete, she ran across the yard. Luckily, it was neither dark enough to set off the security, nor was the store locked. So she sat down in her new home for the night and tried to think. What was her next move? But at least, for now, she was safe.

28

Harris stood at the front of the briefing room, next to a flip chart, in front of the whiteboard, brandishing a black jumbo marker pen. In front of him, variously sat on chairs or on the tables, were Brooks, Fowler and Smith, plus an assortment of other officers from both the unit and other sections. Among the black lines joining ovals and rectangles that adorned the wall were written clues to the case. '*The Red Room*', '*The Brotherhood of the Righteous*', '*Karen Parker*'. A vague picture was starting to emerge, but they were all waiting for the big one. The next episode.

It was Harris' job to educate the assembled officers on what they knew.

'What we have so far is some sort of show that takes place somewhere on the deep web,' started Harris, before being cutting off immediately by the first question.

'The deep web? So it could be anywhere in the world then,' asked an officer.

'Quite right,' replied Harris, patiently. 'Although, if you'd read the brief you would remember that the three people whose disappearances we can link to the show all live in the U.K. This means that we can be reasonably certain that this show is also filmed somewhere in this country.'

Brooks and Fowler turned and rolled their eyes at the stupidity of the question as the officer who asked it slunk into his chair, blushing with embarrassment.

'Anyway,' continued Harris, 'from what we can gather, the group running this go by the pretty sanctimonious name of the 'Brotherhood of the Righteous'. The footage that was emailed into CCU appears to show the group killing convicted paedophile Gary Sweetman by slitting his throat. So it doesn't take a huge leap of imagination to assume that this group abducts these people and then broadcasts the videos of the murders online. And they're clearly very professional. Apart from the production values in the video, they left absolutely nothing to go on with the respective MISPER investigations. They have access to advanced technologies, namely the ability to clone the surveillance tag that Karen Parker was wearing.'

'So, do we know anything about them?' asked Smith.

'Nothing concrete, just assumptions. They must have access to serious resources, funding, and so on. And they must have experience in covert-style operations, given their seeming ability to move around without being seen anywhere.'

'Can we be absolutely certain that they're the ones responsible for the disappearances of Parker and Rankin though?' asked another officer.

'We're ninety-nine percent sure, yes. Fowler?' He motioned to Fowler to come up to the front.

Fowler stood up with his laptop and plugged it in to the USB connector of the smartboard, transforming the big whiteboard into a huge PC monitor. A cacophony of sniggers broke out in the room as Fowler's enormous Batman symbol desktop appeared up on the wall.

'You lot are only jealous that you haven't got one,' he started. 'Anyway, thanks to our trawling through the depths of sub-internet webspace, we stumbled across this.'

He clicked on the JPEG file to display what appeared to be a photo of the Red Room entry screen. It appeared to have been taken on a mobile phone. A large white patch where the flash had reflected on the screen obscured part of the Red Room sign, but the words were still visible.

'We don't know who uploaded this file, but it is date stamped for last Friday. Clearly, Parker and Rankin are referenced as that evening's "special guests". But it's just a picture, the web address at the top of the screen has since been removed. It's either the mother of all coincidences or—'

Just then, Harris' phone, which had been sitting on the table in front of him, lit up and vibrated across the surface, nearly sending it off and onto the floor. He grabbed it and opened it to the home screen. There was a message flashing up on his mobile TOR app.

'Do you need to get that?' asked Fowler, as Harris' attention to the room dropped briefly. 'Harris?'

'Sorry,' replied Harris, still scanning his phone. 'It's a message telling me to check the Enter The Dark forum. I'm assuming the next episode has been put on there.'

Fowler grabbed at the laptop and began typing into the browser as the room watched in quiet anticipation. This would have been the first time quite a few of the regular officers had even heard of the deep web, let alone seen it. As the blocky, retro style browser turned over, Harris began talking again.

'Our sources have indicated that this "Brotherhood" use a chat room called "Enter The Dark" to advertise the show. So if you'll just bear with us for a moment we might have something.'

The room began chatting amongst itself as Fowler and Harris hunched over the laptop.

'There,' shouted Harris, pointing at the screen, at which point the room fell silent and attention switched back to the board. At the top of the list of various chats entitled '*Miscellaneous*' sat a thread entitled *TRATD*. Fowler clicked in to find a link; seemingly random numbers and letters. Underneath were various responses from users indicating that they had already clicked on the link. 'Let's see where this takes us.'

Fowler clicked on the link. 'It's not doing anything. There's no hyperlink attached to it.'

'Smart move, means there's no back trace. You'll have to copy and paste it,' replied Harris, as Fowler began typing into a new browser window.

'Is that it?' asked an officer, as the non-descript white screen, with an input box and statement *Entry 1BX*, flashed up on the board.

'What does—' started an officer, before being cut off by around ten other people in the room all shouting 'Bitcoin,' in unison. 'Sorry,' replied the officer, 'this isn't really my realm, all this nerdy stuff. I'm more of a beat bobby.'

'And you're here because?' asked Brooks.

'I was transferred here to help with the Parker case, since it was me who found the tag. I don't really know why I'm here either,' he responded, to stifled chuckles within the room.

'That's enough,' said Smith, standing up to address the room. 'OK, everyone, thank you for your time. I think we'll call it a day for now. My team and I will carry on with this Red Room investigation, but I want everyone to be on stand-by in case it throws up anything urgent.'

As the mumbling, chattering officers stood to leave, Brooks went and joined Fowler and Harris by the laptop.

'So, chaps, this is it then, I assume. Shit or bust.'

'Well yes,' replied Harris. 'But let's not lose sight of what we're dealing with here. If our assumptions are correct, this page will give us entry to view the live killing of a real person. This is slightly more than just happy slapping or a bullying video posted to Facebook. I hope you're all ready for this, it could be disturbing.'

'Sir, I think we're going to need to plunder the petty cash.' Smith had joined their little huddle and was typing something into his phone at the same time.

'Fine, do what you need to do. But look, I'd rather keep this on the down low just for the time being. You saw most of the people in this room just now. Apart from the ones who weren't really sure why they had even been dragged in, a lot of them just thought we were dealing with some sort of elaborate hoax. Do what you've got to do. Keep as many records as you can, screenshots and so on. Whatever happens, we need to be in that show when it goes out.'

As they left the room, Smith pressed send on his message. *Getting closer. They've found the site.*

Back in the office, Harris sat at his desk with a cup of coffee. He picked up the drinks coaster from next to his keyboard and spun it around between his finger and thumb. It felt like ages since he had spent any proper time with his daughter.

'Go home, Pete,' said Fowler, as she placed her hand on his shoulder. 'You look like shit, smell like shit, but even so, Olivia still needs you to be her dad every once in a while.'

'I promised I would take her to Legoland this weekend,' he replied, staring into the hypnotic blur of the coaster as it spun in his hand.

'Well, that was a schoolboy error,' she chuckled, perching on the edge of his desk.

'I know. I'm probably going to have to cancel if the shit hits the fan with this investigation.'

'No, I mean it's the weekend. Legoland will be absolutely heaving. There's not an awful lot more that we can do here now, especially if his lordship wants us to keep this under wraps for the time being. Why don't you get an early one?'

Grace walked away, placing a friendly hand on top of his before she went. He appreciated the support and knew that, really, he should be listening to her.

'Fowler, can we sort this bitcoin payment out?' Harris shouted across the office.

'Already on it,' came the reply. Harris put the coaster down and walked over to his colleague's desk. 'I've gone to the link to deposit the bitcoin. I've authorised the transfer. I'm just waiting for the transaction to be completed.'

After a few more minutes of waiting, the confirmation message eventually appeared on the screen.

FAILED

'How has it failed?' asked Harris.

'No idea, let me try again,' replied Fowler. He input all the transaction details, the wallet I.D., the transfer key, double checking each digit as he went. Ten minutes later, the same message appeared. Failed.

'I don't understand,' said Fowler, randomly clicking around the screen. 'The details in the transaction screen are correct, we both saw that. There's more than enough credit in the wallet; Christ, it's only one single coin. I don't get it.'

'Could they be blocking us?'

'That would be practically impossible. The transactions are authorised anonymously by users around the world called miners. There's no way that they can backtrack through a transaction before it's even taken place, and there's absolutely no way of telling who's going to mine a particular transfer. Even the miners don't see who it's come from or where it's going to, they just see numbers.'

'So what does that leave?'

'It's possible to put levels of security on the bitcoin account to prevent payments to certain destinations. A bit like blocking certain incoming addresses on your emails.'

'But that would mean ...'

'Correct. It's someone here blocking us from making the transfer.'

29

Amanda stared into the mirror. As she carefully applied the eyeliner onto her left eye, a teary streak of black ran down the other cheek. The puffiness in her lips had lessened and the scabs at the corner of her mouth had healed well. But it still took a lot of eyeliner, foundation, and mascara to cover the bruising that surrounded her eye. The other parents at preschool already gave her looks, looks that told her they were better than she was. She was always conveniently missed off of round robin emails detailing class nights out, school updates, coffee mornings. And if Mo ever received an invitation to a birthday party it was out of obligation to invite the whole class, rather than the parents actually wanting him there. The looks, the stares, she had put them all down to Saeed's reputation; they all believed they knew his history.

The mistake she made had been confiding in someone who she thought was her friend, but all that she'd achieved was to provide this person with a nugget of prized gossip. Armed with this knowledge, the 'friend' could now worm her way into the playground 'it-crowd' at Amanda's expense. But when turning up to the school playground for drop-off with a face like a boxer who had just fought fifteen rounds and lost horribly, when that doesn't elicit any more reaction than any other normal day, that was when it started to hurt deep inside. Every time she looked in the mirror she cried for her boys, trying to cover up the truth about their father, wishing she could find a way out.

A mug sat on the window sill. She picked it up and took a large gulp, grimacing as she struggled to swallow the now room temperature liquid.

'Mummy,' came the shout from outside the bathroom. 'Mummy, Shan's spilt his cup of milk all over the floor.'

Amanda hastily touched up the smudged make-up. She sniffed, wiping her nose on the back of her hand.

'I'm coming, darling.' It was time to run the daily gauntlet of the playground.

Another morning come and gone, and all that Amanda had to look forward to now was an afternoon locked away in her house with her boys, waiting for Saeed to walk back in through the door. He hadn't come home last night, which wasn't unusual, but usually he would at least text a couple of words.

There had been more stares than there generally were today, the not-so-subtle discussions from huddles of women all laughing at each other's jokes and patting each other on the arms. Amanda was the last to find out why, as the teacher gave her a white envelope when she handed Mo over at home time.

As she sat down at the kitchen table and opened the envelope, her boys already sat in front of the television, she poured herself another glass of white wine from the fridge, her second of the day. Or maybe the third. The letter was from Mo's teacher and, in a blunt and to the point couple of paragraphs, confirmed Amanda's worst fears: that Mo was anything like his father.

She caught her curved reflection in the side of the wine glass, and even with the faintly green tint, she could see the black lines running down both cheeks. Nowadays, she sometimes cried without even realising it, but not this time. She read the letter, about how mothers had been complaining of Mo punching and biting their darling little ones, how they were forced to keep Mo isolated for periods of the day to 'chill out', and how they claimed to have raised the issue with her a number of times at pickup. They may have done; she was usually in such a rush to leave there as quickly as possible that she had probably blanked it from her mind. Her sobbing became louder and she took bigger and bigger mouthfuls of wine with each sentence she read.

She had always made it a priority to shelter the boys from the corrosive environment that they were forced to live in. And seeing reports of her little boy being violent at such a tender age, before he could even read, made her hate herself even more; as did anything that reminded her that Mo and Shan were Saeed's, and, even worse, that they might turn into him. This was it, time to call it a day.

Screwing the letter up, she swallowed down the last of the glass, coughing as the harshness of the alcohol caught the back of her throat.

'Mo,' she shouted, 'run up to your room and grab as many cuddly toys as you can put in this bag.'

She handed him a small rucksack as he ran past, not even attempting to hide his discontent at having to leave his favourite television show. Grabbing Shan from the lounge, she followed him upstairs and into their bedroom. She grabbed at clothes, shoes, filled a washbag with essentials, and stuffed it all into one big holdall.

Racing back down the stairs, she took coats off the hooks in the hallway and placed Shan on the bottom step.

'Can you put his shoes on please, darling?' she said, tossing a pair of canvas trainers to Mo.

'Where are we going?' asked Mo.

'Out,' she replied.

'Are we going to Grandad's?'

'Possibly. Will you just put your coat and shoes on, please?'

Amanda opened the door, picked up the holdall, and ushered the two boys outside. She patted her trousers, then her coat.

'Shit,' she whispered to herself. 'Mo sit here, hold onto Shan, make sure he doesn't walk off. I need to find my phone.'

She placed the bag down on the path, walked back into the house, checking the hall cabinet, then in the kitchen.

'Come on, where the hell are you?' she muttered.

A message alert echoed from the lounge. She lifted one cushion and then another from the sofa. Eventually, she found it under the coffee table, still with Mo's favourite game open. Closing it down, she walked out, checking the message as she went. Spam again, telling her she could claim thousands of pounds for an accident she'd never had.

As she walked out into the hallway and turned towards the front door, eyes still down on her phone, she felt a hand on her shoulder, blocking the way.

'Going somewhere?'

She inhaled violently as she looked up to see Saeed standing in front of her, with the holdall in his other hand.

'Sae,' she exclaimed, quickly trying to regain some composure as her heart raced. 'Er, no, not all. We're just taking some old clothes to the charity shop.'

'Really? Interesting,' replied Saeed, calmly. 'Kids, inside. I'd quite like to see what clothes you're getting rid of. Let's open the bag, and we can see what you've decided is no longer good enough for you. Shall we? We'll do that, shall we?'

He closed the door behind him as the boys ran in to the lounge.

'Give it here,' shouted Amanda, trying to grab the bag from him as he held her off with one arm.

'No, don't be silly. Come on, let's see,' he said, as he started to open the holdall, before holding it upside down and emptying its contents all over the floor. 'So, you think charity shops want a washbag full of toothbrushes and toothpaste, do you? Or your skanky nightie?'

He walked over the pile towards her, trampling it deliberately as he tried to stop her running off into the kitchen.

'Get off me. We've had enough. You can't keep us here like this,' she shouted, as she ran around the opposite side of the kitchen table, making sure not to lose sight of him. Slowly, he walked into the room, like a predator stalking an injured prey.

'You really think you can just walk out of here? Just like that? You really are a stupid waste of space, aren't you?'

'No, I'm not. You're the useless one. You're a bully and you know what bullies are? Cowards. They're cowards and you are the worst.'

Saeed laughed, almost in disbelief at what he was hearing. He walked over to the table and saw the empty wine bottle. As he picked it up, he turned it over and looked in the top as nothing came out.

'So, this is what you've lowered yourself to?'

'It's the only way I can deal with living with such an arsehole.'

'So leave then. Go and run to Daddy, find yourself another man. But you won't though, will you?' he said, as he rolled the bottle across the table towards her. 'Because you're damaged goods. You're sullied. As if anyone would lower themselves to take you—'

Before he could finish the sentence, Amanda picked up the wine bottle. As years of pent up anger and frustration boiled over, she hurled the bottle as hard as she could straight at Saeed's head.

As Saeed ducked out of the way, it felt as though someone had punched a hole through her chest and ripped out her heart. She heard the 'Mummy' first and then her eyes focused on her son stood at the doorway as the bottle struck him on the top of the head.

'MO!' she shouted, but it was too late. She dropped to her knees, holding onto the table for support as her whole world came crumbling down. Saeed quickly got to his feet and ran to the doorway. Mo lay prostrate on the floor, out cold, with blood gushing from his head.

Amanda began hyperventilating, and the words she wanted to shout stuck in her throat.

'Get … get … away from him, you bastard. This is all your fault.'

Saeed turned around and smirked at her. He shook his head as he scooped Mo up in his arms before heading to the lounge and collecting Shan. Amanda tried to stand, but her legs felt like jelly and she could only watch helplessly as Saeed walked out of the house with her two boys.

'How does that feel?' asked the doctor, as he snipped the twine after the last stitch.

'It hurts,' replied Mo.

Saeed let out a little giggle and ruffled his hand through Mo's hair. 'It will do, mate, that was quite a bump you got there. You should really be more careful. Some of those books on the bookcase are really heavy.'

'Well, Mister Anwar, it'll take a couple of weeks for the swelling on his head to go down. Luckily, he seems to have avoided any serious concussion, but just keep an eye on him. If he seems unwell, or the bleeding starts again, bring him back to A and E and we'll fix him up again,' said the doctor, before turning his attention back to Mo. 'And as for you, young man, no more climbing up the bookcase. You were lucky it was attached to the wall.'

He handed Mo a lollipop and left. After a few moments of silence, they heard a familiar shout down the corridor.

'Mo Anwar, is he here?' came the desperate shout. 'I'm his mother, I need to see him.'

Saeed pressed his finger against his lips and whispered, 'Ssh'.

But the silence was broken by the curtain being wrenched across, almost right off the runner.

'Mo, Mo, Mo,' she screamed, as she ran towards him, barging Saeed out of the way and stopping short of giving Mo a massive hug only after catching sight of the wound she'd caused. Her arms out wide, she stopped abruptly, not wanting to cause him any more pain. Gently, she caressed his cheeks as tears rolled down her own.

'You did that,' whispered Saeed, as he leaned in close to her.

She swallowed hard. 'What did you tell them?'

'I told them precisely what happened,' he replied, calmly.

At that moment, the doctor returned. 'Is everything alright in here? I heard the shouting at the front desk. Are you Mrs Anwar?'

'He's lying,' she pleaded, stuttering and pointing her finger at Saeed. 'This is his fault. I didn't mean to hit Mo, the bottle...'

'The bottle?' asked the doctor, confused. 'But I thought you said it was a book. Right, excuse me a moment. I need to get someone else in here.'

Saeed grinned and stroked his beard as the doctor turned to leave the cubicle. Realising what she had just done, Amanda turned to Saeed, her face red with anger.

'What did you tell them, you bastard?'

'I was trying to protect you,' he replied, shrugging his shoulders. 'I tried to tell them that it was an accident. You were the one who went shooting your mouth off.'

'You bastard,' she shouted, her eyes bloodshot and filled with tears. She pulled back her fist and, just as the doctor walked back into the cubicle, punched Saeed with all her might, sending him sprawling backwards onto the floor after bouncing off a chair.

'Get her out of here!' the doctor shouted to the accompanying security guard. He pulled Saeed to his feet and helped him down onto the chair as the guard dragged Amanda, kicking and screaming, down the hallway. 'Are you OK?'

'Yes, thank you, Doctor. It's fine, I'm used to it. She gets like that after she's been drinking,' he said, wiggling his jaw from side to side with his hand.

'Is that true what she said about the bottle?' the doctor asked.

Saeed hung his head like a naughty schoolboy. 'Yes I'm afraid it is, Doctor. We were having an argument. She was drinking straight out of the bottle and waving it around. I was trying to calm her down and the bottle slipped from her hand. Sorry I wasn't straight before, but we're trying to work through it, her issues I mean. Where is she now?'

'Security have her, but I will have to get the police involved. They'll take her to the station and she'll probably get away with a caution, but I wouldn't be surprised if Social Services want a chat. I'm sorry, but I have a duty of care to these boys.'

'I understand,' he replied. 'Can I take the boys home now? I think Mo could do with going to bed. I promise you I'll take care of them and, in the morning, we'll get this little matey a massive present. What do you say, champ? How about I buy you that Transformer you wanted?'

'Yes, I suggest that you do,' said the doctor, as Mo's headache seemed to miraculously disappear. 'Then can I suggest that after you sort your wife out down at the station you make sure that she gets some serious professional help.'

'I will, Doctor,' replied Saeed. 'I'll make sure she gets everything that she needs.'

The doorbell rang and Saeed pressed mute on the television remote control. He opened the door to find a female police constable holding Amanda by the arm.

'Good evening, Mister Anwar. Thank you for your assistance earlier on,' said the policewoman.

'My pleasure,' he replied, taking hold of Amanda and leading her into the hallway. 'I'm only sorry I couldn't come down to the station. We've got two small children. One's just been to hospital and I had no-one to look after them.'

'That's fine. I explained to your wife that you had chosen not to press charges and we appreciate that this has been a difficult day for all concerned. She's lucky to have such a supportive husband as you, Mister Anwar. I hope you give her all the help that she needs.'

'Oh, I most certainly will,' replied Saeed.

'Well, goodnight, sir.'

'Goodnight, Officer.'

As the officer left, Saeed looked up and down the front of the house before slamming the door behind him.

30

The day had arrived. Joe sat at his desk, staring out into the warehouse as the last of his staff packed up their belongings and left for the weekend. They always packed up at two o'clock on a Friday, and most could be found in the pub barely ten minutes later. Usually, he was glad beyond belief that he was sat on his side of the desk, sheltered from the mundane, low-paid monotony of their largely insignificant jobs. Whilst his job had its crap side to it, at least he could decide how much he paid himself. But at this precise moment in time, he coveted their blissful ignorance and would have given his right arm to switch places. And as his thoughts dwelt more on the events about to unfold, losing his right arm seemed like one of many potential outcomes.

He watched through the window as the final convoy of cars drove away, leaving him alone in his warehouse. He could just lock up, drive home as quickly as possible, grab Ellie and their passports, and disappear out of the country. The company could run itself for a few days whilst the dust settled. His daydreaming began, and he searched for 'cheap flights to Spain'. Two tickets from Heathrow to Malaga only £186.00 return, but he would have to leave now. He grabbed his wallet and keys, shut down the computer, and stood up from his desk to leave the office.

But it was too late. Around the corner came a curtain-sided Britten Rashford delivery lorry, which disappeared around the back, to the yard. Joe sat back down and restarted his computer. As the two men walked in through the far entrance of the warehouse, the least he could do was to appear slightly nonchalant about what was about to happen. His feigned relaxation certainly wasn't apparent on the inside, especially when he saw that the two men were not the same ones he had been in contact with up until now.

'Good afternoon, Mister Henderson,' said Stan, as he walked into the office, accompanied by Eric. 'I'm Dave and this is my colleague, Alan.'

Joe stood up and held out a hand, which was roundly ignored by both men, who began walking around the office, taking in every little detail and propping open the door to the server and communications room. Cue a failed attempt to make small talk.

'You two look a lot alike. You could almost be twins,' he joked, nervously.

'Almost,' replied Stan.

'I was expecting to see Mister Ziff and Mister White. Will they be here later?' asked Joe.

'No they won't,' said Eric, abruptly.

'OK, well is there anything I can do to help? Can I get you anything? Cup of tea perhaps?' Joe asked, thinking he should maybe sound like a gracious host even if he didn't feel like one.

'No,' replied Stan, equally abruptly, jabbing a finger into Joe's shoulder. 'In fact, the less you do, the better. Leave this to us, don't touch anything, and you shouldn't fuck it up. Again. That way we all leave here on time tonight, OK?'

'Yes sir,' said Joe, rubbing his shoulder.

Another lorry swung around the corner and pulled up outside the shut doors. Out stepped two large men, carrying various covers, plastic sheeting, and tools. Joe was sure he recognised them from the last 'episode', although at no point had he ever seen their faces. He went out into the warehouse, and as the men walked towards the large expanse that had been selected for the stage, he managed a half-wave, half-bow, and greeted them.

'Hi, I'm Joe,' he said, but the men just walked straight past as if he wasn't there. 'Good choice.'

A goon turned around and looked at him with some sort of primeval death stare.

'Er, I mean, er …' Joe stuttered, 'setting up all your equipment in that part of the warehouse. Well hidden from, well, anything.'

'It's close to the tools. Especially the saws,' came the Eastern European drawl, which was the most the goon could muster.

'The saws, yes of course, how silly of me.' By now Joe just wanted it to be eight o'clock. Get this thing over and done with. At least these people had it in their own interests to clear up and get the hell out of there as quickly as possible.

Joe walked back into the office, where 'Alan' was busy in the comms room. He had a laptop wired into the CCTV system and was busy typing in endless reams of indecipherable code.

'Will you be shutting the system down? I know my father checks in every now and again from home. Just to make sure that everything's OK. Not entirely sure what he would do if he looked on his computer at home and saw a man dressed as a clown slitting some bloke's throat in his warehouse,' said Joe, half-jokingly.

'No, we're not shutting it down,' replied Eric, unamused. 'We've patched together some old footage of the warehouse where nothing happens. Once I've reprogrammed the time and date stamp on the footage we'll play it during the broadcast. That way, not only will your father not realise anything is taking place in his warehouse, but if, and I mean if, the police ever have reason to check, they'll find that nothing happened either.'

'Great, I think I saw that once in a …' started Joe, before thinking better of it. 'Never mind.' He walked over to the window, just as a shiny black executive saloon car pulled up into one of the parking spaces out by the front entrance. 'Holy fucking shit!'

'What is it?' asked Stan.

'It's my fucking dad,' he replied.

'We're in,' said Fowler. 'But this is my own bitcoin account, I'm going to want reimbursing.'

'Fine,' replied Harris. 'Just submit an expenses form. Why have you got your own bitcoin account anyway?'

'I trade them. I can make more money in a week dealing in these than in a couple of months at the pitiful rate of pay in this place.'

Harris raised his eyes in surprise, mainly because he couldn't really argue with his logic.

The two of them were joined by Brooks, with another round of coffees. Harris read out the inexplicably long list of letters and numbers that made up the web address as Fowler typed. The payment screen came up and Fowler typed his wallet ID and password into the fields.

'I thought the bitcoin wallet had been tampered with?' asked Brooks.

'Yes it had. This is Danny's account. Turns out he's something of a George Soros in the world of underground virtual currencies. There's not really time at the moment to sort out the force's one, we'll look into it after this is all done.'

The three of them waited a few minutes before, finally, a confirmation message appeared on the screen to say that the payment had been completed. Fowler clicked on the link that appeared.

Appearing tonight – it's the gangland enforcer who everyone loves to hate. It's Cramer McAllister. 2 BX entry.

The face of the Host next to the blinking Red Room sign hung on the screen like a creepier version of the old BBC test card.

They stared at it for what seemed like ages, somewhat in disbelief at precisely what they were seeing.

'This is it,' said Harris. 'Looks like that first payment was for the privilege of getting to this point. Hope you've got plenty of pocket money in that wallet of yours.'

Fowler grunted a reluctant affirmative.

'I'll start checking anything on the system to do with McAllister, see if we've got any missing persons files for him as well,' said Brooks.

'OK, good job. I'll let Smith know that we're in,' replied Harris. 'Fowler, can you start setting up the tracking algorithm.

I doubt very much that we'll be able to start any sort of trace until the transmission begins, but best to be ready for when it starts.'

'Do you think you will be able to track them?' asked Brooks.

Fowler twirled a pen in each hand and spun around in his chair, arms outstretched.

'Come on, Grace, this is me we're talking about. Of course I will.'

Stan and Eric looked up from their respective tasks.

'So bloody well get rid of him,' said Stan, through the set of pliers he was holding in his mouth.

'Now,' reiterated Eric.

'Right, yes. Shit, shit, shit,' said Joe, as he dithered around the desk before walking out of the office.

'Christ, I knew this was a bad idea,' said Stan. 'Why did we have to involve a bloody amateur?'

Eric shook his head in agreement. 'Although we did sort of suggest it.'

The entry buzzer sounded as Joe left the building.

'Dad, what are you doing here? I thought you and Mum were still in Devon,' he said, hastily, as his dad slowly got out of the car.

'We had to come home, her haemorrhoids are playing up something rotten and she refuses to see anyone other than Doctor Southgate,' replied the old man. 'Plus, I needed to get a few files to work on over the weekend.'

'I'll get them for you,' replied Joe. 'It's the ones on your desk to do with the Conway Precision takeover, right? Great, just a minute.'

'I can get them myself, I'm not an invalid.'

'No it's fine. Actually, whilst you're out here, perhaps you could take a look at the flowerbeds and lawn. The landscaper's coming on Monday, so I can let him know if there's anything you want him to do,' said Joe, as he ran back into the office.

'Everything alright, Mister Henderson?' asked Eric, looking decidedly unconvinced by Joe's double thumbs up response as he collected the files from the desk before running back out.

But a few moments later, as the saloon drove away from the warehouse, he allowed himself a small sigh of relief.

'Right, so that takes care of him,' said Joe, excitedly, trying his best to be part of the team.

'Shut up, Mister Henderson,' replied Eric. 'The rest of our group will be here in a couple of hours, so just sit down and do nothing.'

Those couple of hours seemed like days. With the sun beginning to set behind the line of trees, Joe stood in the yard as a white van emerged around the corner, followed by a pristine black limousine.

The goons emerged from the van and walked over to Joe. Before he could do anything, he felt his arms pressed to the side of his body and a hood placed over his head. He tried to struggle, but it was pointless. His arms were pulled around his back and cuffed. After everything he had been through with these people already, this was the first time that he actually feared for his life. Real, total panic.

'So what have we got?' chewed D.C.I. Smith through a mouthful of lasagne, as they each tucked into their respective plates of food.

'We've made it through the preliminary payment level to what appears to be the main portal to view the show,' replied Harris. 'What we expect is, after we've stumped up another couple of bitcoins, we'll have access. Danny has been working on the tracking algorithm, so that any cracks in their firewalls should hopefully show up. Although I would expect them to have the mother of all security systems, since I imagine we aren't the first people, law up-holders or otherwise, who will have tried to find out who this group are and where they come from.'

'Excellent. I can't imagine it will make comfortable viewing, but we need to keep an eye out for any sort of clue, no matter how small,' said Smith. 'What have you found out about this Cramer McAllister?'

'He's a nasty piece of work,' explained Brooks. 'From what I could find, he is some sort of enforcer for an equally nasty bloke named Curtis Slater. He's well known in the drugs underworld but we've never been able to touch him. McAllister has done a fair bit of time, but nothing significant, especially when you consider what he's been accused of. He must have an exceptionally good lawyer.'

'Wasn't there a problem making the payment though?'

'Yes sir, but we found a work-around,' replied Harris.

'It's Danny's account,' interjected Brooks.

'Right, OK,' said Smith, rubbing his chin. 'That's good then. Like I said, try and keep this low-key as much as you can. We need to make sure that we collect as much information on this as possible, but too many cooks spoil the broth and all that.'

Harris and Brooks looked at each other. 'Yes indeed, sir. Shall we come and get you once it starts?' said Harris.

'No,' replied Smith, 'I've got a very important engagement this evening that I cannot back out of, Commissioner's orders. Hearts and minds, you know the kind of thing. Keep me updated, although I'm sure you can handle it,' he added, as he mopped his mouth with the paper napkin and stood up. He pulled his phone from his jacket pocket and walked out, head bowed, flicking across the screen.

Once she was certain he had left the canteen, Brooks leant into Harris and Fowler. 'Do you think he had anything to do with the bitcoin wallet? He seems a bit weird.'

'I can't believe he would,' replied Harris. 'But we'll look into it after this is all done. Let's get back there, it's show time in fifty minutes.'

'I'll get some popcorn on the way,' said Fowler, collecting a donut and walking away.

Harris stood up to leave, but was stopped by Brooks' hand and sat back down.

'Pete, you've been here nearly all week, you probably haven't seen Olivia for days. Are you sure you're up to doing this tonight? Why don't you go home; we can assign another team to this,' said Brooks, her face a picture of quiet sympathy.

Harris rubbed the bridge of his nose. He knew she was right, but this was far too important to him. It was more than just about catching these people, it was about proving to himself that he wasn't a failure, that he could still cut it.

'I'm fine,' he said, looking Brooks square in the eyes. 'I've spoken to Olivia every day. When I arrive home, the first thing I do is lie in her bed and cuddle her. She knows I'm there. She enjoys spending time with her gran.'

'It's not the same though,' replied Brooks. 'She needs her dad. Anyway, you promised her Legoland this weekend.'

'I know, that was a bit foolish. After tonight and this weekend I'll be upgrading that to Disneyland.'

'Well, as long as you're sure.'

'Of course, I've always wanted to go to Disneyland. No, I'm sure, I promise,' replied Harris, although clearly he wasn't. 'Are you ready for this?'

'As ready as I'll ever be.'

'Please don't hurt me,' Joe sobbed. 'I've given you everything you want.'

'Mister Henderson, calm down,' said a soft voice. 'We're not going to hurt you. This is just a necessary precaution. So, if you would like to take a seat over here, we can do what we need to do and then be out of your hair. By the way, we transferred the fifty bitcoins into your wallet as promised ... Well, what do you say?'

'What?' came the muffled response.

'What do you say?'

'Thank you?'

'Exactly,' replied the man, as Joe felt a light tap on his cheek. 'Manners cost nothing. Now, if you would just sit here and be quiet, that would be much appreciated.'

Joe was sat down on a chair behind a large black curtain, the opposite side to the bank of computers and television cameras that had hastily been erected during his conversation. The noise in the warehouse wasn't blocked out completely by the heavy hood, but it was muffled, and he only just about made out the sound of a message arriving on someone's mobile phone.

'Shit,' said Gilbert, as he read and re-read the message that had just appeared.

'What?' asked Alistair, now looking somewhat concerned.

'Look,' Gilbert said, handing the phone to Alistair.

We are in and we are monitoring you. Be careful.

'So what?' Alistair replied, alarming Gilbert with his lack of concern. 'I'm surprised it's taken them until now to start, to be honest. Jarvis, is this going to be a problem?'

'Not really,' answered Jarvis, sharing his boss' attitude. 'I can't see that their monitoring systems will be any better than all the others that bombard us during the episodes.'

'OK,' said Alistair, now standing in the middle of the warehouse, looking around into the dark voids of space that surrounded him. 'Gather round, everyone.'

Gilbert, Jarvis, Eric, and Stan joined him, along with a couple of the goons.

'We're going to have a few uninvited online guests this evening. CCU has finally decided to join the party. But we carry on as normal, as if we have absolutely no idea that they're watching us. It won't take as long this time, but we need to maintain our focus throughout. Everyone clear? Good. To the Brotherhood.'

'The Brotherhood,' they replied in unison.

'Let's go get Cramer. It's show time.'

31

Harris and Fowler sat back in their seats, watching on their respective screens as the large, light-encrusted Red Room sign zoomed away from the camera. They had seen the disclaimer on the entry screen.

'Presumably that's why there's very little trace of this online. They've asked nicely for people not to record it. Looks like there is honour amongst thieves then,' said Fowler.

'Or they treat it like some sort of exclusive club,' replied Harris. 'Look, I think our clown friend is about to put in an appearance.'

The double doors opened, the white light shone through the smoke, and out stepped the Host, arms outstretched. In front of the entrance, he stopped and performed a pose with one arm straight, one arm bent, both pointing in the same direction, like a lightning bolt. The spotlights came up as the doors closed behind him, and as the smoke began to clear he jogged down set to face the camera.

'Good evening, my deep web friends. Welcome to another edition of the Righteous and the Damned here in the Red Room.'

'Snappy title,' commented Fowler.

'We've got a fantastic show lined up for you this evening. So without further ado, let's bring out tonight's volunteer.'

'Well, this clown fellow sounds like a delightful chap,' Fowler added, as he and Harris watched the camera zoom past the Host to the doors.

As they opened, a large goon in a red tracksuit stumbled through with an equally massive body clamped firmly in a headlock under his arm. Two more goons carried him, by a leg each, down to the chair stationed by the Host. As they began the process of trying to clamp the powerful hostage down, fighting against his struggles, the Host decided to offer them a helping hand. He walked over to the chair and placed a hand around the back of the volunteer's head. With his other hand, he thrust two fingers firmly downwards into the soft tissue just below the Adam's apple. The technique took an instant control, causing all the volunteer's muscles to go limp, while the goons finished securing him.

'OK, let's see who we've got today. Tonight's volunteer you may not be very familiar with, but I can guarantee that the minute you see him you will take an instant dislike to him. His official job title would be something like "gangland enforcer", but the only way we can think of describing him is "a total and utter shit". He's well known in the underworld for removing people's teeth with pliers or snipping their fingers off with bolt cutters. Oh, and I should point out that he doesn't care who he does it to. In fact, our little friend here has even been known to coerce his targets by holding their young children's heads in a vice and threatening to crush them unless they do what he wants. Like I said, a real nasty shit.'

'But despite this, his slimy lawyers have always had the knack, whether it be through intimidation, bribery, or both, of making sure that he gets away with his crimes. Well, not tonight, ladies and gentlemen. Please say a warm hello to our guest, Mister Cramer McAllister.'

The goons whipped the sack off of McAllister's head. Clad only in white underpants and a tight white vest, he instantly began shouting, swearing, and spitting.

'That'll be him then,' said Harris. 'How is the trace going?'

'It's still in there, but their system is solid as a rock. These people really know their stuff when it comes to security.'

As McAllister continued his tirade, the Host stood behind him with his hands on the man's head. He began massaging as McAllister flicked his head from side to side, as if trying to swat a fly with his chin.

'Calm down, Cramer. Or actually, how about I call you C-Mac?' said the Host, softly.

'How about I fucking smash the lot of you to shit! Don't you fucking know who I am? Who I work for? You think you're tough guys; you know nothing. You want to get sucked into my world? I'll suck you in, pathetic little maggots. I'll suck you in so far, I'll have to shit you out in pieces at the other end. You've got no—'

Before he could finish his sentence, the Host smashed him around the side of the head with the gold clipboard, shutting him up briefly.

'Thank you, C-Mac, for that lovely introduction,' said the Host. 'But let us just get one thing clear. We know precisely who you are and we know full well who you work for. In fact, we might send your good buddy Curtis Slater a little video of this. You never know, he might even be next to sit in the hot seat. But just in case our viewers out there don't know who you are, here is a little montage of newspaper clippings and photos for their reference.'

A clip started to run showing headlines such as *McAllister Walks Free Again, Enforcer's Victims Slam Judge*, and it ended with a photograph of McAllister kneeling down behind the rent boy with his trousers around his ankles.

'Sorry, Mac,' said the Host, as the camera returned. 'Not sure how that one got in there.'

'You don't get to judge me, you little prick, hiding behind your stupid little clown mask.'

The Host jumped and landed on McAllister's lap, quickly grabbing his throat and ramming his head back against the seat whilst pointing at the camera with his other hand.

'Quite right, Mac, I don't. But those people out there do. Start the bidding.'

On screen, the large monitor lowered down from the ceiling and the names and numbers began flashing up.

'So that's what this bid box is for,' said Harris, rolling his cursor over a box on the side of his screen.

'OK, let's see who the first winner is tonight,' said the Host, looking up at the screen. 'And it is … UpsetDad, with a cracking seven bitcoins. Sorry you're upset, Dad, let's hope that Cramer here can cheer you up.'

The message began to appear on the monitor.

I have no idea who you are, but I am pretty certain the world will be better off without you. Can you ask him why he did what he did to children?

'So, C-Mac, you heard the man. Why did you threaten to torture children?'

'Fuck you, arsehole. You think that the people I was employed to go after were all sweetness and light? Most of them were drug-pushers.'

'Who happened to owe you money for the drugs that you supplied them, so that they could be drug pushers, you mean?'

'They took liberties and they paid the price. We're not here to be pissed around,' said McAllister, arrogantly. He had never been one to play the lesser man, and submitting to anyone simply wasn't in his nature.

'But children, Cramer? Children,' replied the Host, waving his hands at McAllister. 'How could you stand there with a child, who has absolutely nothing to do with their parents' activities, and hold their head in a vice? I'm struggling to even say it. A vice, Cramer. You put a small, innocent child's head in a vice and threatened to crush it?'

McAllister smirked. 'Yeah, and they fucking paid up pronto. Stupid little junkie pissheads.'

'I think we've all heard enough about the type of character this man is. UpsetDad, pick your punishment please.'

Host, I'd like an angle grinder to the knee please.

Harris and Fowler looked at each other. 'Get that tracer in there, now. We have to find out where this is.'

'I'm trying,' replied Fowler, slightly annoyed. 'But this site is practically impenetrable. We can't make it go any faster than it's going.'

Harris began biting the top of his biro as he watched one of the men in red tracksuits hand the clown a small electric cutting disc, which the Host proceeded to rev up in front of McAllister's face. McAllister started to turn pale and shook his head violently from side to side. Forcing himself to watch, Harris took a large swig of water as he realised his mouth had dried like sandpaper without him noticing.

Both men winced as the Host ran the spinning disc of the angle grinder just below McAllister's kneecap. Through gritted teeth, McAllister tried his hardest to stand the pain, but it all became too much. As blood poured down McAllister's leg, the Host put the grinder on the floor, before stamping on the top of the knee, causing the bright white patella bone to slip out of the gash and onto the floor. McAllister screamed. And swore a lot. As blood gushed from his leg, he started to slow his breathing, in an attempt to prevent himself going into shock. He had learnt a few tricks himself from torturing people. A goon threaded a belt under his leg, before fastening it tightly across his thigh.

'We can't have you bleeding to death now can we, Cramer?' said the Host, resting his elbow on McAllister's shoulder whilst continuing to talk into the microphone. 'Not before your viewers have had more of a chance to speak to you.'

'Fucking … arseholes,' shouted McAllister, as saliva sprayed out in all directions.

'He doesn't seem very happy, does he?' said Fowler, as a matter of a fact.

'No,' replied Harris, curtly. 'Grace, are you getting this?'

'Yes,' shouted Grace, from over the desk partition. 'The recording is running, but there is so little to go on. The camera movements are very carefully orchestrated, never veering outside of the set. This is obviously a very well-rehearsed routine.'

'What about the sound?'

'Again, not sure what type of audio filter they're using, but this "Host" person's voice isn't coming up with anything in our database. Doesn't help of course that he's wearing that mask.'

'Bugger,' replied Harris to himself, turning to concentrate back on his monitor. 'There must be something.'

On screen, he watched as the Host grabbed McAllister's head under the chin and pointed it at the large screen.

'It's exciting isn't it, Mac?' said the Host. 'See those names up there? Those are all people who truly despise what you have done. And they want you to pay for your crimes.'

'I've not been convicted of any fucking crimes,' he gasped through the pain, struggling with the words but still valiantly managing to get them out in short bursts. 'You really think that you'll get away with this? I know people, nasty people. They'll hunt you down and when they find you—'

'Find us?' laughed the Host. 'If you're talking about that weasel Slater, whose dirty work you do, I hope he does. But what makes you think he gives a flying monkey's about you? Also, just to clarify, you *were* convicted of crimes, just not jailed, thanks to that slimy lawyer of yours. We've decided that you did not receive the punishment that you deserved and that is why you are here. Got it?'

'Who gave you the—'

'Anyway,' interrupted the Host, stuffing his hand into McAllister's face. 'Let's see who the next winner is. And, with a huge fifteen bitcoins, Mac say hello to MafiaMama. Evening, MafiaMama, what would you like to say to the big C?'

Buonasera Host. This man is un grande bastardo as we say. I want to know, who does he prefer to torture, adults or children?

'This is crazy,' said Fowler. 'People are queuing up to win this. That's the best part of ten grand that 'MafiaMama' just paid.'

'So what does that tell us?' asked Harris.

'That not just anyone can take part in this. You need a serious amount of wedge.'

'Quite. These viewers are probably high earners, professionals, well-educated. What makes someone want to pay that much money just to watch a criminal be tortured?'

'You're forgetting the other people like us who have had to pay for the privilege and aren't bidding. There could be hundreds, even thousands of viewers. And I would imagine they're lapping it up,' replied Brooks.

'Agreed,' said Fowler. 'Why else would they go to this amount of risk unless they were pulling in a lot of viewers and a lot of cash?'

'He seems to have absolutely no hesitation in doing what he does. Does he really see himself as some sort of internet vigilante doing this for the good of the world?' asked Harris, as he watched the Host poking McAllister in the wounded kneecap with the corner of his clipboard.

'Hurry up Cramer, for Christ's sake,' shouted the Host. 'MafiaMama asked you a question and she would like an answer, please.'

'Fuck you. You think I'm going to answer any more of your questions, you stupid little clown prick?' McAllister replied, defiantly.

'Come on, Cramer,' said the Host, continuing to poke the kneecap. 'I know this hurts.'

'Fine,' spat McAllister. 'But come close.'

The Host moved to put his head near McAllister's and held the microphone nearby so the viewers could hear.

'Children,' said McAllister, with a smirk on his face. 'Children. I love fucking up the children. You do an adult and they recover. You do a child and it stays with them for life. Like a little part of me is with them forever.'

Even with a mask on, the Host seemed somewhat taken aback.

'He's not going to like that,' said Fowler. 'It looks like he wants to do him in himself.'

'McAllister, if I could, I would choose the next punishment for you.'

'Told you …'

'But MafiaMama has the honours. It's time to see what she wants to do with you. Mama, make it a good one.'

Can't believe what I just heard. Crowbar, Host, for the children. Anything. Make it hurt.

As a goon handed him a black metal crowbar, the Host pulled a long thick cable tie out of his pocket, which he proceeded to wrap around McAllister's wrist. McAllister looked down, confused, and then at the Host.

'What the fuck are you doing?' he asked.

'Well, Cramer,' said the Host, as he pulled the cable tie as tight as he could. 'I once heard someone say that there is nothing in the world that cannot be fixed with one of these.'

'You're bloody mental—'

Before he could finish his sentence, the Host threw the crowbar up in the air and caught the flat end, plunging the hook deep into McAllister's thigh, causing him to scream out in pain. He wrenched the hook out, spun it in the air again, and then smashed it into the side of McAllister's face, then back the other way, before finally slamming it straight into the man's mouth.

McAllister groaned as his head dropped forward, a trickle of blood pouring out the side of his mouth and down his t-shirt. By now, the cable tie had caused his hand to turn a bright shade of purple and swell up like a giant beetroot. The Host placed the hook of the crowbar on top of it.

'He's not, is he ...?' asked Harris, in hope more than expectation.

The Host brought the crowbar up, before smashing the hook down into McAllister's swollen hand.

'He is,' replied Fowler.

The pressure build up in his hand caused it to explode, sending blood and tissue over his now-limp body, leaving a gaping wound at the top that dripped over the arm of the chair and onto the floor. McAllister passed out with the pain and drooped forward.

'Not entirely sure that cable tie fixed his hand, ladies and gentlemen. If anything, it appears to have made it worse. We've just got time for the last question. Start placing your bids.'

The Host went off camera and took a drink of water.

'I don't think we should change exit nodes for the finale,' said Jarvis, not removing his eyes from the screen.

'Are you sure?'

'Yes, it's too risky, given who's monitoring us. It just might give them the window of opportunity that they're looking for.'

'Fine, do what you have to,' replied the Host, placing the water bottle down and securing his mask.

The Host reappeared in front of the camera as a goon wafted the smelling salts under McAllister's nose and slapped him around the face. After a few seconds, he started to groan again, and the show continued.

'OK, let's see who our final highest bidder is. Well, Cramer, you will be pleased to hear that you've generated a lot of high bids. People have certainly taken a disliking to you. The winner is—'

Just at that moment, the Host and everyone else's attention was drawn to a huge clatter off-set, which echoed around the large expanse of the warehouse. Without speaking, he motioned with his hand and two of the goons ran off to investigate.

'Sorry about this, people,' said the Host, directly into the camera. 'We'll be back with you shortly.'

The goons hunted around the racking with flashlights, searching for anything that could have made the noise. One then spotted three large bars of metal stood on their end and another that was lying on the floor, just rolling to a stop. They nodded at each other and walked back to tell the Host.

'Panic over, everyone,' said the Host. 'Just a slight environmental mishap. So, let's go back to the scoreboard …'

As the Host spoke, no-one in the room heard Joe's chair tip over, or him, muffled both by the curtain and his hood, as he shouted,

'Someone just knocked me over. There's someone else in here!'

32

'An environmental mishap?' asked Harris. 'That doesn't sound like these people. They seem too thorough to have mishaps. But it certainly seemed to catch them off-guard. Grace, did you get anything on the audio?'

'No, nothing, other than a loud crash like someone dropping a bowling ball on the floor,' she replied. 'Although, hang on a second.'

'What is it?'

Brooks scanned through the audio signal of the seconds just after the crash noise. 'There. Did you hear it?'

'No,' they both replied in unison.

'Wait a minute, let me enhance it. There.'

'Is that a scream?'

'I think so, just it's drowned out by the noise reverberating around the warehouse and Mister Host speaking to camera, but it's definitely there.'

'Another victim off-camera suddenly becoming aware of their fate, perhaps?' asked Fowler.

'Possibly,' replied Harris, turning back to the show.

'As I was saying,' continued the Host. 'The winner, with a huge eighteen bitcoins, is our good friend Boxof Brains. Great to see you, my man, we've not seen you here for a few weeks. What would you like to ask Cramer? He's just about got one more answer left in him.'

Evening, Host, good to be back. I'd like to know, does he now regret his life?

'Excellent question, Brains. So, Cramer, given the situation you now find yourself in, if you could go back in time, would you do things differently?'

McAllister was seriously flagging now, his head raised for mere seconds before slumping back into his chest. He managed a few grunts, when the Host raised his head up with the clipboard.

'Cramer, Mister Brains would like to know …'

'I heard what you said, you piece of shit,' he spluttered. 'The answer is yes, I'd do it differently.'

'OK, so perhaps a little remorse creeping into the C-Mac? A few regrets maybe?' the Host said into the camera.

But before he could carry on, McAllister continued, 'I'd torture more kids, fuck more rent-boys, but most of all, I'd find you, rip your heart out, and stuff it beating into your mouth while looking you square in the eyes.'

'I'm honoured that you would single me out for special attention, Cramer, but I think it's time to end your sorry little existence. Just for the privilege of our friends around the world watching this, I want a close up of your face. So the people can see as deep into your eyes as I can while I tell you that you deserve every tiny amount of pain that you are in. You made people's lives a misery, but more than that, this pointless excuse of a justice system let you get away with it. Do you understand that, Cramer? We are righting the wrongs. I hope you feel even a little scared and can maybe see just what you did to people. Brains, choose an ending.'

Thank you, Host. I think we can all be satisfied that justice has been done tonight. I think Cramer just chose his own ending.

'Thank you, Brains, I think we'll all enjoy this.'

'No. Fucking. Way,' exclaimed Fowler. 'Are they seriously going to—'

'I think so,' replied Harris, glued to the screen. 'Just keep the tracker going, keep the recording going.'

'The tracker is there. It had god knows how many layers to penetrate, but it got there in the end. It just can't get past their final firewall.'

'Damn, come on,' whispered Harris through gritted teeth, as he watched a goon hand a pristine silver serrated hunting knife to the Host.

He placed the clipboard and microphone down on McAllister's lap, put one boot up on his thigh, and plunged the knife into the sternum. McAllister began convulsing, and as the Host sliced the blade up through his chest, frothy blood came foaming from his mouth.

'Goodbye, Cramer,' the Host whispered. 'It's been a pleasure.'

With that, he dropped the knife and plunged his hand deep into the opening below the ribs. Before he could finish, a huge scream ripped through the set. He pulled his hand out and the goons began running around in all directions, trying to find the source. Suddenly, small metal objects came flying from the darkness; a hammer, a wrench, a screwdriver, anything. One after another.

'What on Earth is going on?' asked Brooks.

'There,' said Harris, pointing on the screen to what appeared to be a young girl. She was running around, faster than the goons could keep up with. With one last throw, a large spanner landed in front of Jarvis, striking the console. Harris, Fowler, and Brooks' screens all went black.

'Bollocks,' shouted Harris.

'No, wait a sec. Bugger me, we're in,' shouted Fowler, excitedly. 'Whoever that was, it looks like they knocked the main server. It must have disconnected it somehow from whichever machine was running the security program. The tracker's worked.'

'Get as much as you can, IP addresses, physical location, anything,' replied Harris.

'Already on it. Wait a minute,' he paused, examining the incoming data. 'For fuck's sake.'

'What is it?'

'The information's coming through, but again, it's all encrypted. Christ, these people were paranoid. It shouldn't be too hard, but it will take some time.'

'Bollocks. I'll get word to the Super. He'll want to know anyway.'

Eventually, the intruder was surrounded, restrained, and hooded. Despite wailing like a banshee, kicking and thrashing for all she was worth, it was no good. The goons had them.

'Get this lot cleared up, we're moving out in ten minutes,' shouted Alistair, as the main warehouse lights lit up a scene of carnage.

The goons began clearing up the set, cleaning up the blood, and removing the dead body with the efficiency of soldiers dismantling a field gun. Eric and Stan headed straight for the comms room to undo all their earlier work.

'Where the hell did she come from?' Alistair asked.

'No idea, she must have been hiding in amongst all the racks,' replied Jarvis. 'Maybe you should have gotten these imbeciles to check a little more thoroughly.'

'Alright, you've made your point. What's the situation?'

'Transmission went off air when she hit the console with the spanner. Chances are people all saw the commotion, but I need to get back to the house to check everything.'

'OK, pack everything away as soon as. Have Eric see to Mister Henderson,' said Alistair, walking around the back of the curtain before shouting at the goons still wrestling with the prisoner. 'In my car. I want a word.'

The goons nodded and dragged the prisoner out of the warehouse and into the yard. Alistair bent down and lifted Joe back upright, before walking off to the exit and getting into his car. Eric came out of the back office with an armful of manuals, wires, and tools, which he placed in a transit van that had now reversed into the warehouse. He untied Joe, pulling his mask off. Joe squinted as the bright LED light burned into his eyes.

'Mister Henderson, we're all done,' said Eric, pulling Joe to his feet. 'Once we've gone, everything here will be back to normal. I suggest you lock up as quickly as you can and get the hell out of here. We'll be in touch imminently.'

'What?' asked Joe, with a mixture of concern and annoyance. 'I did my bit, you can leave me alone now.'

'We need to debrief you, just so you're well-prepared for what might happen, especially if the police become involved.'

'The police?' exclaimed Joe. 'I thought you lot were supposed to be experts in making sure they wouldn't get involved.'

'We are, but it's always a good idea to plan for any eventuality,' replied Eric, patting him on the cheek.

As the last of the vans closed their doors and left the yard, Alistair, Jarvis, and Gilbert climbed into the back of the limousine, where their captive was firmly buckled to the seat.

'Let's see who we have here,' said Alistair, as he removed the hood. The three of them looked in surprise at the young girl staring back at them; surprised at how young she looked and surprised at how little she appeared to be scared of them.

'What's your name?' asked Gilbert.

'Daisy,' replied the girl.

'Well, Daisy,' said Alistair, taking a large Cuban cigar from a compartment in the arm of his chair. 'You're coming home with us.'

33

Back in the computer room at Clifton Hall, Jarvis trawled through reams of data being churned out by his printer. Whilst he liked to think that he considered the environment, there was something nobler about reading data off of a huge pile of green-lined continuous feed dot matrix paper.

Somehow, it took him back to his childhood, when his father would bring computers home from work to repair. Early and primitive PCs that covered the entire dining room table, with screens smaller than a modern tablet computer. They worked on pure code, and he would sit for hours with his father, reading out lines and lines of the stuff whilst he typed indiscernible rows of letters, numbers, and punctuation marks, until, at the end of it, he could sit back in wonder and watch as he controlled a small spacecraft flying around the screen blasting aliens.

After a while, the code became as natural to Jarvis as English. He thought in code and would write ingenious lines down on whatever scrap of paper he had to hand when they randomly popped into his head. And watching his father fix the machines had given him an early interest in networks and hardware. He was well-acquainted with private packet networking and internet protocols long before the rest of the planet even became aware of what would come to be known as the World Wide Web.

Like many of his ilk, he was looked down on by his peers and laughed at as the archetypal nerd. As he withdrew further into the world of programming, he had developed what he liked to think of as games, although they were more like pranks. His particular favourite was to hack into his halls of residence server and transmit adult movies onto the computers of anyone logged on in their dormitory. He was aware of a few black eyes dealt by disgusted girlfriends.

His talent and aptitude in both programming and hardware interfacing had brought him to the attention of the belligerent and slightly obnoxious young entrepreneur, Alistair Goodfellow. Whilst Jarvis had jumped on the bandwagon of the infant internet, his new acquaintance had a vision that the future lay in large, grey brick-like telephones that people could carry around in their pockets.

'People won't buy stuff on the internet, they won't trust it,' Alistair would say.

'People won't want to carry around a telephone the size of a book,' Jarvis would counter.

After a couple of years of drunken nights in the pub discussing their respective technologies, it dawned on Alistair that they could combine the two into something special. Alistair would be the driving force and public face of the new online mobile phone shop with Jarvis happy to stay out of the limelight and stick to the programming and techie side of things. Soon, Alistair's vision had turned into a very successful and, above all, highly lucrative reality. It was always Alistair's company and it made him wealthy beyond imagination, but Jarvis had stayed with him, heading up the IT sections of his empire, happy just to tinker away with newer and newer technologies. And to take the stock options and high-end six figure salary.

But when Alistair sold the company, the excitement was gone. Jarvis could no longer motivate himself to work for a faceless board of nobodies in America, people more concerned with keeping the shareholders happy than really embracing the spirit that had created the success in the first place. He knew that Alistair felt the same, that he needed something to focus his boundless energy into, to give his life meaning again. It was all very well owning a house with fifteen bedrooms, but when it was just you and a bunch of house-keepers it was largely pointless.

Over a game of snooker in Alistair's new country house, the one he now found himself stood in, they had begun discussing a court case that was featuring prominently in the news. A husband and wife were jailed for trafficking young girls from Eastern Europe, with promises of work and education in the United Kingdom, only to force them into sex slavery. Their solicitors and barristers were able to twist the testimonies of the girls involved; so much so, and invoking so many mitigating factors (their own children's wellbeing and the woman's elderly mother who required round the clock care being just two), that they received relatively pitiful sentences. And taking into account the time they had already spent in custody, the pair basically walked free from court. The tabloids had a field day and there was general uproar, especially when the photographs were published of them leaving the courtroom, holding hands, laughing, and swearing at the assembled throng of journalists.

After a couple of whiskies, Jarvis asked the hypothetical,

'If those two were stood in this room right now, and you could do anything you wanted to them without being found out, what would you do?'

'I'd want to hurt them,' he replied. 'Not because I like hurting people, but to make them realise just what they had done. Having clever lawyers might make them believe, in their own minds, that they're not guilty, but I would want them to see that they are. And that is one of the fundamental problems with the justice system in this country ...'

Jarvis recalled zoning out as the rant went on for quite a while, going through his own answer to his question in his head. But at the end of the night, they had had a plan. A purpose. Jarvis would have access to whatever funds he needed to procure all the necessary technology, and Alistair would call in a few contacts.

'We'll need a name,' Jarvis had said, semi-drunkenly, as he made for the door to go to bed. 'What with us being the new saviours of the righteous and all.'

'Quite right,' Alistair replied. 'All brotherhoods like ours need a name.'

Jarvis had never imagined, on that night two years ago, what their little project would turn into. But they had so many plans for it that they couldn't happen fast enough, as far as Jarvis was concerned.

And concerned was precisely what Jarvis now became as he spotted it on about the thirtieth page of the print-out: a breach.

'Oh. Bollocks,' he said to himself.

He pressed the internal dial button, waiting for Alistair to pick up. Nothing; he would have to walk it. He ripped the page off of the printer and hastened up to the main quarters. This required a fairly urgent meeting, but more importantly, it needed Alistair to pull all his strings to stop the whole project going down the pan.

34

Alistair reclined in his favourite leather armchair, resting a crystal tumbler of whisky on one arm and picking at a brass stud on the other. He watched on the CCTV monitor as Daisy paced up and down in her room, periodically trying the window and door again just in case they had somehow become unlocked since the last time she'd tried. There was something about this girl. He had encountered many troubled teenagers during his charity work, but she seemed to have a spark that he liked.

The door to the room unlocked and she turned around to face it as Gilbert entered, carrying a large tray full of food. He set it down on the table and poured a glass of water for her. She stood with her back against the wardrobe, whilst Gilbert motioned for her to sit down.

'Come, my dear,' he said to her, pulling a chair away from the table. 'It's roast chicken, roast potatoes, stuffing, vegetables, and sausages in bacon; everything that you asked for. It's perfectly fine, we're not going to poison you. In fact, chef would be quite offended at the mere suggestion.'

Deciding it was time to get to know the new guest a little better, Alistair put his drink down and walked down the hallway to Daisy's room. He passed Gilbert on the way.

'She's an interesting one,' said Gilbert. 'She's really not giving much away. Given the set of circumstances she's found herself in, she seems remarkably calm.'

Alistair nodded and continued past. He knocked on the door and, after waiting a few seconds for a reply that never came, let himself in.

'Good evening, Daisy,' he said.

Daisy glanced up from her plate, chewing on a large mouthful of food. As much as she hated being detained against her will, she had to admit that not only was this the nicest food she'd eaten for a long time, it was probably the best she'd ever eaten. She once again found herself in a place that she didn't want to be, but in the big scheme of things, this was about as good as her life had been for as long as she could remember. But these people were murderers, why were they being so nice to her?

'May I?' said Alistair, pointing to the chair opposite.

Daisy stared at him blankly. Why on Earth was he asking her if he could sit down?

'Yes, OK. I guess,' she replied, slightly confused, as Alistair sat down. 'Have you come here to kill me?'

'No, of course not. If that was our intention we would have done so by now,' he said, half-jokingly, sitting back with one leg resting on the other knee. 'So, Daisy, tell me a little about yourself.'

'No, I don't believe you. I think you'll try and find out what I know then kill me,' she answered.

Alistair stifled a laugh. 'Seriously, I'm not here to kill you. After all, you haven't even finished your dinner yet. Plus, blood is a nightmare to get out of these tablecloths. Please, tell me about Daisy.'

She eyed him suspiciously. Although he seemed nice, she thought she should probably do what he asked for her own safety.

'So, like what?'

'Like how did you come to be in that warehouse? You might have caused us a lot of aggravation you know.'

'I saw you kill someone,' she said, through a mouthful of food. 'Give me one good reason why I don't call the police.'

'Because you can't,' he replied, curtly. 'Anyway, you didn't see *me* kill someone, now did you? It was, how shall we say, unfortunate that you were witness to that unpleasantness. It most certainly wasn't for your eyes, and for that you have my sincerest apologies. But like I said, how did you come to be in that warehouse?'

'I was squatting in it. The idiot who owns it used to leave the back open while he went around the backyard locking all the gates. I would run in when he wasn't looking and hide among the racks. When you lot all turned up, I jumped into this big wooden crate that was lying on the floor. The screaming got too much at one point and I tried to escape but I think I knocked something over. After that, I just panicked when I saw what was going on and started throwing whatever I could find to hand. Then your big fat friends caught me and bundled me into your car.'

Alistair smiled at the side of his mouth; he was warming to this kid. For the next hour or so, they spoke as Daisy ate and drank. Daisy told him all about her escape from the house, how she had been held there and plied with alcohol and drugs, living in the woods and then ending up on the trading estate. Alistair probed more into her past, her family, how she had ended up on the streets, careful to avoid seeming as though he was simply after the gory details.

Once she realised it was unlikely that he wanted to murder her, she began to relax a little. And then it all became too much. She began sobbing; the pain and anger that she had fought so hard to suppress for the last few weeks exploded from her like a volcano of emotions. Thumping her fists on the table, she pushed the chair away, picked up the glass decanter, and launched it across the room, shattering it against the wall into a thousand pieces. After kicking the chair against the table, she sat down on the edge of the sofa with her head in her hands, crying. Alistair, who had quietly remained seated with his arms crossed whilst Daisy had her moment, looked at her for a while, slightly unsure how to deal with this creature.

'That was a twelve hundred pound Lalique decanter, you know,' was the best that he could muster.

'I hate myself,' replied Daisy, not really listening to what he said. 'I hate them for what they did to me, but I hate myself for letting them affect me this much. I thought I was getting over it, but it's still there. When I close my eyes at night, when I walk into an empty room or down a dark road. They're there, inside me, eating away.'

Alistair stood up and walked over to her, handing her a white napkin with which she wiped her face.

'You seem a lot stronger to me. Far stronger than you probably believe. Look at how far you've come just since you escaped that house. You have a strong will to survive. Not many people have that.'

Daisy scrunched the napkin up and held it against the side of her face. It reminded her of a small pink rag bear that she'd had as a child, something that gave her comfort amongst all the turmoil in her surroundings.

She was still struggling to make sense of this man. Compared to the people she had run from, he seemed like a saint. But she had witnessed something that she couldn't imagine even her previous captors being capable of.

'You remind me a lot of my sister,' continued Alistair, as Daisy stopped crying, sniffed, and glanced up at him. 'She had a troubled time during her teenage years. Not for the same reasons that you've told me about, I hasten to add. Compared to your upbringing, she practically wanted for nothing. We had nothing like this growing up, but we had a secure, loving, modest home.

'My parents saw it as her "going off the rails" or falling in with "the wrong crowd" and they weren't really sure what they had done to cause it. She started skipping school, dabbling in drugs. Pot and speed mainly at the beginning. But then she started living in a thoroughly squalid little squat with a bunch of other drop-outs. "Anarchists", they called themselves. Any rally against anything and they would turn up, just to make trouble. But really they were nothing more than unemployed junkies.

'One day, her boyfriend, off his face on some drug or another, beat her absolutely black and blue. I remember seeing her in the hospital bed, all the tubes and wires coming out of her, and how much it seemed to destroy my parents. The helplessness, the feeling of failure despite giving her nothing but love. It was made all the worse when she decided not to press charges. I went around to the squat to find the scumbag that did it, but ended up being arrested because I tried to kick the door in to gain entry. The whole hypocrisy of the situation was what angered me the most. That the law favoured these worthless members of society who are happy to break the law when it suits them, but then expect the law to protect them when they want it. This was just as I was starting out on my business ventures and I vowed then that if I ever had the means, I would start doing something about it.'

'But you murdered someone …'

'Who enjoyed torturing children to extort money from their parents. Who thought nothing of brutally raping young men for his own enjoyment. Who carried out the violent orders of his drug lord boss with an almost childlike glee. Anyway, we don't see it as murdering, more punishing.'

'But what makes you think that you can judge people?' asked Daisy.

'Nothing,' replied Alistair, nonchalantly. 'But does that make me any less qualified to judge people than those actual judges who let these people off? Look, the first episode we did of the Red Room had an audience in the low teens. But news spreads quickly nowadays and we'd struck a nerve with people. The last episode, it was in the thousands. You always hear people talk about how 'they should bring back hanging'. Well that's all we're doing. We've brought back hanging, just updated it slightly for the twenty-first century.'

'What if you get caught?'

'Well that's the million dollar question, isn't it?' replied Alistair, with a slight glint in his eye. 'Over the course of running this show, we've come to know a little about our audience. You know what type of people watch?'

'Criminals?' replied Daisy, with what she assumed was a fairly obvious answer.

Alistair chuckled. 'No. Well I say no, some of them are. They seem to enjoy it actually. But mostly our audience consists of doctors, businessmen, scientists, lawyers, even the odd senior police officer or judge. And not just from this country, people tap in from all over the world to watch. Anonymously, obviously. Could you imagine the uproar if word ever got out that a senior judge was taking part in something like this? But that's the beauty. It's people who, on the face of it, have to play by the rules and within the boundaries of society, whilst secretly yearning for something more. We just offer them a playground in which to do so.'

Daisy stared at him blankly as he smiled back. She stood up and went back over to what was left of her drink, wiping away the last remnants of her tears. For a moment, there was silence.

'So, what happened to your sister?' she asked, gently.

'She's doing OK, thank you,' replied Alistair. 'We took her out of the life in which she had found herself and moved her back with my parents. Unfortunately, the strain of it all took its toll on my mother. She died about a year later from sepsis resulting from complications with her stomach ulcers. That was the wake-up call for my sister. She has her own life now and has carved quite a successful career for herself, but we are very close and like to look out for each other. Her relationship with my father is still a little rocky, but he's coming around slowly.'

Daisy nodded in understanding, not really sure what else to say. At that moment, the silence was shattered as the large wooden doors shot open, slamming back against the wall and causing Daisy to jump and nearly drop her glass.

'Jarvis,' said Alistair, calmly. 'Don't worry about knocking, it's fine.'

'You need to see this,' a bright red, sweaty Jarvis replied, ignoring the sarcasm. Seeing Daisy across the table, he motioned for Alistair to come outside. 'It's probably best if we do this in the hallway.'

'OK,' replied Alistair, rising to his feet. 'Oh, Daisy, this is Jarvis. He is what's known as a tech guru. Hence why the slightest amount of physical exercise lends him the appearance of an asthmatic in an iron man competition.'

Daisy smiled as the two men left the room and closed the doors behind them.

'What is it?' asked Alistair.

'We had a breach in the firewall during the last episode,' said Jarvis, pointing at a portion of the read-out.

'How did that happen? I thought it was absolutely watertight,' said Alistair.

'It was. I think it may have happened when your new friend in there caused her little fracas,' said Jarvis, looking towards the room.

Alistair stroked his goatee, contemplating. His ability to think quickly had always been his greatest strength.

'I'm going to need to make a couple of phone calls. Gather everyone in the dining room.'

'What about her?'

'Make sure she stays in her room. She may be of some use to us.'

35

The phone on the arm of the settee began to vibrate, slowly shifting towards the edge before falling off the side. It continued shuffling around on the laminate flooring as the ringtone began. Joe continued staring at the television, as he had done for the last half an hour or so, the ice cube in his glass of Jack Daniels long since melted. As the strains of Eye of the Tiger mixed with the buzzing sound of the handset against the hard floor filled the room, he pulled his gaze from the empty screen and bent down to pick the phone up.

Unknown Number

He swiped the icon to the left to reject the call and placed the phone back on the arm. Returning his stare to the television, a message alert sounded. He quickly grabbed the handset, hoping it was a message from Ellie. The message preview on his home screen simply said,

You missed a call from Unknown Number

It had been nearly an hour since he had replied to Ellie's message, begging her to come home. Her text had said that she needed to go away for a few days, clear her head. It told him in no uncertain terms not to contact her and that if he went anywhere near her parents' house, he could forget about ever seeing her again. When she returned home, she would call him to discuss how they were going to split their belongings.

He thought back a couple of weeks. To how ordinary and boring his life was, stuck in one big rut stumbling from one weekend to another. At this precise moment in time he would give anything to go back, to slip back into that rut. Ordinarily, at about two o'clock on a Saturday he would be mowing the lawn, or coming back from the hardware store with a few shelves to put up. The rest of the day would be taken up watching the football scores come in before working out which pub he was meeting his mates in, whether Ellie was coming or if she was off out with her own friends. But at two o'clock on this particular Saturday, he was sat staring at a television screen with nothing showing, thinking about how he had messed his life up to such an extent. His head wasn't sure whether to dwell on the fact that his fiancée had left and threatened to never see him again, or on the fact that someone was murdered in his family's warehouse the night before.

The unknown number rang his mobile again. He picked it up and stared at it as it vibrated in his hand, his right thumb hovering over the red circle. A few seconds later he switched to the green icon and swiped it right. After all, it wasn't as if his life could get much worse.

'What?' he snapped, abruptly, at the handset, switching the sound to speaker.

'Is that Joe Henderson?' asked the caller.

'Yes,' he replied, curtly.

'Good afternoon, Mister Henderson. My name is Detective Sergeant Peter Harris from the Metropolitan Police Cyber Crimes Unit.'

Joe rubbed a sweaty palm across his face. 'Fuck me gently,' he muttered to himself, as he realised his life probably *had* just become considerably worse.

'Excuse me?' came the voice on the phone.

'Nothing, sorry. What can I do for you?'

'Well, perhaps you could tell me.'

'Pass. No idea what you mean.'

'Really, Mister Henderson? You have absolutely no idea why I might be ringing you?'

Joe held the phone at arm's length, stuck his other middle finger up at the screen and mouthed an exaggerated 'Fuck you'.

'OK, Mister Henderson – or can I call you Joe? How about if I tell you that last night we were monitoring a webcast on the deep web called the Red Room, during which a man called Cramer McAllister was tortured and then murdered at the behest of a paying audience.'

Best option now was to keep quiet and hope this bloke went away.

'Then what if I told you that during that transmission, something happened that allowed us brief access into their server, which subsequently let us trace their physical location to an industrial estate. Or more precisely to a warehouse on said industrial estate. More precisely still, to a warehouse owned by your family.'

Joe's head started pounding. The abrupt man at the warehouse, Dave or Alan, he couldn't remember which, had warned him that they would need to debrief him in case the police became involved. But they hadn't, at least not yet. Why not? Did they know this was going to happen and it was easier just to throw him to the wolves to let him take the rap for it? After all, it wasn't like he knew who they were and, in the heat of all the nerves and anxiety, it was unlikely that he would be able to identify or even describe them.

'Joe?' came the voice, after a short while.

'I'm still here,' he just about managed. As he waited for the voice to carry on talking, the doorbell rang. 'For god's sake. Look, hang on a minute.'

He dragged himself out of the sofa, gulped down the last of his bourbon, and opened the door. Stood on his porch were two men. One of the men had a phone held to his ear, and both held police badges in their outstretched arms.

'Won't be needing this anymore,' said Harris, as he put the phone in his inside suit pocket. 'Can we come in?'

Joe said nothing, but stepped aside as the two men walked past and went straight into the lounge.

'How about you stick the kettle on, Joe? We have some very important matters to discuss, matters of such gravity that they must be accompanied by a nice cup of tea.'

A few minutes later, Joe returned to the lounge with two mugs of tea. 'You don't seem like you're here to arrest me. I've seen TV, how come you didn't smash my front door in with a steel battering ram?'

'Perhaps you would like to begin with telling me how this show came to be filmed at your warehouse? You seem like a fairly normal person, certainly not the sort to be capable of pulling off what we saw last night,' said Harris, as he flipped the top page over on his notepad.

'Thanks, I suppose I should take that as a compliment,' replied Joe.

The two men stared at each other. A raise of the eyebrows from Harris was sufficient for Joe to realise he was backed into a very tight, inescapable corner.

'Alright,' he sighed, finally breaking down. 'It all started a couple of weeks ago when I went back to my mate's flat after the pub and he showed me Tor. Before that, I'd only heard about it in the newspapers. The usual Daily Mail shit about how illegal immigrants are selling machine guns to children on the deep web, or something. After he showed me the first video, I felt compelled to look further into it, despite the sick stuff he showed me. Nothing, you know, dodgy with kids or anything. Eventually I stumbled across the Enter The Dark message board forum where they advertised, and something just made me do it. I can't explain it. It was as though not knowing what it was made it more compulsive.'

'Even though it could have been "dodgy with kids"?' interrupted Harris.

Joe nodded. 'I didn't think of it like that at the time. Maybe I was just being naïve, and assumed, hoped even, that they wouldn't be so brazen in advertising it on a message board if it was that bad.'

'So, what did you think it would be then? Funny videos of babies falling asleep into their bowl of cereal?' asked Harris, sarcastically.

'No of course not. But look, it just somehow took over me. Everything about it, the mystery, the secrecy, the virtual currency. It just made me forget for a bit quite how dull my life had become.'

Joe began to sob, and the knots in his stomach ate away at him as the enormity of his situation sank in. It took all his effort to pull himself together and continue his account of the night when his whole world had come crashing down around him.

'So, just so I'm clear. You had taken part in the bidding of the previous episode, your bid failed and they essentially held you to ransom. They forced you to provide the warehouse for them to stage the episode and, now, have just let you go? Seems an awful risk for them,' said Harris, running the pencil back over his notes.

'They're very persuasive, and can track my every move, know everything about me. They knew I would have too much to risk to go to the police. To be honest, I just wanted the whole thing to be over last night, so I let them get on with it. And after seeing what they were capable of, I wasn't about to go making more trouble for myself.'

'But you didn't see any of them?'

'Not really, they hooded me up and handcuffed me to a chair. The only people I saw were these big burly bouncer type blokes who, as far as I could tell from their accents, were Eastern European, and the two who came to the warehouse to set it all up. When the big car arrived, I guess the people in charge, I didn't get to see any of them. And once it was all finished and they finally untied me, they'd more or less all disappeared.'

'I see,' said Harris, as he finished scribbling notes down. 'OK, look, we could arrest you this instant. Take you down to the station, process you, and you could go to jail for a few years. But we know you're not the brains behind this. You're of more use to us if they think that we haven't caught up with you. So you have a choice essentially, either—'

'Help you or go to jail,' interrupted Joe.

'Exactly,' replied Harris. 'Although chances are you might go to jail anyway. Let's be honest, a person was murdered on your property, with your prior knowledge. But if you help, that would stack very heavily in your favour. By heavily, I mean you would be a fool not to help us.'

Joe sucked the droplet of blood that had pooled on the side of his thumb. A message popped up on his phone sat on the coffee table, and from where he was sat he could see the preview of the reply from Ellie, simply saying '*No*'. He knew that, once again, he had very little option.

'OK, I'm all yours.'

'Good. I should warn you that very few people know we're even here. We are maintaining what is known as a cloak of total "plausible deniability" around this case. If anyone asks, or anything happens to you, we can just deny any knowledge of meeting you.'

'That's alright,' he replied. 'I imagine my fiancée is doing much the same at this precise moment. So what do you want me to do?'

Fowler decided it was time to join the conversation. 'The chances are they've discovered by now that we managed to infiltrate their systems. Which means that they will almost certainly assume that, a, we know where the show was taking place and, b, were able to trace it back to you. Did they say that they would be in contact with you? I can't believe that they just packed up and left with the intention of leaving you to get on with your life.'

'One of the blokes did say that they would be in contact shortly to "debrief me",' Joe replied, making air quotes with his fingers. 'Although I wasn't quite sure what that meant, I'm pretty certain it didn't mean that they were going to present me with a nice thank you gift for all my help.'

'Kill you, perhaps?' piped up Harris.

'That did cross my mind,' replied Joe.

'I think they would probably have preferred a little time to go through this there and then,' said Fowler, as he began rummaging around in his black padded case. 'It would appear that whatever little cock-up happened at the end made them rethink their plans and concentrate on getting the hell out of there. And the fact that they haven't sought you out already would indicate that they have yet to discover the breach. Or they are biding their time. Either way, I think we need to kit you out with one of our little toys for when they do.'

Harris stood up and started to walk around the living room as Joe's eyes followed him. In a weird way, Joe had feared the police becoming involved more than anything, but now he saw these two officers as his best hope of coming out of this rather sticky situation in one piece. Harris picked up a photograph from the mantelpiece and looked at it for a few seconds.

'Is this your fiancée, Joe?' he said, turning the picture of Joe and Ellie stood on a beach, holding two enormous cocktails.

'Yes, Ellie,' he replied, solemnly. 'She walked out on me a few days ago after she found out I'd spent practically our entire wedding fund on this show. Not that I did of course, I still have the bitcoins, but it was better to make her think I'd spent it than say what I'd planned to do with them.'

Harris tutted and shook his head. 'Still, it could be worse, I suppose. She could know what you did last night.'

'I had considered that, yes,' Joe replied. 'But however she reacts will be nothing compared to when my parents find out. They'll disown me.'

Harris placed the photo frame back down and walked over to Joe, placing a semi-reassuring hand on his shoulders.

'Well, yes, whichever way you look at it, you are in a considerable amount of deep shit. So deep in fact that you could be looking at a very long stretch inside. But, like I said, if you help us, we can help you. There's no reason why you won't just receive a big slap on the wrist and be told not to be such a huge dickhead in the future.'

'Thanks. I think.'

Fowler pulled a small black earpiece from his case and handed it to Joe. 'When they arrange this debriefing, just place this as far into your ear canal as you can and it still be comfortable. Just before you place it in, squeeze it together to activate it. That will let us know that it's on and is working properly. Try it.'

Joe took the earpiece between his finger and thumb. He gave it a small squeeze and placed it in his ear. The small black unit that Fowler was holding lit up blue and bleeped.

'OK, you should be able to hear me coming through the piece straight into your ear?' asked Fowler. 'We can't hear my voice outside, but when you speak we'll be able to pick it up on here. Understand?'

'Yes, I've got it. It's not very comfortable, is it?' replied Joe.

'And this is a tracker,' said Fowler, ignoring Joe's complaints. 'Wear a shirt to your meeting and tuck this into where the stays go.'

'The what?'

'The stays. The stiffeners. No? The bit at the front of the collar where the two bits of plastic go that keep the collar stiff.'

'Oh, I see,' said Joe, as he examined the tracker. 'I'm not sure I have any shirts that have those.'

'No, not a lot of people do nowadays,' replied Fowler, tossing a shirt wrapped in clear polythene from his bag. 'That's why we have these.'

Harris sat down and sipped from the teacup, spitting the nasty cold tea back and wiping his mouth. 'When they contact you, arrange to meet them at your work. Then give us the time so we can be ready to monitor you. All we need you to do is keep them talking as long as possible, so that we can record as much incriminating evidence as possible before we come and take them down. Got it?'

'Yes, I think so,' replied Joe.

Harris and Fowler packed up their things and walked to the front door.

'Remember, Joe,' said Harris, 'we'll be monitoring you. Any sign that they are about to pull anything and we'll be straight in there. You can do this.' He stood closer to Joe's face and his manner changed, 'But if you do choose to fuck with us then you can kiss goodbye to any hope of coming out of this with anything less than a serious jail term. And looking at you, you wouldn't last five minutes in the nick. OK?' Harris smiled at him and left, closing the door behind him.

Joe breathed a sigh of relief and slumped down on the sofa, closing his eyes to try and regain some composure. But the silence was quickly broken by the vibrating handset on the coffee table, followed by the loud ringtone. He picked up the phone, half hoping to see *Ellie Mobile*, but instead his heart sank as he saw the letters *BR*.

'Hello, Joe,' came the voice on the other end. 'It's time we had a little catch up.'

36

The triangular conference phone in the middle of the dining table rang only a couple of times before it was answered. 'Yes?' came the voice over the loudspeaker.

'Yes? Is that all you can say?' said Alistair, as Gilbert, Jarvis, Stan, and Eric sat around the table, variously twiddling pencils or stroking their beards. 'I assume you know precisely why I am calling?'

'Of course.'

'Well did you not think to contact me earlier? You managed to send me a text on Friday just before the show started. Instead, we had to discover that your lot managed to break into our system for ourselves.'

'There's not a lot I can do about that,' replied the voice, the background noises suggesting they were walking to somewhere a little quieter, where they couldn't be heard. All of a sudden the voice became louder and more talkative. 'I risked exposing myself enough with that text. You cannot expect me to contact you every single time they get any sort of breakthrough. It would be blatantly obvious that you were being fed information.'

'Fine,' said Alistair, curtly. 'Who is the main officer looking into this?'

'Harris.'

'Really?' replied Alistair, a little more enthusiastically, as the others all looked up and at each other. 'So he's back in work is he? How far along are they?'

'They worked out where the episode was filmed from, that was fairly straightforward. Maybe you should ask Jarvis to use McAfee or Norton as a firewall next time if his is so easy to penetrate.'

The others let out stifled laughs, except for Jarvis, who mouthed an expletive at the phone.

'Enough,' said Alistair, impatiently. 'Go on.'

'They are on their way around now to see your little friend, and they'll make him an offer to help them. If I were you I would leave it a while so as not to arouse too much suspicion. They are obviously aware that you either already have discovered, or very soon will discover, the breach. But also, they will assume that you will work out the fact that they have contacted Mister Henderson, given how easy that is. They aren't stupid, Alistair, you will need to play this very carefully. I would say that your best bet is to contact Henderson now but delay meeting him for a day or so. That way, they might just believe that you were either ludicrously slow at discovering the breach or that you are arrogant enough to believe that it doesn't matter. Either way, make sure you have some leverage in place. Shouldn't be too difficult given Harris' current situation. Anyway, there's people coming, I've got to go.'

And with that, the phone clicked off.

The men sat around the table in silence as Alistair stared at the table, stroking his beard. They all knew that it was better to let him work it out in his own brain first and then for them to pick his plans apart; although he was rarely wrong, and in this instance it didn't take long.

'We need to move and move fast,' said Alistair. 'I know the perfect person for leverage, as they put it. And by happy coincidence we have the perfect guest to help us capture him.'

'The girl?' asked Stan. 'How in the hell is she going to help?'

'Leave that to me,' replied Alistair, rising from his chair and making his way to the large oak double door. 'You call our friend Joe and arrange to meet him on, say, Monday morning. In the meantime, we'll set about collecting some bait, then we set the trap and, once we have our detective sergeant, we can close this out once and for all.'

As he shut the doors behind him, he heard the ringing tone, and then heard someone pick up at the other end.

'Hello, Joe. It's time we had a little catch up.'

A little further down the hall, he stopped at Daisy's room and knocked, before turning the key and entering. Daisy was lying on her side on the sofa, reading one of the books that she had found on the bookshelf. Alistair walked over, grabbing a footstool on the way, and sat down next to her.

'Oliver Twist,' he said, looking at the book in her hand. 'One of my favourites.'

'I never read it,' replied Daisy. 'He seems to be a sorry boy, always treated badly, yet he tries to do the right thing.'

'Indeed, and it does have a happy ending. When he finally gets what he deserves.'

Daisy put the book down and looked at Alistair. 'How long are you going to keep me here?'

'We need your help,' replied Alistair, dodging the question. 'The man who held you captive, Saeed Anwar, we need him.'

Daisy sat bolt upright. She had been trying her damnedest for the last weeks to erase that man from her mind. The mention of his name made her uncomfortable, visibly so, and Alistair saw it.

'I know how you must feel, hearing his name again after what he did to you. But that's why we need your help. We want to right his wrongs.'

'Kill him, you mean?' replied Daisy.

'Well, we need to do what we need to do. Your little stunt last night has put us in a very difficult position. The police are on to us and one particular officer has us in his sights. Anwar would be the perfect person for us to, how shall we say, tie up all the loose ends. After that, you are free to go.'

'What, walk out of here, just like that?' replied Daisy, unconvinced. 'How do I know that you won't hunt me down and put me on your show?'

'How do we know you won't walk out of here and go straight to the police?' said Alistair, immediately. 'I had hoped that we had developed an understanding and I had made it clear that we don't want to hurt you. I explained to you very personal things about myself, about why we do what we do. We're both in a situation now where we need to trust each other. Just think about Anwar. Think long and hard about everything he did, not just to you, but before you. We are offering you the chance to have your revenge. To help stop him doing to others what he did to you and the other girls in the house. You don't need to take part if you don't want, but I am sure it would help provide you with a little closure.'

Daisy thought about this. It didn't take long.

'I'll help,' she said. 'Just promise me one thing.'

'What?' replied Alistair.

'Make sure he suffers,' said Daisy, as she lay back down, resting her head on her hands and closing her eyes.

37

The door of the small mid-terrace opened, and out walked a small boy closely followed by the front wheels of a black three-wheeled buggy.

'About time,' said Stan, placing a half-eaten Cornish pasty into the door compartment. 'I thought for a minute we were never going to see any movement.'

Daisy and Stan had been sat in the car parked down the street from Saeed's house for the last couple of hours, waiting for any sign of life coming from his home. Amanda followed Mo, pushing the buggy down the path and through the front gate. Once they reached the pavement, she grabbed her son's hand and walked off down the street.

'That must be his wife and children,' said Daisy. 'They're probably completely oblivious to the sort of person he is.'

'I don't know,' replied Stan. 'Judging by the state of that woman's face, either she's incredibly clumsy or she's well aware of his character. And the boy, he's got a bandage around his head. If you were having any doubts about this, maybe now you see you're not the only person in this world whose life he's ruining.'

'I'm not sure what's worse; having no father or having one like that. I would prefer it if he didn't have any kids at all,' said Daisy, with an air of doubt.

'They've got their mother,' replied Stan, quickly. 'Eric's going to go and check he's in. Just watch when he opens the door so you can confirm that it's him. OK?'

Daisy rested her hand on the door's window sill and put her head on it, watching as Eric walked up the path with a large parcel in his hand. He rang the doorbell and waited a few seconds, looking up and around the row of properties, before the door finally opened.

'Delivery for Mrs White, sign here please,' he said.

'Who?' came the curt response.

'Mrs White. Are you Mister White?'

'Do I fucking look like Mister White?'

'Alright mate, calm down. Does Mrs White live here?'

'No, she doesn't.'

'Is this number sixty-four?'

'Yes.'

'But Mrs White doesn't live here. And presumably you haven't ordered anything from …' continued Eric, rotating the parcel to see the sender, 'er … ValueSexToys.com?'

'Are you having a fucking laugh?' replied Saeed, trying to slam the door in Eric's face.

'OK, sir,' said Eric, planting his foot in the door. 'It must be for your wife then.'

The door flew open and Saeed launched through the doorway, grabbing the parcel from Eric's hand and throwing it down the path. He grabbed Eric by the lapels and pulled him close to his face.

'What did you say, you jumped up little prick?' spat Saeed. 'Think you're funny, do you? Well let's see how funny you find it when I smash your fucking face in.'

Eric pushed away and stumbled backwards, holding his hands up. He turned and ran for the end of the garden.

'Jeez, are you some kind of bloody nutter? I was only joking. You've got serious issues, pal.'

But Saeed had already slammed the door behind him. Eric dusted down his delivery company uniform and held his finger to his ear.

'That's him alright. I think I successfully pissed him off, so he shouldn't be too hard to entice after us.'

Eric made his way a few houses back down the road to his parked car to wait. Stan turned to Daisy, who had turned ashen at the sight of the man who had caused her so much pain and misery. She concentrated hard to control her breathing, which had become fast and shallow, sipping water to calm her nerves.

'Are you alright?' asked Stan, trying his hardest to sound fatherly and concerned. Over the course of his career in special operations he had been in situations of mortal danger and in the company of some of the most dangerous people walking the planet, but dealing with teenage girls was somewhat outside his usual remit. And having to work with them was even more of a cause for concern.

'Yes,' Daisy replied. She could feel the hatred that she held for Saeed swelling inside her, and mixed with the intoxicating nervous energy, it made her feel as though she were in the middle of some sort of out of body experience.

'You need to stay calm, and you need to stay focused,' said Stan, clicking his fingers in front of her face to snap her out of her apparent trance. 'As soon as he takes the bait, i.e. you, you need to leg it back to the car. I'll be watching and I'll make sure that I'm close at hand for when you need to get out of there. Once you're back here we'll lead him away, Eric will follow, and then we'll pick our moment.'

'But why do you need me to get him to chase us? Why don't you just get him to come outside again and then bundle him into the car?'

'Because it's broad bloody daylight,' replied Stan, before quickly realising that his young charge wasn't quite as experienced in this kind of activity as he was. 'Sorry. We need to lead him away so we can take him down without the risk of being seen. His neighbours probably won't bat an eyelid to him having a barny with someone on his drive, but they would if they saw us Taser him and throw him in our boot. This matter has become urgent and we have to sort it now. We'll be keeping a close eye on you, you'll be fine. Everything clear?'

'Yes, clear,' replied Daisy, taking a last mouthful of water before stepping out of the car. She walked along the pavement, past the parked cars, past the black BMW that she remembered from the first time he took her out. A tunnel vision engulfed her, all the other houses blurring into one, and her focus was entirely concentrated on his house. She felt strong now. Nothing like the shadow of herself that she was the last time he saw her. She had played this moment over in her mind on numerous occasions, but never with an experienced backup to protect her. It was finally time to make him pay. If anything, his family would probably thank her for doing them a favour.

She strode up the path, her hands in the pockets of her light grey jogging trousers, her zip-up hoodie done up to the top. Pausing for a minute, she looked back to check the positions of Stan and Eric, before pressing the doorbell. Waiting a few seconds, she rang it again, holding the button down longer this time. Still no answer. She decided it was time to try another tack and smashed her fists four or five times on the door. Finally, through the frosted glass window, she saw movement, stepped away from the door, and turned to face away from the house.

She heard him swearing before the door opened.

'What the fuck is it?' shouted Saeed, as he stared at the back of the hooded person stood down his pathway.

Daisy opened her eyes and slowly turned around, pulling the hood from her head. For a moment, the two of them just stood there, frozen to their spots, staring into each other's eyes. It took a moment to register, but eventually Saeed's mind returned to the squalid room in the house where he kept his girls, where he had stared at this piece of meat through the crack in the door after having taken what was his. This didn't really seem like the same pathetic creature from a couple of weeks ago, but no worries, he knew he had a hold on girls like this. Once he had them under his control there was very little they could do. And this one returning to his house just proved that even when they wanted to escape, they couldn't.

'Hello, Saeed,' said Daisy, not taking her eyes away from his.

'Daisy,' replied Saeed, an arrogant smirk written across his face. 'What a nice surprise. I say surprise, of course I knew you'd come crawling back. Scrubbers like you always do.'

'Absolutely, because you are such a big man, aren't you, Saeed?' said Daisy. 'But the truth is, I came back to kill you.'

Saeed looked at her blankly, and slowly his face changed into a picture of pure amusement. A snigger at first, followed by a huge bellowing laugh.

'That's brilliant,' he said, after regaining his breath, as Daisy stood stock still, her face emotionless.

'Not only kill you,' she continued, 'but make you suffer. For what you did to me and for what you did to all the other girls as well.'

'Like I give the slightest fuck about anything a pathetic little skank like you has to say.'

'Oh, Saeed,' said Daisy, softly, as she moved closer to him, gently cupping his cheeks in her hands. 'Perhaps you should.'

The two held eye contact, gazing deep into each other's souls, just the two of them in silence. Then, mustering all of the hatred that had built up in the last few weeks, Daisy thrust her knee into Saeed's groin, as hard as she could. He yelped in agony and dropped to his knees, grabbing her leg as he fell. She fought against it, pulling her leg away as hard as she could. Saeed held on as he fought against the pain radiating through his stomach.

'Shit, get in position,' said Eric, as he saw the commotion unfold. Within seconds, Stan was moving his car closer to the house.

Daisy turned and fell. Seeing the safety of the car a few metres away, she tried to crawl away, grabbing hold of anything she could find – fence posts, branches – but Saeed resisted as he waited for the pain to subside. Finally, he regained enough of his strength to grip her legs with both hands and pull her back towards him, before manoeuvring himself on top and pinning her to the path.

'I'm going to enjoy this,' he smirked, raising a hand and slowly and very deliberating making a clenched fist, ensuring that she could see exactly what he was doing. 'As if a pointless piece of gutter trash like you could come round here and threaten me.'

Before he could land his punch, his head was rocked backwards as the toe of a boot connected with his chin. He lurched back, grasping his face.

'Quick, get up,' said Stan, grabbing Daisy by the arm, 'and get in the fucking car, now.'

Daisy didn't need asking twice and stumbled to her feet, running through the open passenger door of the car parked behind the black BMW.

'Come on, you little fucking pussy,' said Stan, bending over Saeed. 'Let's see what you've got.'

He slapped him mockingly around the face, before following Daisy into the car. Saeed's anger boiled over, and the surge of adrenaline quelled the pain in his stomach and face. He rose to his feet and watched as Stan's car slowly pulled away down the road. Pulling his keys from his pocket, he ran to his own car, leaving the house's front door wide open, pulled the car door shut, and quickly took off in pursuit.

Daisy turned around to look out of the rear window. 'He's taken it. He's coming after us.'

'Good, you'd better put your seatbelt on.'

Stan drove as quickly as he could whilst trying not to draw too much attention to their cars. In the rear view mirror he could see the bright xenon headlights of Saeed's BMW catch up quickly and then drift back as he braked. A few cars further back, Eric's was weaving in and out of traffic, fighting to make up the distance. Then his progress was halted as an articulated lorry pulled out in front, too long to make the turn properly.

'Come on, you arsehole, keep coming. Keep coming,' Stan mumbled under his breath. 'OK, here.'

Having driven a few kilometres out of the town centre, Stan suddenly swung the car around a sharp turning into a single track country lane. Daisy clung on to the door handle tightly as Stan threw the car down the bumpy, hedge-lined road. Blind corner after blind corner came and went as Saeed followed, the bumpers of the two cars sometimes touching. After a kilometre or so, the lane opened out into a forest. The hedges that lined the side transformed into a tunnel of tall, overhanging trees.

As they drove, shards of light from the setting sun pierced through gaps in the canopy and shadows danced across the glass of the windscreen. Stan accelerated but, as the road widened, Saeed's more powerful car started to edge up alongside, until the two drivers were level.

Stan switched his concentration from the front of the car to out his side window, where he could see Saeed doing the same. He waved his hand sarcastically and blew a kiss in Saeed's direction. But the smile on his face vanished as Saeed's left hand raised, and he found himself staring down the barrel of a pistol.

'Shit,' he shouted, as he slammed his foot on the brake just as the passenger side window shattered, a loud shot ringing out.

Saeed's car flew in front by a good few metres, and Stan saw the back of his car light up bright red as he braked hard. As Stan swerved to avoid the BMW, the front wheel hit a large tree stump just off the road, sending the car spinning into the middle of the road. Trying to compensate, he swung the steering wheel back the other way and found himself heading straight for the back of Saeed's car. At the last moment, Saeed swerved hard as the road took a sharp bend to the right.

The fraction of a second wasn't enough for Stan to react, and the car smashed straight into the trunk of a huge oak tree. Both airbags exploded in a shower of white powder. The seatbelt dug into Daisy's shoulder and she screamed in pain. Next to her, Stan lay unconscious, dazed by the impact of the airbag. The front of the car had crumpled, crushing his legs and trapping her right foot between the seat and the central console. As she fought to free herself, she saw the black BMW skid to a halt before reversing back up the road. She shook Stan by the shoulder and he groaned as his chin rolled on his chest.

The BMW stopped, and her breathing increased as she saw Saeed slowly leave the car and walk towards the wreck. He was pulling his black leather driving gloves on. He tapped on the driver's window, staring in with a psychotic grin. Daisy struggled to release the seatbelt and all of a sudden the silence was broken as Saeed's fist punched through the window. He grabbed Stan by the throat and held his head up.

'Who the fuck are you?' he shouted at Stan's face.

Stan groaned and struggled to open his eyes. Through his bloody, powdery eyelids he saw Saeed's features, contorted with anger, staring back at him.

'We ... are ... your ...' He struggled to get the words out. '... worst nightmare ...'

'Ha, I don't think so,' Saeed spat back. His face twisted with effort as he squeezed his hand harder.

'NO!' shrieked Daisy, as she tried to snatch Saeed's hand away, but her shoulder injury left her powerless to do anything. She watched with a sense of utter helplessness as the life ebbed from Stan, until finally he gargled his last breath and slumped forward, dead.

'Your turn,' he said to her, starting round to Daisy's door, as nonchalantly as if moving around a table having just poured Stan a drink.

She switched her attention back to wrestling with the seatbelt buckle until, eventually, it released. Saeed began trudging around the back of the car, all the time shouting threats of what he would do to her, how worthless she was and how she was now, basically, screwed. Daisy screamed as she pulled her leg against the mangled console, her desperation growing along with the pain. It had to be now, and with one last concerted effort and a final scream of pain, her foot slid out of her trainer, releasing her leg.

As she turned to open the door, she screamed again, her face within inches of Saeed's as he crouched down, peering, waiting at her window. He opened the door and reached inside, grabbing her by a mixture of hood and hair, and pulled her out, throwing her onto the damp, leaf-covered mud. She held her right shoulder and her right leg dragged straight out behind her as her good leg worked its hardest, pushing against the soft, yielding channels of mud, barely managing to propel her along the ground. The sound of Saeed laughing echoed through the forest as he strolled behind her, stalking her like a cat toying with an injured mouse.

She gave up and turned to look at him. He approached slowly, hands in pockets, and he shrugged as he planted a foot deep in the mud either side of her waist. Turning onto her back, she watched his shoulders moving up and down in long deep movements as he smiled at her. The sound of his heavy breathing was drowned out by the thumping of her heart and the pounding of blood through her head. She closed her eyes and waited for the inevitable.

She heard a shout.

'You fucker!' shouted Eric, as he launched himself at Saeed, smashing a knee into Saeed's head. Daisy felt his boot in her ribs as he fell sideways, and she mustered enough strength to push herself backwards a few yards, out of harm's way.

Eric grabbed Saeed and pulled him to his feet, throwing him against the car. He landed blow after blow into Saeed's ribcage. Saeed threw a wild swinging haymaker in an attempt to defend himself, missing by miles. As his arm flew across his front, Eric pinned it to his chest, opening up the whole of Saeed's right side, into which he thrust his knee again before slamming a huge fist into the side of his head. Saeed slumped to the floor in a heap.

'That's for my brother, arsehole,' shouted Eric, as he spat into Saeed's face. He pulled out a handful of cable ties and wrapped them around Saeed's wrists, pulling them tight. 'Come on, we've got to get out of here before the police arrive,' he told Daisy, helping her to her feet. 'I parked up the road a bit so he wouldn't hear me come. Wait here with him while I get the car.'

'Will those things hold him?' asked Daisy, looking at the flimsy pieces of plastic that were all that restrained him.

'They hold anything,' replied Eric, as he ran off up the road.

* * *

A few minutes later, Daisy slumped back in the passenger seat as Eric drove out of the forest. She glanced back out of the window, flames rising from the crashed car, and she shielded her eyes as it exploded in a blinding flash.

On the back seat lay Saeed, unconscious, with his hands fastened behind his back. She carried on staring out of the front as the hedgerow sped past and she was overcome with tiredness, and closed her eyes. With one hand, Eric dialled the phone attached to the dashboard, as the ringing came through the car's hands-free speaker.

'It's me,' he said, as the phone answered. 'Did you get my message?'

'Yes, the goons have your position and will be there in a minute or so to collect Mister Anwar's car. Is he restrained?'

'Yes. Fucker's fast asleep,' replied Eric, as he sped his way out of the country lane and back onto the main road.

'Right, get back here as quickly as you can,' said Alistair. 'Oh, and Eric? I'm sorry about Stan. Once you get him back here, we'll give him the send-off he deserves. And I promise you, my friend, as sure as night turns into day, you will have your revenge.'

38

'Carefully does it,' Harris whispered to himself, staring at the screen, squinting with one eye as the crosshairs flew around his target. His fingers twitched nervously as he tried to zero in; he took a deep breath and pulled the trigger. Missed.

'Daddy, you really are useless at this,' said Olivia, grabbing the controller from his hand. 'Look! The Joker's killed you now. I'll do it.'

'Sorry, sweetheart,' he replied, taking a sip of beer from the pint glass resting on the coffee table in front of him. He put his arm around his daughter and kissed her tenderly on the top of her head. 'Sorry we didn't get to Legoland. But hopefully, an afternoon of Lego Batman has made up for it, even if I am rubbish with a batarang.'

'That's OK. Can we play Minecraft now?' she replied, just as the doorbell rang.

Harris got up and answered the door to find Grace standing on the step, holding a glass casserole dish between oven gloves.

'I figured that since you're so crap at cooking, you might like something proper for you and Olivia,' she said, barging past him. They had gotten used to her impromptu arrivals, usually laden with food of some description, and it always made a welcome change from the standard fast food and microwave meals. 'Hey, Liv,' said Grace, as she walked into the living room, stopping only to place the dish down on the table and give Olivia a high five.

'Aunty Grace has brought us our dinner. Do you think we should ask her to stay and eat it with us?'

'I guess so,' replied Olivia, without moving her attention away from the multitude of coloured cubes on the screen.

Grace smiled a slightly uncomfortable smile at Pete and went into the kitchen with the dish. Pete sat down on the sofa and put his hand on Olivia's knee, taking the controller from her hand.

'Is Grace going to be my new mummy?' she asked.

'Oh, heavens no,' replied Pete. 'She's just a very good friend who's looking out for us. Don't you like her?'

'Yes I do. But I miss Mummy,' said Olivia, snuggling under her dad's arm.

He hugged her harder. 'I miss Mummy too. But I'll make sure that we never forget her and no-one will ever replace her. I promise.'

She looked up at him and managed a faint smile as he kissed her on the forehead.

'Anyway, I think you've got creepers to kill,' he said, handing back the controller.

He heard the clattering of crockery coming from the kitchen as Grace made her way through the cupboards, searching for the dinner plates. As he wandered over to join her his mobile rang. *Joe Henderson.*

He quickly answered it, speaking loudly enough for Grace to know from the other room who was on the line.

'Yes, Mister Henderson. Do you have some news for me?'

Grace came out from the kitchen and stood with Pete in the hallway, as he held the phone out and put it on speaker. There was very little sound coming from the other end, except what sounded like glass clinking against glass, and a few coughs and sniffs.

He tried again, 'Mister Henderson?'

After a loud slurping sound, and another cough, Joe started to speak at the other end of the line.

'Evening, Constable,' he slurred, as Pete and Grace glanced at each other, raising their eyebrows. 'I thought you might like to know that I've been in contact with the Righteous Brothers and they very kindly agreed to come and see me at work tomorrow.'

'Mister Henderson, have you been drinking?'

'A little. I decided that, since you bunch of wankers and that other lot have pretty much ruined my life, I was going to spunk as much money as I could today on the most expensive wines I could find. I've already polished off the Petrus and now I'm working my way through the Chateau Lafite. It's a cheeky little—'

'Mister Henderson, you need to pull yourself together,' interrupted Pete, impatiently. 'I need you to concentrate. What did they say exactly?'

'They said that they needed to give me a debrief in case the fucking police got involved.'

'OK, and did you tell them that we'd been in contact with you?'

'No, I didn't, cos I'm smart you see,' replied Joe, taking another large mouthful of wine. 'I acted like I hadn't never met a police guy so far since Friday. Or something like that anyway.'

'OK, Joe, I need you to listen to me very carefully,' said Pete, sternly. 'Tomorrow, assuming you manage to drag yourself out of bed, go to work as usual. Usual time, usual route, everything. Do nothing differently. Got it?'

'Yep.'

'You still have the items we gave you?'

'Of course. In fact I'm wearing the shirt you gave me now …'

'Christ, are you sure this is going to work?' whispered Grace over the top of him, as Pete silently waved away her concerns.

'… only I spilt a bit of Petrus down it. But I'm sure they won't care about that.'

'Joe, shut up,' snapped Pete, his patience now bordering on zero. 'Put the transmitter in as soon as you get in your car, before you drive anywhere. We will be in contact with you from that point, and make sure that you put the tracker in your collar so that we can monitor your position on your way to work. My colleagues will be in contact with you from the office and I will be waiting on your estate for when they arrive. Once they arrive, we will be able to listen in on your conversation and advise you on what to say. Do you understand?'

'Yes.'

'I will phone you at about six thirty to make sure that you are awake. Do not answer it, just let it ring and then decline the call. Have you got all that?'

'Got it.'

'OK, and please stop drinking. We could do with you being reasonably compos mentis in the morning.'

'No problem.'

'And Joe? Try not to worry about it,' said Pete, attempting to reassure Joe that his situation perhaps wasn't as bad as he thought, in the hope that it might make him more compliant. But all it appeared to do was draw a grunt of sarcastic non-belief. 'We will be watching you and assisting you. You just need to make sure that you do absolutely everything we tell you.'

'Well that's made me feel tonnes better, thanks. Guess I'll see you in the morning. Bright and early,' replied Joe, as he hung up the phone.

'Why don't we just bring him in?' asked Grace. 'The boy's a bloody liability.'

'No, it's too risky. Despite what he says, I doubt very much that our friends in the Brotherhood are under the impression that we've had no contact with him. If we bring him in, we lose the chance of reeling them in. If we let him just carry on, there's obviously every chance he could screw it up, being the buffoon that he is, but at least we have the opportunity to catch them. Look, we should eat and then you'd better go. I need you to be in at silly o'clock tomorrow. I'll call Danny and make sure he's up to date with everything.'

After dinner, Pete packed up an overnight bag for Olivia and sat down with her on the sofa to watch one last episode of 'The Simpsons' before it was time for her to go back to her grandmother's house.

'Right, munchkin, I need to take you back to Grandma's. I've got an early start in the morning so she'll have to take you to school.'

Olivia looked up at him, her expression in stark contrast to the jolly happy child she had been all afternoon.

'I heard you talking on the phone. Do you have to go and catch some bad people?' she asked.

'Yes, I do.'

'Is it dangerous?'

'No, of course not,' replied Pete, doing his best to sound convincing. 'It'll be a piece of cake. Then next week, I promise, we'll go to Legoland.'

The mere mention of the place was sufficient to bring the smile back to her face and she leapt up from the sofa and went to put her shoes on.

'I can drop her off if you like,' said Grace, putting her coat on. 'Your mother's house is on my way.'

'Are you sure? Liv, would you like Aunty Grace to take you to Grandma's?'

'Yes, please!' replied Olivia, excitedly.

'Great,' said Grace, putting her arm around the girl and zapping the car through the front door. 'Tell you what, you can sit in the front seat. Well, Pete, thanks for dinner. I'll call you in the morning when I'm in.'

She leant forward and gave him a friendly kiss on the cheek. He smiled back at her as she left, closing the door behind him. Back on the sofa, he picked up his mobile and dialled Danny.

'Evening, Daniel. We're on for tomorrow. You might need to skip breakfast though, I need you in for five.'

39

'Everyone set?' said Harris, munching on a petrol station cheese and bacon slice, rapping his fingers on the steering wheel as he surveyed the scene out of his windscreen.

'Yes, we're all ready,' replied Fowler, over the radio. 'The tracker indicates that he's still in his house, and I've got no signal from his transmitter yet.'

'Alright, he should be leaving any minute now. I rang him about forty-five minutes ago, so it can't take him that much longer.'

Grace returned to Fowler's desk with two cups of coffee and two doughnuts, before sitting at her own.

'How's life on the road? Must be a bit like being a travelling salesman.'

'It's alright. Coffee's shit, worse than in the office,' he replied, just as he heard the receiver come alive. Joe had activated his transmitter. 'Thank god for that. At least he managed not to cock that up,' he whispered to himself.

'Come in the police, come in the police,' said the voice over the radio. 'This is Joe, repeat, this Joe.'

Brooks and Fowler looked at each other and shook their heads.

'Mister Henderson,' said Fowler, 'you really don't need to speak like that. We can hear you perfectly, can you hear me?'

'Yes, I can hear you perfectly. Over.'

Harris interjected, hoping to save his colleagues from dealing with this imbecile. 'Joe, seriously, just relax and talk naturally as if you were talking to us in the room. Hopefully after a while you'll forget that you even have this thing in your ear. I'm parked just down the road from your warehouse so

I'll clock you when you get here. We're going to switch the transmission to one-way temporarily, so we'll still be able to hear you but you won't hear us. OK?'

'Yes.'

'Good, now just get here. I'll see you in a bit.'

Joe turned on the engine and pulled out of the drive. It still sat very uncomfortably with him that his employees would be turning up to work in a place that was now technically a murder scene. He had returned to the warehouse on Saturday morning, first thing, to make sure that the estate was empty, just to double check that everything was how it had been when they all left on Friday. The Brotherhood people had done a perfect job of clearing away any evidence, but he still gave the floor a good going over with the bleach.

Quite why the police hadn't impounded it as a crime scene he wasn't sure; would he be in more trouble for trying to cover it up? He convinced himself that he didn't really care, since very little could make his situation any worse. As he pulled onto the pavement opposite the local convenience store to pick up some milk for the kitchen, it occurred to him that his mind had been wandering into a daydream, and he couldn't really recall anything of his journey for the last fifteen minutes. He could have run over any number of old women crossing the road and not realised it. Still, the milk was important. Just do what you always do, they had said.

Joe got back in the car, threw his orange carrier bag onto the passenger seat, and started up the engine. As he pulled away, he turned up the car stereo as loud as he could manage. Might as well give the officers something better to listen to than the sound of his breathing. About a mile down the road, he pulled up at a junction. As he waited in the queue to turn, he felt a hard object press against his ribcage. His heart jumped as he turned to see a hand holding a gun against his body.

'Don't say a word,' came the voice; Joe could now see the person hiding under his coat behind the driver seat. 'Leave the radio on, and drive where I tell you.'

Joe struggled to breathe but did what he was told.

Back on the monitor, Fowler watched as the car got ever closer to the warehouse.

'About five minutes away, I reckon,' he said to Harris. The red dot on his map stopped. 'Looks like he's hit a bit of traffic, probably a tractor or something knowing that road.'

After a minute or so, the dot began moving again.

'Shit,' exclaimed Fowler.

'What is it?' replied Brooks, looking over his shoulder at the screen.

'He's moving, but in the other direction.'

'Bollocks. Pete, did you hear that?'

'Yes,' said Harris, throwing the last of his coffee out of the window and driving off at speed. 'Fucking hell. What is he doing? Can't you hear anything over the transmitter?'

'It's muffled, like he's covering it over.'

'Bloody hell. Where's he going?'

'He's on the main road heading out of town to the motorway. But you'll need to hurry, he's going at a fair speed.'

In the back of the van, Eric pulled his hand away from Joe's ear and pressed his finger to his lips.

'OK, Joe,' Eric said, loudly and deliberately. 'If you'd just like to pop the earpiece out, you won't be needing that anymore. I'm sure Detective Harris is now well aware that we have taken you on a small detour.'

Harris nearly choked as he heard his name. 'How in the hell does he know that I'm on this?'

'It must have been Joe,' said Brooks. 'He must have told them all about your visit on Saturday.'

'Shit,' shouted Harris, as he swerved to avoid an old man on a bike. 'I knew he wouldn't be able to keep his mouth shut. Where's Smith, he should be watching this.'

'He's just arrived,' replied Fowler. 'Sir, you need to see this.'

Smith joined them around Fowler's desk. 'Fill me in, Harris.'

'Sir, Joe Henderson was supposed to be meeting a member of the Brotherhood at his warehouse this morning. I was stationed on the industrial estate, waiting for everyone to arrive. It would appear that the Brotherhood was suspicious of our knowledge of the meeting and intercepted him en route.'

'Do we still have communication with Henderson?'

'No,' replied Brooks. 'The man knew he was wearing an earpiece and had him remove it. He also made it very obvious he knew that he was being listened to. He mentioned Pete by name.'

'And the tracker?'

'Still in there, sir,' answered Fowler.

'But why? Surely they would suspect that too? Why not just ditch the tracker and vanish?' asked Smith.

'Exactly, I think they want me to follow them,' interrupted Harris. 'I think they know that I'm after them and this is their way of trying to lure me in. Make it look as though they haven't found the tracker, as though they've made a mistake. Danny, send the tracker to my phone, I want to make sure that we don't lose them. They seem to know our every move.'

'What, you think they're being tipped off?' asked Fowler. 'Hang on a sec, be quiet, there's something coming through on the earpiece.'

'Where are you taking me?'

'Joe, you have nothing to worry about. The information that you gave us about Harris' visit to your house on Saturday was invaluable.'

'What? I didn't give you any information. You're fucking lying. Yes they came round mine, and then you phoned just after they left. I never said anything about what we spoke about.'

'Oh, Joe, you were a bit pissed though weren't you? You probably don't remember.'

'No, not then I wasn't. I remember I didn't say a word.'

'I think he's too shit-scared of going to prison,' said Harris, 'I don't think he did tell them we went round. If you ask me, they found out from somewhere else.'

Smith, Fowler, and Brooks all looked at each other. The operation had been kept as hushed up as it could be.

Smith cleared his throat, 'Harris, you carry on following. Grace, you and Danny keep monitoring Pete's progress. See if you can get a positive I.D. on the voice and cross reference it with any possible locations that they could be heading to. I need to put in a call to SCO-nineteen, have them on standby in case.'

He pulled out his mobile phone and walked out of the office.

'Pete, they've pulled off the motorway and are heading across country. You're about two miles from the junction.'

'OK. Grace, do you have anything on the voice?'

'Working on it. Just coming through now. Got it: Eric Wolfe. Fifty-seven-year-old, ex-intelligence service. One of Six's more maverick agents by the look of it. He was discharged about five years ago, and nothing has been seen of him since.'

'Why appear now?' muttered Harris.

'I would guess, given the type of work that he specialised in, he's gone freelance,' replied Brooks. 'I doubt he's the brains behind this whole thing though.'

Harris turned off the motorway, following the red blip on his smartphone screen, which was attached to the dashboard. As he passed through the large town, he stared at the hordes of suited office workers carrying their maroon cardboard coffee cups, briefcases, and umbrellas. The mums, laden with book bags and PE kits, dragging their kids behind on scooters. This was a life he had never known, the mundane drudgery of the rat race, serving no purpose other than to create wealth for a faceless board of company directors. He had a job, sometimes sat in an office behind a computer, but he had a reason. It was because of people like him that these wage slaves could go about their business without worry. But now, he was entering a part of the job he had never encountered before.

It was rare for him to be out in the field at all, let alone on the chase for a group of murdering internet stars. He believed he could handle himself, but the more he thought about it the more it bothered him. The questions raced through his mind. Why had this operation been kept so quiet? Why were they not sending a whole army of squad cars to chase this Wolfe? How did the 'Brotherhood' manage to stay one step ahead? Questions for later. This was it, do or die time. And as far as he was concerned, realistically, those were the two options. His strength welled inside him. He needed to make damned sure that it wasn't the second option. For Olivia's sake.

After a few miles of winding country lanes, the red blip came to a stop.

'It looks like he's turned into an old disused farm,' said Fowler. 'There's various buildings there. He's stopped over by the largest in the far corner.'

'Pete,' said Grace, softly, cupping the handset so Fowler couldn't hear. 'Be careful. We need you to come back.'

'I'll be fine,' said Harris, as he pulled into the farm, slowing down to a crawl to reduce the tyre noise on the crunchy, pothole-riddled path. 'Just get firearms here.'

He stopped behind the next door building and turned the engine off. Peering around the corner, he could see the white van parked up but no people. He went back to the car, opened the glove compartment, and nervously took out the telescopic baton that he had borrowed from the stores. Not that he thought it would do much good against these people, but at least it made him feel a little better.

As he snuck up to the large building, pressing his back against the wall, he reached the van. Extending the baton, and holding it ready to strike, he pulled the rear door handle. Locked. But the noise had alerted the occupant to his presence.

'Let me out!' a voice shouted from inside.

'Mister Henderson?'

'Yes, let me out for fuck's sake.'

'I can't, it's locked. Just stay in there and keep quiet. Keep quiet,' he reiterated, more forcefully. 'Help will be on its way. I don't know how long, so just keep your mouth shut.'

He turned away towards the building and stopped dead in his tracks. There, on the door in bright red letters, was scrawled, *Pete Harris, it's show time.*

40

Saeed Anwar sat, completely disorientated, trying to gather his thoughts. All he knew was that his hands and legs were fastened to whatever it was that he was sat on. The hood over his head had not been removed once since the minute it was forced on him in the forest. He was tired and his thirst had made him weak.

Suddenly, the hood was ripped off and a startling white light flooded into his eyes. As his vision became clearer, a face came into focus: hers.

'Hello again, Saeed,' said Daisy, her face bruised and cut.

'What the fuck do you want? What are you doing with me, you stupid little whore?'

Daisy laughed and slapped him hard around the face. 'Still giving it the big man. You seem to be somewhat clueless, Saeed. Do you not realise what is about to happen to you? You are going to die.'

'You haven't got the bottle,' he snarled back at her.

'No, you're quite right. I don't,' she replied, pointing over her shoulder at the camera set-up. 'But they do. I'm going to enjoy watching you suffering, you pathetic excuse for a man.'

Saeed turned away as much as he was able. Daisy grabbed his face and turned it back towards her own.

'This will be for everything you ever did to me. To all those girls whose lives you ruined. Come on, Saeed. Pin me down on the bed now. Hold me down with all of your weight and force yourself into me.' She slapped him around the face again. Once, twice, again and again. The anger and hatred overwhelmed her as she channelled it all through her fists and into his face. As she brought her fist up one last time, it was grabbed from behind.

'Stop, enough. We have to go. Our guests will be here soon. Leave him to them. Start the transmission.'

It all went dark as they placed the hood back over Saeed's head, followed by a bright white spotlight illuminating the inside of the thick hessian. He heard what appeared to be thick heavy chains lowering something above his head, clattering to a stop. Then it went completely black. The silence was broken only by the sound of a door shutting, followed by the crunching of tyres driving off into the distance. All he could now hear was the sound of his own breathing, nothing else.

* * *

Back in the office, a message popped up on Fowler's screen.

'Grace, look at this,' he said, as he clicked on the link.

'No, no, fucking no,' she cried, 'get Pete out of there. Not him, it can't be.'

The Red Room logo had appeared above the words *A very special edition of the Red Room. Today's special guest – Saeed Anwar.*

41

Fowler stared at the black screen, rapping his fingers against the desk, waiting for something to happen. It had been a few minutes since they'd arrived on this page, with nothing to see but the Red Room logo. Brooks hung up and threw her mobile down onto the desk.

'Nothing,' she said, ruefully. 'I can't reach him. He must have turned his phone off.'

'Well, I doubt he wanted his ringtone going off as he's trying to sneak up on his unsuspecting targets now, does he?' replied Fowler. 'Either that, or they've killed him already.'

Brooks punched him on the arm. 'Don't say that, you arsehole. If anything happens to him—'

'Look,' said Fowler, cutting her off and pointing at the screen. 'Something's happening.'

The screen faded to total blackness, which was all of a sudden broken by a bright spotlight of white, silhouetting a hooded figure strapped to a chair. There was no music, no dry ice, nothing of the usual production values, just a solitary figure, hooded, sat alone in the middle of stark, grey concrete floor.

'Weird,' said Brooks. 'They haven't gone full in for the blockbuster style of previous episodes. That must be Anwar.'

'They never usually broadcast on a Monday morning either. No, I think this was something of a rush job. And I wouldn't mind betting that this is for our benefit only,' replied Fowler.

Then, on screen, the camera panned around to show the familiar form of the Host walking towards the front of the chair. He stood behind it with his hand on the hood, placed the microphone to his mouth, and spoke.

'Good morning. Welcome back to the Red Room. Sorry for the impromptu and somewhat hastily constructed episode, but since this is only being viewed by a very select group of people, we decided to dispense with the usual formalities and get straight down to business. Our first guest today is your good friend, Detective Inspector Peter Harris.'

He whipped the hood off of Harris' head.

Fowler and Brooks looked at each other, stunned, as the camera zoomed in on Harris' face. Apart from a few red marks across his face and some little cuts, he seemed fine. But as the shot moved closer, his eyes burned with fire, a thousand yard stare that seemed to break through the monitor and straight into the souls of the viewer; he knew he was being watched.

Harris allowed the light to flood into his eyes, to become more accustomed to his surroundings. He had seen the show, he knew the drill and his journey to the chair had been a lot more rapid than previous occupants'. They had known he was coming and lay in wait as he carefully tiptoed through the lightless corridors of the building. When it came to it, he was no match for the two large brick shithouses that jumped him in the dark. He let them take him; better to conserve his energy in the hope that he might just survive long enough for the armed response to arrive.

'But,' said the Host, 'in a break from tradition, Pete here isn't one of our volunteers, he is going to be … wait for it… my assistant.'

'I've got a bad feeling about this,' said Brooks.

'Can you get a match on the clown's voice?'

'I'll try.'

Harris looked up at the Host as the two goons unfastened his restraints. He waited until the last ankle strap was released and leapt up, aiming to grab the Host by his boiler suit. The Host easily moved out of the way and Harris fell to the floor, unprepared for the toll that his capture had taken, before being pinned down with the weight of the two goons pressing into his back.

The Host knelt down next to him and spoke softly. 'Look, Pete, there's no point in trying to fight your way out of this, so if I were you, I would just go with it. You never know, you might find you enjoy it. So, come on, Pete, back on your feet! Did you like that? I know I did. Get him up.'

The goons pulled Harris upright and pushed him a few feet forward.

Harris stood and rubbed his shoulders, looking around, trying to take in his surroundings. All he could see in front of him was the powerful spotlight encasing him in a circle of white. Past it, he could just about make out the silhouettes of two, maybe three bystanders, but nothing more. He glanced in the direction of what he assumed was a door, but the slightest movement of his body implying an attempt to escape and the goons moved closer. The message was clear, he was going nowhere.

'Pete, Pete, Pete,' said the Host, as he took Harris by the arm and led him slowly to a large item, in darkness until the spotlight moved to illuminate it. 'Why don't you grab the bottom of that sheet for me?'

He gestured to the dusty black piece of fabric covering what Harris could now see was another person. Harris kept his gaze on the Host, who, after a few seconds of reciprocal staring, motioned again with his hand for Harris to pick it up. Reluctantly, Harris bent down and grabbed the edge of the sheet, stood up, and walked backwards. Slowly, the sheet slid back to reveal what it had been hiding. Harris stared in disbelief, his heart racing.

'That's right, Peter,' said the Host. 'Please accept this little gift as a token of our esteem. The man who killed your wife and unborn son. Mister Saeed Anwar.'

Fowler and Brooks watched on the screen as the colour fell from Harris' face. He looked around, helpless, as though searching for guidance from the people he knew were the other side of the screen. The silence in the Red Room was palpable, broken only by the loud dripping of water from somewhere in the building. The Host stood with his hands on his hips, watching Harris struggle to think.

Anwar looked up from his seat and shook his head with an air of almost arrogant disappointment, whispering, 'For fuck's sake,' as though nothing more serious had happened than he'd left his mobile in the car.

'Cheer up, Pete,' encouraged the Host. 'Look what we've got. The man who killed your wife. Here, on a plate. Look at him. He doesn't even look like he gives a shit.'

'What do you think he's going to do?' asked Fowler, squeezing his grip strengthener so hard his fingers had turned white.

'I don't know,' replied Brooks, who had now started biting her fingernails. 'Call Smith, find out how far away he is with armed response.'

Fowler made the call and was met with a very abrupt 'Fifteen minutes,' before the line went dead.

'Stay with me, Pete,' she whispered. 'Just keep it going a little longer. Don't do anything stupid.'

Back on the screen, the Host grabbed Anwar by the jaw and forced him to look at Harris.

'Pete, look at him. This man took away the most important thing in your life. He mounted the pavement because he couldn't be bothered to wait for a van turning right and ploughed straight into your wife. It was only by the grace of God that she had just left your daughter in nursery. Doesn't that make you angry?'

The words were cutting through Harris like razor blades; his breathing increased as he struggled to maintain his self-control.

'Doesn't it make you want to kill him that he was jailed for a pitiful six months?' The Host's voice was rising, now more of a shout than speech. 'Despite having only been in the country long enough to get some tart up the duff. Despite having no license. For Christ's sake, Pete, get angry.'

Anwar began to laugh at Harris. 'You fucking pussy,' he shouted, 'you're not man enough!'

Harris turned away, head bowed and mind spinning, the white lights disorientating him. He saw the faceless goons, the clown face, the face of his worst nightmare. Whoever else he thought he had seen earlier was no longer there.

'He's laughing at you, Pete. Just like he laughed at the system when it was powerless to deport him, thanks to his 'human rights',' said the Host, making exaggerated air quotes with his fingers. 'But what about your rights, Pete? They were pissed all over by the courts. But now you have the right. You have the power.'

He grabbed Harris' arm and thrust the handle of a large hunting knife into his hand.

'If you won't do it for your wife, do it for the dozens of girls he's trafficked since his release, his beaten wife, the countless lives wrecked by his drugs.'

Harris held the knife in his hand, watching his reflection in the blade as he rotated it around in front of his face. His breathing was almost hyperventilation, and specks of saliva pebble-dashed the blade as he seethed through gritted teeth.

'Fuck you lot,' shouted Anwar. 'I went to prison for what I did. So what if I killed your wife? So what if I beat my wife, she's mine. She belongs to me. Those stupid little whores that I took, they were worthless, who cares? The kids buying my drugs, fuck them. They buy more, they use more, I give it to them. This whole fucking country is weak. The people who live here are weak, pampered nobodies. If this was the other way around I would already have slit your throat you fucking little piss-stain. If your wife was still alive she would be—'

Before he could finish his sentence, Harris leapt forward, thrust his forearm into Saeed's throat and pointed the tip of the knife at his eye. As Saeed struggled for breath, he still managed a smirk as the two men locked eyes. After what seemed like a lifetime, Harris let go of his throat, stood up, and threw the knife away.

'Armed response will be here any minute,' he said, quietly.

'Seven minutes to be precise,' interrupted the Host.

'How the hell does he know that?' asked Fowler, as he and Brooks stared at each other in slight bewilderment. Brooks shrugged her shoulders.

Harris continued, somewhat taken aback. 'They will be here soon and, thanks to this lot, whoever the hell they are, we have your little confession on record. This is what separates people like me from people like you.'

He turned to walk away but his path was blocked by the goons.

'Sorry, Pete,' said the Host, 'unfortunately we can't just let you leave.'

He pulled out a gun and aimed it at the back of Harris' head. Just as the words came out, a loud clatter in the corner of the building distracted everyone's attention. Seizing his chance, Harris spun his arm around, knocking the gun away from his face, then grabbed the Host's arm and kneed him in the chest.

Back in the office, the screen went black as the transmission cut.

'What the fuck is going on? Was that our boys going in?' said Fowler, clicking at various windows and links, trying to retrieve the feed.

'I hope so,' replied Brooks, as she went and sat back at her desk, taking a large swig of water.

When the gunfire started, Harris ran and jumped behind a large pile of pallets. The Host, reeling from the blow, was then struck by shots in the shoulder and stomach. He turned, ran in the direction of Harris, and was shot again in the back. As he fell feet away from the pallets, Harris ran out, grabbed the Host by the arms, and dragged him to safety behind the makeshift barricade.

'They're early,' spluttered the Host.

Harris looked up to see the two goons get riddled with bullets, blood and scraps of their red tracksuits flying through the air until finally they slumped in a heap on the floor.

Two men strode out of the darkness and stood in front of Anwar.

Harris struggled to regain his breath, before finally quietly replying, 'I don't think that's the police.'

42

The man stood in front of Anwar, aiming a small machine gun directly at his head.

'Hello, Saeed, my brother,' said the man, as he peeled off his balaclava.

The sound of his voice made Anwar sit up and shift nervously in the chair as much as the restraints would allow. Behind him stood another, larger man, weapon slung over his shoulder, unsheathing a large knife.

'Aleksander,' Anwar laughed, nervously. 'My friend. Thank god you are here. Untie me quick. The—'

The butt of the machine gun struck him on the side of the jaw before he could finish the sentence.

'You think we are here to save you?' laughed Aleksander.

'How did you know I was here?'

'That stupid little whore who you let escape after you left us for dead, Daisy or whatever the fuck her name was. She contacted us and told us that we could find you here. I told you not to do something you would regret, you pathetic little piece of shit. Now, we are going to make you realise your mistake.'

'Come on, brother,' begged Anwar, nervously. 'It was just business. Let me go. The drugs, the house, the girls, I'll give you the lot.'

Aleksander took the knife from Janusz and held it to Anwar's throat. 'I already have them.'

Harris watched through the cracks in the pallet. He had to do something. As he went to make a run towards the men, a hand grabbed his top and pulled him back.

'Don't do it,' said the Host. 'Let them take care of him.'

Harris struggled to free himself but the fatigue stopped him. The Host held him tight and he looked up to see Aleksander slowly plunge the knife, point-first, into Saeed's neck. Saeed convulsed backwards and forwards as the blood frothed up in his mouth and he began to suffocate. Aleksander took a step back, spraying Saeed's body with bullets until, finally, his head slumped forward as the last breath left his body.

The two men stood looking at Saeed for a short while before spitting on his body and turning to leave. Just then, a small black projectile landed between the two men and the chair. Aleksander and Janusz looked at each other but, before either could react, a blinding flash and deafeningly intense bang knocked them both off their feet.

Harris rubbed his eyes, his ears ringing after the explosion, and through the smoke he could see beams of light tracing around the area, searching for their targets. A dozen figures clad in black and carrying machine guns ran into the room. As Aleksander and Janusz began firing their weapons, they were picked off by precision shots to the head and fell to the floor. The smoke started to clear and, briefly, there was silence. The men fanned out and began scouring the room.

Harris looked down at the Host, who was lying on his back, struggling to breathe. Harris knelt beside him and propped his head up on a folded-up sheet. Taking a deep breath, he grabbed the top of the clown mask and slowly removed it.

Eric stared up at him, coughing as fluid accumulated at the back of his throat.

'First time,' he spluttered. 'First time I take on Host duties and I fucking get shot. I only did it because that wanker killed my brother. What are the chances?'

'Who are you?' said Harris, grabbing Eric by the jaw.

Eric's stare penetrated deep into Harris' eyes. 'I am the Righteous.'

Harris let out a small laugh as Eric's eyes closed and his head rolled to the side. Harris stayed kneeling in silence for a few moments longer, as if in deep contemplation, before feeling the barrel of a gun in his spine.

'Get up. Get the fuck up,' shouted the officer. 'Hands behind your head and move away from the body.'

43

'Ladies and gentlemen of the press,' began Detective Chief Inspector Smith. 'I can confirm the following details of the incident which took place here. At around nine a.m. this morning, an officer of the Metropolitan Police Cyber Crime Unit infiltrated this building behind me and was able to smash an international crime ring involved in illegal broadcasts taking place on the so-called "dark web". The sophisticated operation involved the capture and torture of criminals, allowing viewers to bid for the chance to take part. The group had been closely monitored by our team and I can confirm that the group was headed and bankrolled by two Polish criminals, Janusz Kaczmarek and Aleksander Nowak. They were aided in the U.K. by two former British security service agents, who will at this moment remain nameless. Along with a number of other associates of Eastern European origin, these armed and dangerous individuals were removed by our armed response unit during the filming of one of these despicable shows.

'Their latest victim, who is yet to be positively identified, was also found at the premises, but unfortunately we were unable to save his life. We were able to rescue another civilian who appears to have been caught up in their activities and we will be taking him for questioning. I can also confirm that none of our officers were injured in the assault. We consider this to be a hugely successful operation that has brought about not only the end of a dangerous group of individuals, but also of a sinister underground show where people were murdered for fun. We will be making further announcements as and when necessary. That is all.'

Smith smiled and walked away. Amidst the cacophony of questions and shouts ringing in his ears, he heard his phone ring in his jacket pocket.

'Yes?' he said.

'Nice little speech, Detective Chief Inspector, although I do wish you would use the phrase "deep web" instead of "dark web". It makes us sound like a bunch of common psychopaths.'

'Surely that's a good thing? Makes the bunch of bullshit I just spouted about the Polish seem more believable.'

'I do hope so, Smith, for your sake. It was one huge mistake sending that video in to your colleagues.'

Smith went white. 'What?' he stammered. 'What makes you think that was me?'

'I'm surprised you even feel the need to ask. You knew full well what would happen, that it would prompt an investigation. Did you really believe that you could threaten us like that? That we'd just leave our most valuable asset alone?'

'Fuck you,' replied Smith. 'I don't have to listen to—'

'Just make sure that this case is wound up as water-tight as possible. We'll leave our contact in place to keep an eye on you. I would hate to have to release details of the contents of your hard drive, or your bank account, before you've managed to sign this one off.'

'Look,' he said, as firmly as he could without being heard, 'I've done what I agreed, at great personal risk, I might add. You have to keep your end of – oh fuck.' The line had gone dead.

Alistair ended the call and placed his phone on the white leather arm of the seat. Jarvis snapped down the lid of the laptop and placed it in the central console of the back seat of the limousine.

'Well, that seems to have gone better than we could have planned,' said Jarvis.

'Are you sure that they won't be able to trace any of Eric and Stan's recent activity back to us?' asked Gilbert, from across the table.

'As sure as we ever are about anything,' replied Jarvis. 'By their nature, they lived their whole lives off radar. There's no paper trail, nothing linking them back to us.'

'So that's it then,' said Alistair. 'Probably best if we all lay low for a while. It is a crying shame about Eric and Stan, but they knew the game. Apart from that, I think everyone had the outcome that they wanted. Plus, it would appear that we owe a huge debt of gratitude to this brave young lady. It was a truly amazing stroke of genius to involve Mister Anwar's old associates. Although it did somewhat scupper our original plans.'

'I just felt as though I couldn't let anything happen to the policeman. I knew he wanted revenge, but what good would that do for his little girl? She would just end up like me,' replied Daisy, gazing out of the window as the fields flew past.

'That's no bad thing. You have a great deal of integrity, Daisy, which I admire. And I want to make sure that you receive as much help and as many resources as you need to be what you want to be. Because I think that you have the makings of an exceptional person.'

She looked at him and smiled.

'To Daisy,' said Jarvis, as they clinked their glasses together. But she was already back to staring out of the car, head resting on the window as a tear rolled down her cheek.

* * *

Harris sat on a hay bale outside the farm building with his head in his hands. The place was swarming with activity now; uniformed officers, plain clothes officers, everyone. Across the yard at the entrance, a thin yellow line of tape held back the throngs of journalists, which had seemed to arrive within minutes, still shouting questions for the D.C.I. Harris glanced up to see white overall-clad scene of crime officers leaving, carrying a number of body bags. Even at this distance he could hear the multitude of clicks from the cameras with their enormous zoom lenses capturing the all-important action for the evening editions.

A shiny pewter hipflask appeared in front of his face.

'I think you might need some of this,' said Smith.

Harris looked up at him and pushed his hand away. As he got up to walk away he felt Smith's hand on his shoulder.

'Don't feel bad, Pete, there's nothing you could have done for any of these people,' he said.

Harris stopped in his tracks, laughed, and turned around. 'I don't care about these people. They're welcome to kill each other. I could have died today. Olivia would have been left an orphan. But the worst part about it is that I couldn't trust the people who were supposed to be on my side. You're a part of it, aren't you? That's how they were always one step ahead. You could have had armed response here earlier, but they needed to get away. And you have the front to tell me not to feel bad.'

'What are you talking about? I'm not part of anything,' replied Smith, indignantly. 'I'm the chief inspector of this department, and you would do well to remember that before you start making accusations. We will perform a thorough investigation into—'

'Into what, exactly?' interrupted Harris. 'It's utter bullshit and you know it.'

'Sorry, Pete, but you have no conception of what's been going on here. I'm not one of them, I haven't been contacting them. If anything, I should have the credit for bringing this to an end. You probably don't believe me but that's your problem.'

'You're right, I don't believe you,' replied Harris, getting to his feet. 'And no, it's not my problem. Not anymore.' He took his badge from his back pocket and threw it into the mud at Smith's feet. 'You'll get my official resignation in due course.'

'Pete …' Smith began, hoping to make Harris understand as he turned away.

But Harris just waved him off and continued his long walk through the crowd of people. They turned and looked at him as he passed, including a sorry-looking figure huddled under a brown blanket, sipping a cup of water.

'Mister Henderson, how are you?' he asked.

'How do you fucking think? I could have been in one of those bags,' replied Joe.

'Well just be thankful that we didn't arrest you on Saturday. At least now you have something that you use in your defence. Have a nice life, Mister Henderson. And if I can give you one piece of advice, stay away from the deep web.'

Joe sniffed a sarcastic laugh and resumed gazing down at his feet.

Harris walked to the squad car, where an officer was already holding the door open for him. He would be questioned for certain, but after that there was something that he needed to do.

44

'Here's to Billy and his remarkable concrete-like head,' said Joe, raising his pint of ale. Foam and beer splashed over the table as Rosco, Mike, and Billy all smashed their glasses against Joe's. 'I can't explain how good it is to have you back, mate, it really is.'

'Shut up,' replied Billy, the red scars from his car crash still obvious across his face. 'I'll think you'll want to start touching my arse or something.'

'So, Joe,' said Rosco, 'glad to be free I bet? That was one close shave. Tell me again why an international criminal gang chose a little twat like you to kidnap.'

'I think I was just unlucky,' said Joe, checking to see if Billy was looking at him. 'But luckily, the police seemed to be on my side, and because I was able to provide them with so much useful information, they let me go with a warning.'

'But how the hell did you convince Ellie to come back, given that you managed to take the wedding of her dreams and royally fuck it up?' asked Billy.

'What's he fucked up now? Budge up,' said Ellie, as she barged Rosco along the bench.

'Nothing, ignore them,' said Joe. 'Anyway, now that we're all here, there's something that I want to say.'

'Great, another bloody sentimental speech. Is it going to take long, only I need a piss?' moaned Mike.

'No, not really. So, one thing that I never got around to before, when we were doing the wedding the first time round, if that makes sense, was to ask you three arseholes if you would do me the great honour of being my groomsmen.'

'What, when you eventually get married? Of course, dickhead, it would be a pleasure,' said Mike, now a little more excited as the other two nodded in agreement.

'Billy, I would actually need you to do something a little more important. I need a best man.'

Billy clinked the ring on his finger against the pint glass a few times before answering, 'I'll think about it.'

Joe and Ellie looked at each other.

'Of course I will,' he said, finally, shaking Joe firmly by the hand.

Ellie reached over and gave him a peck on the cheek.

'And, finally, I have one last surprise for this beautiful woman here. Not only has she forgiven me for acting like the biggest idiot in the world, she has also helped me calm my parents down. For that I will be eternally grateful. So, firstly, I have here in my man-bag the actual real-life booking confirmation from the travel agent for our honeymoon. Two weeks, in a five star resort in the Maldives with first class return flights.'

Ellie got up and wrapped her arms around him, squealing excitedly. 'But how can you have booked the honeymoon? We don't have a venue or a date.'

'We do now,' replied Joe, smugly. He reached into his bag and pulled out a glossy brochure which he handed to Ellie. 'This came through the letterbox today.'

'Wow, it looks amazing,' she purred, as she flicked through the pages.

'It is,' said Rosco. 'I went there once to do a plastering job. You'll absolutely love it.'

'But I've never heard of it,' she said. 'They were never at any of the wedding fairs.'

'No, apparently they've only just opened up for functions. I rang them today and, luckily, they had our original date. And because they're just starting out doing this, they'll give us the works for a knockdown price, even throw in some photographs. I spoke to the head of the household, Gilbert I think he said his name was. There's a beautiful stone gazebo out in the woods in the grounds of the house. That's where we'll be stood, right in the middle, there on that stone circle.'

Ellie threw her arms around his neck.

'Oh, Joe! It's absolutely perfect.'

45

Harris watched from behind a tree in the distance as the imam threw three handfuls of soil into the grave. Apart from him, he could see only four other people present, two adults and two small children. The lady dressed in black stood next to the grave with her head bowed, whilst the smaller of the two boys swung from her hand in boredom. Next to her, an older man placed a comforting arm around her shoulder. After the ground had been filled and the soil stamped down, the imam led a final prayer before wishing the lady well and leaving.

After a few moments of contemplation at the graveside, the four of them walked back in Harris' direction.

'Mrs Anwar?' Harris said, softly, as he stepped out into their path. The four of them stopped and Amanda looked at him.

The older gentleman's posture suddenly changed to one of protection.

'Please, could I have a word?' asked Harris.

'Boys,' replied Amanda, switching their hands from hers into her father's, her gaze barely leaving Harris. 'Go with Grandad, please. Dad, it's fine, I promise.'

Once the boys and their grandfather were far enough away, Harris begun to speak. 'Mrs Anwar—'

'Please, I'd prefer it if you called me Amanda,' she replied. 'I assume you're here to tell me how glad you are that he's dead?'

Harris looked at his shoes. She was right, he was glad. But this wasn't the time or place.

'I'm sorry, I didn't mean that,' Amanda quickly added. 'It's been a stressful last couple of weeks.'

'It's fine, you have no need to apologise. I wanted to tell you in person that I'm sorry I couldn't save him. As much as it brought everything back, I would always have tried to be the bigger man. If I could have stopped it, I would have done, regardless of what he did to me.'

Amanda looked him in the eye and a tear rolled down her face. Gently, she placed a hand on his cheek and caressed it with her thumb.

'Mister Harris, words cannot express how sorry I am for the pain that my husband caused you and your daughter. Since the time that I met Saeed, I could not believe that he was this monster he'd been made out to be in the papers. Of course I knew what had happened, but he had a way of making it seem as though he was the victim. And I fell for it. But now I have those two to think of. Just as you have your daughter. I'm supposed to mourn him, but I will not. I only hope that my boys do not remember this day. When they're older I will talk to them about him. But for now, my job is to undo the damage that he has done.'

'I think we can both sleep a little easier now he's gone. I'm just sorry it was in such circumstances,' replied Harris.

As he stared at her face, the black puffiness under her eyes, the remnants of cuts across her forehead, he could see that she was as much a victim of Anwar's as he was. He had started to move on, but for her it would be a much more painful journey, with her two sons at her side. As much as they were her world, they were also his legacy, a constant reminder of the abuse she had suffered at his hand.

'Thank you, Mister Harris, you are a good man,' she replied, softly, as she took his hand, before they each went their separate ways.

'How did she take it?' asked Grace, as she picked up the large glass of red wine from the coffee table. She sank back into Pete's large leather sofa, tucking one leg under her body and resting the glass on the other.

'I think it helped,' replied Pete. 'The man was clearly deranged and seemed to hurt everyone he came across. It certainly helped me. It sounds a little clichéd but the whole thing has provided me with a degree of closure.'

'So what are you going to do? We miss you.'

'I can't go back, I just don't have the energy to battle against it any more. It's rotten, Smith's rotten, and it's like constantly having to fight with both hands tied behind your back. The whole thing stinks. Apart from you, of course.'

'Well of course. So what's the plan?'

'I saw a guest house on the Isle of Wight up for sale. It's right by the seaside, a nice little town. It'll be perfect for Olivia and Mum to make a fresh start,' Harris said, rubbing his finger around the top of his wine glass.

'Are you sure? That doesn't sound very you,' replied Grace, slightly amused.

'It's not. That's what makes it ideal. No more worrying about the corrupt internal politics of work. No more searching for shadows that are there one minute, gone the next. This whole Brotherhood of the Righteous thing just makes me realise that there are some fights you simply cannot win. Time to keep my head down and blend into dull normality. With maybe a little freelance work on the side ...'

Grace leant forward and placed her hand on his leg, before planting a kiss on his cheek. 'I can't let you just walk out of my life, Pete. I'll be coming to stay whether you like it or not.'

Pete smiled back and winked. 'Of course, I'd be offended if you didn't. I'd better just go and check on Olivia.'

As he left the room, Grace waited a few seconds, until she heard the footsteps on the stairs finish and pulled out her phone. She quickly scanned through her contacts and stopped on *Ally (private)*. Listening at the door, she could hear Pete reading a story in the bedroom.

Eventually, the phone picked up.

'Alistair, it's me ...' she whispered, as loudly as she dared. 'Yes, I'm with him now ... No, of course not, he hasn't got a clue ...

He's moving away to the Isle of Wight ... No way ... No, please, Alistair, leave him alone ... I'll be visiting him regularly, so I'll be able to keep an eye on him ... No I know. Come on, look, you're my brother and I love you, but please do this for me. He's no threat I promise ... Thank you.' She hung up and placed the phone on the table.

'Who was that?' asked Harris, making her jump as he walked in through the other door, holding another bottle of red wine.

'Oh, no-one, someone offering to recoup my payment protection insurance or something,' she stumbled. 'Come on then, are you going to pour that or what?'

The End

A Note from Bloodhound Books

Thanks for reading Enter The Dark We hope you enjoyed it as much as we did. Please consider leaving a review on Amazon or Goodreads to help others find and enjoy this book too.

We make every effort to ensure that books are carefully edited and proofread, however occasionally mistakes do slip through. If you spot something, please do send details to info@bloodhoundbooks. com and we can amend it.

Bloodhound Books specialise in crime and thriller fiction. We regularly have special offers including free and discounted eBooks. To be the first to hear about these special offers, why not join our mailing list here? We won't send you more than two emails per month and we'll never pass your details on to anybody else.

Readers who enjoyed Enter The Dark will also enjoy

Robbing The Dead by Tana Collins

Brick by Conrad Jones

CPSIA information can be obtained
at www.ICGtesting.com
Printed in the USA
LVOW12s1926020717
540139LV00001B/209/P